D1760853

John Needham

THE Exploits OF an 18th Century Entrepreneur

'A Smugglers Tale'

novum 🔲 pro

www.novum-publishing.co.uk

© 2017 novum publishing

ISBN 978-3-99048-724-2
Editing: Nicola Ratcliff, BA
Cover photos: Darkbird77,
Jerzyc | Dreamstime.com
Cover design, layout & typesetting:
novum publishing

www.novum-publishing.co.uk

Introduction

In the famous dictionary of 1765 by Dr Johnson, he describes a smuggler as, 'A wretch who in defiance of justice and laws imports or exports goods either contraband or without payment of the customs.'

Adam Smith, the great eighteenth-century economist and advocate of free trade wrote, 'A smuggler is a person who, though no doubt blameable for violating the laws of his country, is frequently incapable of violating those of natural justice, and would have been in every respect an excellent citizen had not the laws of his country made that a crime which nature never meant to be so.

I will leave you the reader to make your own judgement

Chapter I

My name is Roger Bruce Smith and this is my story, born on the 10th April 1720 into a large family, being the youngest of seven children, four older brothers and two older sisters, with fifteen years separating me and my eldest brother. We were not the richest family but at the same time, we were not the poorest by any means. Our mother and father worked hard doing long hours and with little rest, just to put food on the table and clothes on our backs, but what we lacked in wealth we gained in love. When I look back all those years ago to my childhood, I can say without any doubt I actually enjoyed it. Those carefree years when I had nothing to worry about except maybe those times when I had done something wrong and mother would say "wait till your father comes home you can explain to him what you have done," and when he did come home after work I would be summoned downstairs and I would have to stand there in front of him, not frightened and to be honest not really worried, whilst he sat in his favourite chair in the snug in front of a roaring wood fire, smoking his favourite pipe. Head bowed I would then have to recall in detail what I had done and why I did it. When I had finished explaining, I knew what the punishment was to be, the strap or be sent to bed with no tea just by the look he would give me. Invariably, I would have to go to bed with no tea but there were occasions when I had done something really wrong and I would get the strap and by god that did hurt and I never did whatever I did again, well let's say my parents never found out. But generally life was good. Unlike most children in the area, I had four older brothers and two older sisters who would look after me, protecting me from the local bullies and by god was there a few who would sometimes chance their luck and be waiting for me after school, along the lane hiding in one of the many fox holes littered along the road side. But unknown to them, my older brothers would be also waiting for them and dispatch them with ease, and then we would walk home, knowing a good job had been done that day. Until one day, when one of the fathers of the bullies came knocking on our door with a blood soaked son at his side, sporting a very bloody, broken nose. Father was not at all happy and this time, we all thought we were in real trouble, even though my brothers were now of an age that was beyond being sent to bed without their tea, but when Mother started, it did not matter your age, you just listened to what she had to say. But this was one of those rare times when father backed us up, pointing out to the young lad's father, the errors of their son's ways and what did he expect when they were the aggressor and his son was the target. Then sending them on their way with a flee in their ear. Instead of getting the strap that night, Father thanked my elder brothers for looking out for me and ensuring I was safe, but as I sit here today, all those years later, trying to recall my childhood, I do remember an incident which landed me into very serious hot water and not only with my father. I was around five years old and didn't really know what my father did for a living and to be honest, I did not really care. I knew he worked in the forest as a woodsman but that was about all, but as for his nocturnal activities as a child, I had been shielded from them. The reason being, was what I did not know about I could not talk about. But on this particular day, I was out on my own in Stroud, running an errand for mother. If I remember, I was sent out to get some eggs for breakfast, when I was approached by this well dressed gentleman who said he knew my father very well and he would approve of what he was going to ask me to do. That being, to deliver a small package to the local house on the hill and he even offered me 2d if I would do it. Not seeing anything wrong with his request and being paid 2d to run the errand was a bonus and 2d was a lot of money to me in those days, so I agreed, not really knowing what world I was about to enter into. Anyway, as I said, I did as I was asked and delivered the package on time and to the address the gentleman gave me. It was not far away, only a ten-minute walk across the village. On returning from my errand, I received my payment of 2d for my troubles from the gentleman who, as agreed, was waiting for me outside the 'Bell Inn'. I then ran all the way home proudly giving the 2d to my father who asked me "where did you get it from and tell me what did you have to do to receive such a payment?" I then went onto explain how I had met this well dressed gentleman whilst running an errand for Mother and then I told Father what this gentleman had asked of me, that being to deliver this small brown package to one of the local houses on the hill. I never expected the response I got from my father, he leapt out from his chair making for the front door, Mother came running over and pulled me away, sending me to bed. All I remember was, how I was shaking so badly that I could not sleep that night. All I did was to cry and cry. For god's sake, I was only five years old and had no idea that I had done anything wrong. All I had done was to deliver a package, wrapped in brown paper and I did not know what was in it and I did not think to even ask, not knowing I was doing anything wrong. This at such a young age was to be my introduction to the life of a smuggler and what they would do to get what they wanted. The goods I had delivered was only tea, tea that had been smuggled into the country the night before in a large shipment of wine and tea. When Father returned home later that evening, he came into my bedroom and then he explained what I had done was not wrong but dangerous and I should never do such a thing again and if approached, just politely decline the offer and thank the gentlemen kindly for asking and then come and tell us. My father then explained if I had been caught, I would have been in very serious trouble and my age was no defence when caught smuggling or even with smuggled goods on me. The local paper reported stories of children being caught and sent to the local goal for smuggling and in some cases, even deported to the plantations for seven years. The local revenue officers would more than likely come knocking at our door and that's something we really didn't want. As for the 2d, my father said it was mine and I could spend it as I liked. Of course I did not spend it. I placed it in an old battered money box, handed down from my older brothers and there it stayed until today, as I still have that old money box and in it is still that 2d I earned that day. The very first wages I had ever received. As for the old gentleman, Father had paid him a visit and gently reminded him not to ask me to do anything like that again. The matter was never spoken of again until today, as I re-call those events in this book.

Chapter 2

Looking back throughout my childhood I was a fearless child I would be the one that would go into the farmer's fields pinching carrots or climb the farmer's apple trees and pinch an apple and never once was I caught by the farmer, but I never found out how but mother and father always knew when I had ventured into the farmer's fields or up his apple trees.

But there was one occasion when I was ten years old and looking back, when I did even scare myself half to death and I really thought I was about to meet my maker. The year was 1730 and being ten years old, I was allowed to play as a child down on the beach, not far from Port Douglas, only as long as I told mother where I was going. On this occasion, I think it was Brandy Bay if I remember rightly. But, when the tide was out, I came across a large cave cut into the face of the cliff by the sea. Now me being me, I decided to investigate what was inside and at the age of ten, I was still unsure of how the tides run in the area, but let's just say the tide was out when I entered the cave and access to the cave was very easy. The sea was about thirty to forty feet away from the cave entrance allowing you to easily walk into the cave without getting your feet wet and this was all new to me, so how was I to know that when the tide came in it blocked the entrance meaning only access to the cave entrance was at low tide or by boat at high tide. If you are a smuggler landing and hiding your contraband, all you would need to do would be to sail into the bay and make for the entrance to the cave, lower your boat and then off load straight into the cave, easy, as I was to do later in life. But at age of ten, I had never seen this cave before and as such, never been in it. So, me being me, I decided to play at being a swash buckling pirate. I found a stick that looked like a pirate's sword, laying around at the entrance to the cave and so I pretended to fight the most dangerous Pirate, Captain Pike, of the Rose, who ruled these waters and of course, as always, I won and saw off the pirates and made off with their fortune. By this time, I was now very deep inside the cave in my own little world of pirates and my quest was to rescue the maidens in distress from the pirates and of course, everybody's enemy, the revenue officers. As time went on, I noticed it was starting to get dark and I needed to get home, so I made for the cave entrance, only to be greeted by the sea crashing into the cave and the tide coming in very fast, filling the cave entrance. I was cut off with no way to leave the cave.. My heart sunk into my stomach and I started to panic, how was I to get home to safety and more to the point what must Mum and Dad be thinking. This area was more dangerous than most people realized, much more dangerous than even I realized, at such a young age. All I could think of was how was I going to get home and images of my brothers and parents panicking, wondering what had happened to me and a search party being organized to come looking for me. My mother, well, I could not imagine what she would be thinking, as for Father, all I could picture was his strap coming off. I had to get out of this cave and get home. I then remembered overhearing my father tell a visitor to the house about this cave the smugglers use and how you entered from the beach at low tide and left via a secret exit at the rear of the cave, into the forest that reached down to the cliff edge. Without thinking, I started to move to the back of the cave, soon realizing I was climbing and that I soon would be safe from the incoming sea, as the tide rose which made me feel slightly safer. I carried on walking deeper and deeper into the cave and it soon got very dark, to the point it was pitch black, but then all of a sudden, I thought I was seeing things. As I turned a corner in the cave, I suddenly realized there was a light glowing in the distance and sure enough, as I got closer to the light, the cave opened out into a large cavern, well lit with candles and there, sat around a large fire, with a group of rather bedraggled men, was one rather familiar face. it was my father. What was he doing here, I asked myself, he never noticed me straight away but then one of the men turned and asked "what have we here then?" pointing across at me. I panicked, making a dash for the side of the cave and the exit which was at the top of some very steep slippery steps. But, before I could make it to the top, I slipped, falling back into the perusing man's arms, who grabbed my arms tightly and pulled me over. I started to struggle and pulled myself free whilst screaming at him to let me go, he then drew his knife and pushed me up against the side of the cave and held it to my throat. With his face inches from mine, I could smell the sweat and god his breath stank. Suddenly, as fast as he had moved in on me, he let me go and moved away with the point of a dagger placed firmly in his side. I heard a familiar voice ask me "Well what the hell are you doing here son? And why are you not at home with your mother?" With that he picked me up and turned to the man who had held the knife to my throat and pointed out that if he had harmed me, he would have slit his throat from ear to ear. "For god's sake, this is my son, just go and sit down and leave this to me." A few more words were exchanged and the man turned and re-joined his friends next to the fire. This was to be my first introduction into the true life of a smuggler. It turns out my father was a smuggler and a good one by all accounts. I thought to myself, my father is a smuggler and I had to admit, I was rather proud of that fact., I'd had my suspicions for a few years, but it really was true, he was a smuggler. I was excited with the thought of him being a swash buckling buccaneer, riding the waves in his ship whilst being pursued by the authorities. Looking back, it was a rather childish thought, but I was only ten years old and rather impressionable. He gathered me up and took my arm, telling those around the fire to make way for him and his son. We sat down by the fire where I told him the story of what had happened and how I had got cut off by the rising tide and that evening I was the greatest pirate from Port Douglas and I had seen off a troop of dragoons single handed, making everybody in the cave laugh out loud and the echo of the laughter sounded throughout the cavern, but then I had been caught out by the tide, cut off from the beach and unable to get home. I then told my father how I had remembered the stories being told about a cave, this cave, I believe and how the smugglers used it to hide their contraband and how there was an exit to the forest at the back of the cave, so I decided to see if this was the cave and made my way further into the back of cave, until I found you which I said was really lucky. "Now I have found you, you can help me explain what happened to me to mother can't you please? In which case I shall not be in so much trouble. By now I was wandering around the cave looking at all of the boxes and barrels littered around the cavern and thinking what may be in them, I thought to myself best not to ask or touch anything. Father turned back to the group, finished his business & called me over and we left the cave by the one exit at the rear of the cave, leaving the men to carry out my father's orders; that being the delivery of the hundreds of kegs stored within the cavern to whoever they were to going to. I never did find out where they were to go to or for that matter, what was in them. Like I say, best not to know, then you cannot tell anyone. But the men with Father were more worried about me talking and letting everyone know of what I had seen that night, which Father assured them I would not. On the way home, Father asked me "What will we tell your mother when we get home then? More than likely I will be in as much trouble as you are for once." "No tea for both of us then I said." With that, we both laughed and carried on walking towards home. On reaching home, I remember we quietly opened the front door and standing there waiting was Mother, with a face like thunder and the largest wooden spoon in her hand that I had ever seen. God we were in trouble alright, I thought to myself. Tea was ready and waiting for us. Mother ordered me to sit down and eat my tea, which I did, quietly, whilst Father explained to Mother what had happened. Mother was not happy and if I remember rightly, she slapped Father across the face and shouted across the room that this must never happen again. After I had eaten my tea, I was sent to bed early. The next day, I did try and explain to Mother that Father had nothing to do with me entering the cave and getting cut off by the tide and actually, that it was lucky Father was in the cave at the time, to bring me home safely. But

Mother was having none of it, it was Father's fault for encouraging me to play such games. From that point onwards, I would help Father as much as I could and as much as Mother would allow and you will see, as my life unfolds through this book, smuggling was to play a very large part in my life, in fact, it was my life. I was to become a very well-known and respected smuggler and my family's lives would also revolve around the life of a smuggler. I would also make my fortune this way, allowing me to build a small empire to be proud of and hand down to my children. But, what was to help me on more than one occasion, was my second sense when it came to danger. I was never afraid of following my instinct, whatever hand fate dealt me. It saved my life and my friends' lives many times. It also helped that I had a number of revenue officers in my pocket, feeding me information on the comings and goings of the officers, and my main adversary, John Baites, who was to take over from James Watts who'd retired by the time I brought my first vessel. John was to become such a thorn in my side, causing me many sleepless nights.

Chapter 3

Going back to my childhood and growing up with my older brothers and sisters, with such an age gap between me and my eldest brother, at times, it was like being an only child. I soon found my own company was all I needed. For my mother and father, having me so late in life proved quite a drain on their finances. But knowing how hard times were, I did try and do my bit and would help by running errands for them and helping around the house as much as I could. As I got older, I would go down to the harbour with Father in Port Douglas and earn a penny or two by helping out, cleaning the decks of some of the ships that would frequent Port Douglas. I especially liked working on the ship captained by Captain Flanagan, somebody who would play a great part in my life and would also prove to become a great friend and ally, of which, you will soon get to read about. But growing up in and around the little village of Port Douglas was the best thing that could have happened to me, with so much to do and so much to see. The harbour was a bustling and busy little harbour, with so much coming and going and for such a small lad I was mesmerized, everything seemed so big and exciting. I would ask if I could go on board some of the vessels and on one, I remember meeting a young lad about the same age as myself, the captain's son I believe, dammed if I can remember his name, but we would spend hours playing on board the 'Lynton', climbing the rigging and pretending we were pirates and walking the plank. We had some fun in those days; care free with nothing to worry about. I never did find out what happened to him after all these years. He was older than me by a couple of years from what I remember. My memory today is not as sharp as it used to be, maybe one day I will remember his name then I will have to look him up. I know the name of the little boat; it was the Lynton, a small lugger of around 50 tons. I know I will ask Roger my son to check the list of vessels that are registered to Port Douglas;

you never know he might turn something up. But it's more than likely, she's long gone to the breakers yard, as she was not in the best state back in those days. She was tired and letting in water back then. But for now, let's return to my little story.

Chapter 4

By the age of ten, I knew in my heart what I wanted to do. I wanted to go to sea to be captain of my own boat and in control of my own destiny, traveling the high seas, visiting faraway places, all those places I had learnt about in school, places where the sun shone so brightly and the sea was a beautiful deep blue. Except, as you will read, I did own my own boat, in fact a small fleet of boats, but the furthest I travelled was the Channel Islands to the west and Holland to the East, and on many an occasion we travelled north to deliver a cargo to Liverpool and Newcastle. Not so exciting as the Caribbean, where my future wife's brother was to earn his fortune in the sugar plantations of Barbados. Although my life was just as exciting and fulfilling, but in other ways. At least I did not have to suffer five years serving in His Majesty's Navy, a harsh and unforgiving place, to be at sea for so long with bad food and very harsh and brutal conditions that would kill the average person. Many did not survive the ordeal, only to be buried at sea and even worse for their families, who would never know what happened to their loved ones.

Looking back at my childhood, by the time I was about five or six, most of my brothers and sisters had long since left home, got married and were working to keep themselves and their own families. My eldest brother Sam, joined my father working in the forest and helped at night as a tub man, earning extra money to help towards his growing family, whilst John, along with my two sisters, Elizabeth and Ruth, went off into service in one of the large country houses within the area. John ending up as the butler of the house and Ruth and Elizabeth ended up marrying into gentry, marrying the two sons of the house and became ladies of the house, moving from the lower rooms of the house into a different world, a world of leisure and luxury, never to want for anything again. This was to prove to be of great advantage to me and my family, especially when I needed finance for my business adventures or should I say, for my forages into France and the Channel Islands and every time there was a great party at the house, we would always be invited, as the in laws and it is at these events that I would make great friendships that would be most helpful throughout my life and in my later years, when I had hung up my smuggling shoes and become a respectable citizen, I would become the Mayor of Port Douglas when I would get an invite to these great occasions as the main guest of honour and fun would be had by all and we would dance and drink fine wines; normally wine from my cellars till late into the night, as by then, I was very well respected and regarded as a person to be admired, by those of the younger standing (if only they really knew how I made my fortune, a rags to riches story you might say). The strange thing is much of the wine and liquor consumed at theses occasions was more than likely imported by some less legitimate route, I should know this as those throwing the parties would end up to be some of my best customers.

My other two brothers William and Peter would also prove to come in very handy as my life unfolded before me. William took up an apprenticeship within a local boat yard which would be to my advantage when I needed a fast and sleek smuggling vessel and Peter my other brother took up an apprenticeship within the local blacksmiths only to take over the blacksmiths itself when the owner of the blacksmiths was killed one evening whilst trying to recover a cargo sunk off the coast near Brandy Bay. The story goes he fell overboard bringing in a line of 50 or so kegs whilst trying to attach the line to his boat. More than likely he was drunk, as he was always drunk, and nobody will ever really know as his body was never recovered claimed by the sea. His small boat was seen by someone walking the cliff tops on route to Port Douglas a drift at sea only to be picked up by the Revenue Cutter with the line of kegs still actually attached, which of course they brought aboard and instantly seized. Which I suppose they could not have believed their luck, an easy seizure. The loss and events of that night were reported in the local paper and the seizure was reported within the Ports big red book the letter book, and no doubt this would be a good catch and a good financial reward would be coming to the captain and his crew of the revenue cutter. But sadly no one missed the blacksmith as no one really liked the man, he was always drunk, never at work, and when he was at work all he did was shout and try and beat my brother who sadly just had to take it and except this was the way. On the day of his funeral the only person to attend was my brother which really showed what the man was thought of even his wife and children did not attend the funeral and afterwards it soon came to lit how he treated them and why she too hated him so much. But like my other brother when we needed all the tools of the trade made to sink and recover the tubs or in fact just about anything that we might need we did not have far to go to get them made and at a very reasonable cost.

As for my parents they were lovely people not rich but rich in many other ways. My father was firstly a woodsman working the forest but secondly so much of his time he spent smuggleling, and as I have already said a very successful one too and maybe it was from him that I learnt the trade and from such an early age I knew exactly what I wanted to do with my life. Most evenings he would get a knock on the window or the door and when you opened the door, nobody was there but Father knew what to do, he would quietly pack his bag and around 10pm he would leave the house, only to return the following morning tired and dirty. And sometimes, Father would get a secret message delivered and left in the barn or as in many villages of the time, a young girl would walk around the village and by looking at her and seeing what she might be wearing or for that matter, carrying, you could determine where and what time the vessel was landing its cargo. One of Father's many jobs was to look after the tub-men, who carried the cargo away and up to the waiting carts; or would take the tubs off to a safe hiding place, like the caves in the face of the cliff at Brandy Bay. Yes, the same ones I found myself trapped in. From there, they could be collected at a later date. Working in the forest all day, meant he was very fit and strong, just what was needed to be as a tubs man. In one evening, he could earn more than he could earn in a week working in the forest. He was also known to sign on as a crew member on one of the many smuggling vessels that operated within the area. He would only do this when he was really needed though, when one of the regular crew had been caught by the press gang who roamed these areas and was then impressed into His Majesty's Navy, or because one or two of the crew were so drunk they were unable to go to sea, because they had spent all their money in the local Inn, much to the Inn Keeper's delight. As long as they all behaved themselves, which invariably they did not always do, as the marks on the walls of the inn show, where fights and battles have been fought. Mother hated it when my father went on one of these trips to sea which is why it was rare that he would go, but the money was good if all went well and with such a large family to support, every little bit helped. On these nights, Mother would put me to bed, tuck me in and kiss me good night and then she would just sit in front of the fire in her rocking chair with her shale round her neck, just waiting for the catch to go on the door and for my father to walk back into the house. One night when I could not sleep, I remember getting up and going along to the top of the stairs. I sat down and looked through the slats in the stairwell, watching my mother as she sat in her chair just rocking back and forth. From the light of the fire flickering across the room, I could see she had that look of deep worry on her face and even at such a young age, I could see and feel her worry. All I wanted to do was go down and sit with her, but I couldn't, as I was not really supposed to know what Father was doing. It was as though she had the whole world at on her shoulders but it soon changed in an instant, when the catch went on the front door and my father walked back into the house. She leapt up out of her chair and ran over to my father, flung her arms around him and just hugged him and would not let him go. I am sure she kept thinking that the revenue men would one day catch up with him, take Father away and impress him into His Majesty's Royal Navy, never to be seen again as had happened to my grandfather on my Father's side, all those years ago. As you will find out later, this is where my future brother-in-law would be shipped off, to serve on one of His Majesty's Naval ships. Life aboard His Majesty's War ships, as I have said, was a harsh life, in which many did not survive for very long. My father used to tell me many a story about my grandfather and how he had gone off to sea one evening to the Channel Islands, never to return. The story goes of how the revenue cutters were waiting off the needles, as my grandfather's vessel was returning late one night from the channel islands, with a full cargo of wine and brandy. When they turned around the needles, whilst making their drop off at Brandy Bay, with a group of interesting characters to off load the cargo, they were spotted by the captain of the revenue cutter. The revenue cutter sprung it's trap and fired a volley of cannons across the bows of my grandfather's vessel, making them heave too. Grandfather's vessel was out gunned, out manoeuvred and even if they tried to make a run for it there was nowhere for them to go. The seizure was made with the crew arrested and shipped off to a holding vessel off the coast of Christchurch and then shipped off to one of His Majesty's Naval Ships and finally off to fight one of the Empires many battles and never to be heard or seen of again, leaving my grandmother to fend for herself. We must presume that he died at sea in battle, or died of some disease that would have been rife onboard the ship, only to be buried at sea where he loved to be. But luck would have it, Father was old enough to support the family so he left school and managed to get an apprenticeship working in the forest as a woodsman, working with his uncle and following in the family traditions, where he works to this day and where my brother has followed in Father's footsteps, but not me, I was to follow in my Grandfather's footsteps and go to sea and of course, a career in smuggling.

As I grew up, my father knowing when it was safe, would take me along in the evenings, showing me what he was doing. I was not allowed to get in the thick of it. My job was to act as the lookout, keeping an eye on who was around and signal when anyone approached, but as I got older, I would help where

I could, with the deliveries and moving the kegs around small ones of course. Helping to such a point that I started earning good money which I would take home and try to give to my mother, which she rarely accepted and as clear as I stand here today, I can remember her words "You earnt it, you keep it and spend it how you wish." One of my jobs was to help my father deliver the tea to one of the grand houses in the area and no one would suspect a small child smuggling tea would they, and of course this was done with the blessing of my father who would have been consulted well beforehand and my mother never did find out. God forbid if she ever did, especially after what happened all of those years earlier, and a secret which was to be kept with me and will go with me to my grave. In fact, I never even told Charlotte, my wife. The money I had earned, I would save and I had a battered old money box which was handed down from my brothers, in which I would place this well earned money. But helping my father did cause many an argument between my parents. I can clearly remember one day my mother and father arguing and my mother begging my father not to take me along with him. For a time, he would go along with my mother's request and leave me behind, always leaving the house after I had gone to bed and was fast asleep, but gradually I learnt the ropes and whatever anybody would say, I knew what I wanted to do as I got older. This was to prove a good grounding for me, using my father as a teacher and this is how I learnt many of the tricks of the trade, in how to avoid being captured.

Chapter 5

To give you the reader an idea of why Mother was so worried about me at such a young age, being allowed to go into the thick of the smugglers' world. She would constantly remind Father of an incident that was reported in the local paper that sent shock waves through the community and made parents think twice about allowing their children to be used by the smugglers. The smugglers would use the children as lookouts, being so small they could hide away easily and also, run much faster.

The report went on to tell of a group of smugglers working a beach about 50 miles to the west of here, when without warning or provocation, the revenue officers and a troop of dragoons, opened fire on the smugglers at point blank range from the top of the beach and the revenue cutter 'The Bell' which by now had rounded the headland and entered the small bay, catching the smugglers off guard, and without warning, the Bell, fired a volley of cannons onto the beach, landing among the smugglers, turning the sand and beach red in a matter of minutes. The saddest thing was within the small group of smugglers on the beach were two twelve-year-old boys, two years older than myself and both were there helping their fathers. They did not stand a chance against such fire power, with no way to defend themselves against such an attack and with nowhere to hide, they were killed instantly, stuck in the centre of the beach in the open. All the smugglers on the beach that night died from their wounds and some were so badly wounded that identification was not an easy matter. Their families were called upon to identify them and the cries and screams from the children's mothers, I was told, could be heard throughout the village as they were shown their sons and husband's bodies. The only blessing would have been that they would not have suffered or realized what had happened. It would have been a very quick death for them all.

The story goes that the small group of smugglers had already unloaded the cutter by the time they were cut down or should I say, before they were murdered. They stood no chance against such an attack and neither did the kegs of wine and brandy that was piled up in the centre of the beach. The volley of canons that came from the revenue cutter landed amongst the kegs, sending splinters of wood out amongst the smugglers and this was to do most of the killing, cutting them down like wheat at harvest. The small cutter that was beached did not fare much better, being hit a number of times by cannons from the revenue cutter making it impossible to try and escape the attack. The captain and his men survived and later were to surrender to the revenue officers. They were the only survivors of that night of horrors and their story was to send shivers down the spines of those that listened and would fare greatly in the investigation that was to follow

There was an inquiry of that night's events, but nothing was to become of it. The men and children that were killed that night were classed as criminals and as such, had no rights and were fare game. This sent out a warning to those that took part in such activities, that this was what to expect if you were caught red handed smuggling. Except, in reality, it had the opposite effect. It brought communities together in defiance and acts of violence would erupt against the revenue men and those that supported them.

The men and children that died that night were buried together in their local church, with everybody in the village attending their funerals and the communities around rallied together and looked after the widows and the families of those that were killed. Surprisingly, after a few weeks, the revenue officers who ordered the attack found that they could no longer do their jobs, as nobody would talk to them and they found they were no longer welcome anywhere in the village. They could not buy food or even get a drink from the Inn, they were shunned by all, even their children were turned away from school by the teachers, being told they were no longer welcome in the school. All they could do is take their families and leave, which is exactly what they did and as they left with all their belongings on the back of a horse and cart, some of the villagers spat on them as they moved past. Even worse than that, they started to throw rotten fruit and veg at them, driving them from the village.

Could or would this happen again? I would hope it would not but who can tell. The fight against the smugglers increased and from that day onwards, no one was safe and all were under suspicion. Battles between the two would carry on over the years and from this point on, the smugglers would be better armed and prepared and this was the start of the smugglers' vessels being armed. Albeit, not as heavily as the revenue cutters but it gave them a better chance to defend themselves. Their advantage would soon be speed and manoeuvrability. Whilst the revenue cutters still used old square riggers on loan from the British Navy, which were harder to turn and being heavier meant they were also slower and best of all, had much deeper drafts so they could not follow the smugglers into shallower water which allowed the smugglers to escape capture. If they did try to follow the smugglers into the shallow waters, they would run aground. This was a trick I was to pull myself, in later years, whilst being pursued by a French privateer. What a pleasant sight it was, to see them stuck on the sand bar at high tide, knowing they were not going anywhere, as it was already high tide and they were well and truly stuck in the sand, so they could never float off and for that matter, not go anywhere.

So this is why Mother did not like me going off at night with Father, to help and earn a few pennies, as mother was frightened this would happen to her son and husband.

Chapter 6

Before getting too far into my story I would like to tell you just a little about where I lived and grew up, so let's go back to the beginning, where I was born and grew up and also learnt my trade. We lived in a modest little house on the edge of the great forest, well it seemed such a great forest, as it covered such a great area and I was young and impressionable then remember. I was brought into this world in the front room, in front of the fire. The cottage we lived in, was in a small village called Stroud, it had a large village green, surrounded by a handful of thatched cottages and of course, there was two Inns 'The 'Bell' and 'The Royal Oak', both were known for attracting the local smugglers and a few less desirable characters, who would spend all their time and money at the bar, chatting up the young ladies, thinking they might chance their luck for a night of pleasure or more than likely, after a skin full, no more than having their wallets emptied whilst they slept like babies. The house where we all lived and grew up may have been small and modest, but it was home and a place where we all felt safe, a small cob cottage with thick walls made from clay and straw, ideal for hollowing out and allowing the odd keg or two to be hidden. Inside, the ceilings were low and if anyone was over six foot, they would have had to stoop as they entered through the front door. But it was home, a warm comfortable house with a large inglenook fireplace and a hearth, where Mother would spend most of her day preparing the daily meals over an open fire, and as the family grew, so did the house, starting as a two up two down cob cottage and ending with two extra bedrooms being added for me and my brothers. Now we rented the cottage from the local landowner, a good man by all accounts and as time would go on and as my business flourished, I would end up owning the cottage my parents lived in, allowing them to live there for the rest of their lives rent free, knowing they were safe from the threat of being turned out at the whim of the land owner.

Within the village at its centre, was the local church which without fail, we all had to attend every Sunday morning and if we missed a service, which we did now and then, due to my father's nocturnal activities, the Reverend James Brown would make an example of you and in front of the whole congregation, ask why you were not present at the service the week before, knowing full well why, as the Reverend was one of my father's biggest customers, having wine delivered to the rectory on a regular basis under the disguise of communion wine, and on more than one occasion, the Reverend was to be seen in the rectory at night slightly worst for ware, and if anybody wanted any wine you could always buy a bottle of wine or two from him, supplementing his meagre income. He was a good man though and looked after his parishioners like they were his children, whether they were rich or as most in the villagers were, poor. The reverend was in fact, no better than anyone else in the village, as he would allow the smugglers to use the church to store their contraband within the roof space of the church or within the churchyard, for a small fee of course, usually a few extra bottles of fine wine would be enough, or if he could get his hands on the brandy, then he would allow the smugglers access to anywhere in the church. Yes wine or brandy was all that was needed for the full cooperation of the reverend himself. In the churchyard by the main entrance to the church, stood a number of false raised graves, very ornate and they even had names and messages carved on the headstones and these would be used by the smugglers, with secret compartments which could easily be opened if you pressed in the right place. The sides had a secret door that would open and allow a person easily to pass through into a small compartment with steps down to an underground vault which normally would hold a body, but not these, they would hold the prize of some famous smuggler and these soon would be used by myself and friends, as one of our hiding places which I must admit would be used for many a year and was never discovered. Now these turned out to be one of my favourite hiding places, as the revenue men would not touch these graves, as not wanting to disturb the dead being of consecrated ground, although they must of known what was hidden in them, not a body, but what they had been looking for. In the roof space within the church, could also be found hundreds of tubs of wine and liquor, all awaiting to be moved off up country to awaiting customers. Nearly all of the goods landed within this area would find their way up country to the midlands and the Black Country, the centre of industry at the time and where the working man lived and worked. At each Sunday service, the congregation would look up to the ceiling not praying to our Lord but praying the ceiling would not collapse under the weight of all the tubs stored in the roof space. What a sight it was, to see all our kegs lined up like soldiers in the roof space. As for getting them there, this too was a feet of engineering also. We would haul each keg up the side of the church tower and then through a door in the tower and into the roof space. We dropped a rope down through the centre of the tower, using the bell free and then a group of men on the end of the rope would walk up and down the church isle, pulling the kegs up the tower side. Now this had been going on now for many years, to the point that a groove had been cut in the stone work on the inside of the church and on the outside face of the tower. Much to the disgust of the Vicar. There were also rumours of tunnels that led off from the church and one was supposed to go from the church crypt to the cellars of one of the Inns within the village. I think it was supposed to be 'The Bell' but I cannot confirm this, not having seen them and I have used the church throughout my life to hide the contraband I imported. I can assure you, if they were there I would have found them and used them and been so close to a river and the sea, the water table would have been so high, these tunnels would have more than likely been flooded on a regular basis, making them unusable, but thinking about it, may well have helped the smugglers. They could have floated the kegs along these allusive tunnels, not having to carry them.

To keep away any unwanted visitors from the church and churchyard at night, whilst we went about our business, stories of the headless ghost were circulated throughout the village and once or twice just to back up the stories, we would go up to the churchyard at night and hide behind the gravestones and wait until somebody walked by the church. Then we would moan and groan as though we were the headless ghost and then watch as they turned and ran screaming from the churchyard. We would then sit there, leaning back on the gravestone, laughing, and as children we could earn a good night's wage, while at the same time have some fun with the locals. The next day we would then hear of the visit of the headless ghost which roamed the churchyard the night before and we would turn to each other, smiling. Until one night, as usual, we were hiding among the gravestones, playing our little joke on a pair of lovers who thought the churchyard would be a safe place for a late night meeting, when we too were frightened half to death, when out of the blue a young headless girl appeared carrying her head in her arms and walked past us moaning and groaning, stopping only for a minute, before turning and walking around the church and out of sight. From that night onwards, I would not set foot near the churchyard at night alone, although when I was much older, a few clandestine visits were made when I wanted to be alone with a young lady, but even then I would keep my eyes open for any unwanted visitor, ghostly or not. So maybe there was a certain amount of truth in the stories about the headless ghost that roamed the churchyard at night, or was it an elaborate practical joke, played on us to get revenge for all those evenings we spent in the churchyard, playing our own practical joke on all of those lovers and unwanted visitors, but whatever they might be, it kept people away from the churchyard whilst other nocturnal activities went on.

Within our little village were the two Inns, 'The Bell' and 'The Royal Oak', located on the opposite sides of the green and apart from the local church, they were the centre of the village, frequented by many of the locals and the smugglers or free traders as they liked to be known, who would meet in the back rooms of the two inns. The 'Cook' gang would meet in The Bell, whose leader was a gentleman called James Cook, a gentleman of good means who would finance and run his men with a rod of iron and god help those that stood out of line. Whilst in The Royal Oak, met the 'Smith' gang whose leader was a Robert Smith. He was in a class of his own and would slit your throat just for fun, not a man you would want to cross and they hated each other and once or twice their paths would cross. Fights would break out where someone would be seriously injured. In these back rooms, plans would be made and money would change hands, but more than likely, they would be looking to see what their next move was or their next trip over to France or wherever, to collect yet another cargo of wine and liquor, always trying to be one step ahead of the revenue men, or even worse to decide the fate of an informer or turn coat. Not something I would like to think about, but later in life, a situation which I would also have to face, but not to dish out such harsh punishments as they did. When I look back, they were a motley crew of drunkards and ragger bonds, but let's be honest, being a smuggler did, in some cases, attract the worst kinds of people, those that did not care who they hurt and if anyone was to get in their way, they would not think twice about removing them and worse still, enjoying doing it. When I was twelve years old, I found I had to go into one of these inns, The Bell, to get Father. As I entered, across the other side of the inn, sat around a large wooden table, was a small group of men, one of whom was very smartly dressed. This must have been James Cook himself I thought to myself. He seemed to be the one giving out the instructions, and handing out money, payment I suspect for an act of smuggling or something which, to be honest, I did not want to know about, or maybe he was just the ring leader, the one in charge, the financier of all their smugglers' endeavours, to which, as the years passed, I was to find out who he was and he was to come to my aid a few times as a financier and protector. Although, I suspect he was never seen actually taking part in importing the cargo, he just would reap the financial rewards from the act of importation, as I would do in my twilight years and when needs must, allow me to keep my head down and out of trouble.

One thing you learnt from an early age, was never to look over or stare them in the face, as on the table in front of them, was always a loaded pistol, ready just in case there were any unwelcome visitors, namely the revenue officers. When they were drunk, they had been known to fire off their pistol into the ceilings of the inn, which they did on one or two occasions, outraging the guests staying upstairs in the inn, although you did not argue with them as they had a fearsome reputation for dealing with informers and anybody else that upset them. But also, the landlady of The Bell had just as good a reputation for one who did not allow such acts of violence, or any trouble brought into the inn. She was a fearsome lady and being so young, I was not afraid to say I had no intention of upsetting her, as she had been known to throw out those unruly ones by the scruff of their necks onto the street outside to the great roar of laughter and a cheer coming from the inn.

Looking back, I can clearly remember when I was about twelve, one evening I was sent down to The Bell, to get my father. As I walked into the inn, it went very quiet and one of the smugglers picked up his pistol, took aim and let off a shot, just missing me and to this day, I never knew if he was really trying to kill me or just trying to frighten me. I turned and ran out of the inn to the sound of laughter, with my father following closely behind, trying to make sure I was ok. Father turned back to see the man who fired the shot place his piston back down on the table in front of him and the look my father gave him was enough to know what was about to happen. Father found me outside with my back to the wall of the inn and I was shaking and crying my eyes out, not really knowing how close I had come to losing my life. The landlady was soon behind Father, making sure all was well. The look in her eye told me what she was going to do and sure enough, the word soon got out how she threw him out, making sure he was no longer welcome in her inn. She also gave him a black eye. Being a member of the Cook gang, he could not go in the Royal Oak, so he had nowhere to drink, not that he was going to be able to anyway. Now whilst being comforted by my father, he took me home and explained what had happened to my mother, who I had never ever seen in such a temper. Father explained to Mother that he would take care of this, mother just turned back to him and told him to be careful and watch what he did. After my father had got me safely home and ensured I was ok, he left to go back to the Inn. I am not sure what he did, but he came back two or three hours later with blood on his hands and all down his shirt. He told my mother what he had done, and to this day, I never found out what really had happened to him, except whenever I saw the man from the inn on the street, he would cross to the other side of the road and run away as fast as he could, with his tail between his legs and now he had a bad limp on his left leg. Therefore, whatever my father did to him must have scared him half to death, along with hurting him badly. At this time in my life, I did know my father had a fearsome reputation of being somebody you did not want to upset, so even though I did not find out what he did, I can imagine the man that fired the shot did not come off too well and looking at the state my father came home in, I would say he beat the man to within an inch of his life and the next day, I saw the man who fired the shot and, he took one look at me and turned and ran up the street towards the centre of the village, but before he left, I managed to see his face which was very badly beaten and bruised and as he turned and ran away, he held his side. He must have been in great pain. All I did find out was, he was a member of the Cooke gang, which Father worked closely with and Father knowing James Cooke well, between them, the man must have been served a beating such that he was to have a limp for the rest of his life and would never work within the Cooke gang again, or for that matter, for anyone else in the area. In the end, I heard he had been run out of the village by my father. It's strange really, the smugglers were in fact nearly always the dregs of society, ragger bonds and men that love a good fight, but when needs must, they stick together and help each other in times of need as this was to prove, do not break the smugglers code of practice.

Chapter 7

Now every Wednesday in Stroud was market day, held on the village green in the centre of the village and being a farmers market and a local market, there was a cattle market which attracted people from far afield, bringing their goods to market to sell which gave us a good opportunity to camouflage the sale of many an item and then have them moved away with such ease, hidden within the carts which entered and left the market, all loaded with hay and goods, along with many other strange items and there being so many carts leaving the market, the revenue men could neve search them all. But strange as it might sound, the local revenue officer, James Watts would visit the market every Wednesday and try to catch us all out. He knew what we were doing, but as always, he seemed to miss what was going on right in front of his own eyes. That, or we were good at what we were doing, or, he was being paid to turn a blind eye, as many of the local smugglers had the revenue officers in their pocket. They too, or should I say, some of them, enjoyed the spoils and comfort of a glass of brandy or two, but as for James Watts, he was in no way in the pocket of any of the smugglers. He was one officer who would never turn against his profession, which begs the question, why did he never see what we were doing? Or it could just be that some of his officers, I am glad to say, did change sides and that was the only way we knew what he was planning and what he had in store for us and that included my father. But during James Watts' appointment, we found that few smugglers were caught and few seizures took place, just enough to keep his superiors happy. To keep suspicion away, kegs of liquor would be left in a secret place in the village, only known to the revenue officers, only to disappear the next day. These were used to show that the revenue officer were doing their job and by doing so, they would turn a blind eye when the real work was being done. These kegs would then be presented to James Watts, the local supervisor, as seized goods. The fact that half the time, these were spoiled kegs ones that had been contaminated by sea water and no good to us. The market was also a good meeting place, where deals would be struck and partnerships made, all hidden under the disguise of the market and let's be honest, nearly everybody at the market was involved in some way or other in the trade, so everybody looked after each other and watched each other's backs.

The small village of Stroud was not far from the sea, about three to four miles, as the crow flies, over rough ground of gorse and low trees, just enough though to hide away from the revenue men, if you needed. Small burrows would be cut in the ground and then disguised with the gorse but just enough to hide a few kegs of wine and brandy, along with a few bails of tobacco and these burrows were always located just off the beaten tracks that criss-crossed the area. Being so close to the sea might have been the reason why, as a young lad, I had decided that this was where I wanted to be and where I wanted to work. As time would pass, I would live and eventually die, in Port Douglas, starting out as a fisherman and secondly, a smuggler, till eventually becoming a respectable member of the community with a very successful business and somehow later being persuaded to run for Mayor of Port Douglas and I don't know how, but serving as Mayor for five consecutive years. Somebody must have liked me.

One thing I did love was going down to the quay in Port Douglas where I would sit on the quay side just watching the boats coming in, never knowing what was in their holds and trying to guess what was being unloaded or loaded onto the ships. Sometimes it was easy, just by the smell coming from the ship or just by looking at the crew of the vessel. If their faces were blackened, then I knew the vessel was carrying coal, the worse ones were the fishing boats, as they came along the quay you could smell the fish. But as time went by, I would see the same boats coming in and leaving and they always seemed to be carrying the same cargo but now and then I would be caught out. The little harbour may have been small but it was the life line to the town and surrounding area, bringing in many of the local commodities of life like bricks from London and beer from just down the coast in Southampton and one of the most important items, coal, to keep us warm in the winter months and candles to light the houses at night. But, on the other hand, the sea took away many of the local items manufactured for example, within the area, was a thriving leather works, along with sheep, hundreds of sheep which created much wool and around June each year, there is a hive of activity down by the River Oxo at the sheep dip, where all the sheep were given a good bath and then later sheared. The wool would then be taken down to the harbour and loaded onto a waiting vessel moored in Port Douglas and taken away to an unknown destination, this being allowed as Port Douglas was a Staple Port bestowed on the port a few years ago and mainly due to the amount of wool produced within the area. Just down the road was a tobacco factory which drew much attention from the revenue officers, and all the comings and goings were carried out under the watchful eye from the local revenue officer, none other than James Watts, who I mentioned earlier, a very thorough man who would be seen to rummage through each vessel in turn, looking for that illusive cargo which was not shown on the ship's manifest. When all was finished and he was happy, he would make an entry in his big red book what the ship was carrying and what had been unloaded and loaded, along with the ship's next destination, not knowing if the captain was really telling the truth, as normally they did not like people to know where they were going, so James Watts had to trust what he was being told.

As the years passed and I reached the age of 16, I managed to get my first taste of the sea when I signed on as an apprentice on one of my father's associates' so called fishing boats. In fact, its purpose was not really for fishing but for smuggling, a fast sleek vessel ready to out sail and out manoeuvre any revenue boat on the high seas that dared to cross its path. The captain was of Irish decent, a Captain Flanagan a likable person. I had known him personally for many years, through my father of course and from my cleaning and scrubbing of his decks for the last six years and my father having helped on many occasion to unload the captain's ship on some lonely beach along the coast, as well as signing on a few times as a crew member, when needed. Captain Flanagan was a fair man but also expected nothing but the best from his crew and most of all, when at sea, he would shout orders to the crew in a broad Irish accent which sometimes was very hard to understand, but he was a man you could rely and trust when needed and his reputation was one to be proud of.

Chapter 8

Now, before getting too far into my story, I feel that it's only fitting I tell you a little about Port Douglas, as it will fair quite a lot in my story. As the years unfold in the pages of this book, it would become my home, where I grew up and eventually, where I would bring up my own children and of course, my place of work where my small fleet would be registered and sail from. It will not be an easy place to live, as tragedy and heartache will also befall us on more than one occasion in this idyllic and beautiful village.

Port Douglas was a small fishing village and actually still is, to this day, but mainly it's a very busy little port with lots of comings and goings where everything in the village and surrounding area needed for day to day life or even produced in the area, was to enter or leave by, and it will be from here that my modest fleet would be registered and normally sail from, but not every cargo we carried would be landed in this small harbour. But let's say all cargo transported would be landed within the area, just not legally landed and all of the small coves and beaches along this rugged coast would become very familiar, such that I could walk around at night without any worry or danger.

Now the area being a large wool producer, Port Douglas about twenty years ago was also awarded the status of a Staple Port, something to be proud. This meant that we could import and export wool or should I say, I was to import and export the wool, but in this case, we mainly exported the wool as I was to win the sole rights to use the port for this purpose. A good piece of negotiation if I do say so myself. The wool was to come from the thousands and thousands of sheep that roamed the open land around Port Douglas. The land being common land and as such, open to all to use and around July time, the harbour side would be piled high with fleeces, all ready to be loaded onto one of my waiting ships and taken off up country to one of the many mills that was located in and around Liverpool. Or, to be taken by barge along the canals into Manchester, and do you know I did once give some thought to buying a barge and taking the fleeces myself, rather than paying somebody else to do it for me, but that venture never came to anything. At times, there would be so many fleeces piled on the harbour side that no one would even be able to walk along the harbour front. I can remember loading all my vessels high to the gunnels and then edging slowly out to sea and sailing north. But do you know what, with my age, trying to recall such things, my memory is not what it once was and I cannot remember who the captain was of the other two vessels. I was of course captain of one of the ships, the Valiant, but as for the other two, I still cannot remember. I will have to check the records or ask Roger my son to check for me.

Now, Port Douglas was situated in the bottom of a steep sided valley, with small white washed cottages dotted along its edges and up the sides of the valley. Running through the valley bottom was the River Oxo, a small fast flowing stream, although, all that lived in the village referred to it as a river, but that might be true when the rains came and the rainwater would pour off the sides of the valley and swell the stream to such an extent that the stream would burst its banks flooding the low-lying parts of the village.

There is only one road in and one road out of Port Douglas which made its way from the cross roads on the main route to London which can be found at the head of the valley, about two miles from the village centre. This being a very busy road where the London bound stagecoach would stop, let off any travellers bound for Port Douglas and where usually, there was an old cart waiting to take the traveller onto Port Douglas. That would be old Jack, an old lad. I say old lad, he must have been around seventy years old. He would earn a few pennies taking the travellers down into the village and onto the harbour and an awaiting vessel, where they would board and carry on with their travels. Not sure where, but we would be asked a few times to take a passenger up to Liverpool, normally on a one way trip. When old Jack passed away, the stage coach, instead of stopping at the cross roads, would make its way along the track and into Port Douglas. Not the most comfortable ride as the road was full of pot holes which were gradually filled in by one of the local farmers. The main part of Port Douglas was at the seaward end of the valley, where the land met the sea and the white washed cottages were neatly placed around the small well-kept harbour with steep paths up and down to the cottages, on the valley side. There must have also been around fifty to sixty small cottages crammed into such a small area, facing back from the harbour with narrow paths running between them. Running alongside them all, was the River Oxo, which emptied into the bay, just beyond the harbour wall. The paths that ran between these cottages were so narrow that you could easily have shaken your neighbour's hand, if you stood on your doorstep or even opened the windows upstairs. All these cottages were all well cared for and spotless in their white washed walls. Most of the cottages had a window box that in summer was a blaze of colour making the village a lovely place on a summer's day with the scent from the flowers filling the air. Some of the cottages on the valley side had cut a small garden out of the valley side and started to grow roses and flowering plants that would climb up the side of the cottage, normally this was done to hide a secret entrance to a good hiding place, where a keg or two might be hidden away. One clever person, who shall remain nameless, who worked in one of the local copper mines, was to cut a small cavern in the side of the valley and then hide the entrance by growing a climbing plant over the entrance. To anyone else, all you would see was the cliff face with plants and shrubs etc. growing up the sides, but to me and some others, they knew what was really there. There was no church in the village itself, just a few houses and an inn, located on the harbour and being the only inn in the village, this was a very busy meeting place, where many who came straight off the ships with their pay, would make their first stop, before going home to their waiting wives. On one or two occasions, those said wives would storm into the inn and point out the errors of their ways and then drag them from the inn to a great applause and laughter. The church was located one mile outside of Port Douglas on route to my home at Stroud and the Reverend of the church was the same one as at Stroud. He covered both churches which was interesting on Sundays, as if you wanted to, you could attend both services on the Sunday, if you wished and if you could move as fast as the reverend himself, who would travel at great speed between the two churches on horseback. It was a sight to be seen, a vicar in full regalia, racing through the lanes on horseback. There was a small school, high up on the valley side and its here that I would have to go school. I would walk the four miles from home to school each day and back home again, whatever the weather, and then have to climb the hundred and fifty steps to the playground and the small but welcoming school. Of course, there waiting for us was the teacher, who at 8am each morning would ring the school bell and would herd us all into the classroom and try her very best to try and teach us something. What was her name, uhh let me think, ahh yes a Miss Jenkins, that was it. I spent the best part of eight years at school. At the age of twelve, I left school, after learning many useful things like what was the capital of Spain, not that that came in handy through my life.

We were also very lucky to have a doctor in the village and luckily, he was a sympathizer to the smugglers cause and would be called on many a time, to remove a slug from the body of one of the smugglers, after which, he would not ask for payment for his services. Thing is, if he admitted to helping us and being a sympathizer to our cause then he would be in great trouble and to be fair to him, why should we put him through that. However, he would always wake the following morning to find something on his doorstep. Normally, a small keg of a very good brandy which I am glad to say he would share with anyone who would stop and listen to his stories of his exploits aboard one of His Majesty's ships. Yes, he was a ships surgeon but luckily, no limbs ever needed to be amputated, but many limbs would need to be sewn up, after a clash with the authorities.

I digress, back to the story and Mr Baites the Revenue Officer and my future adversary. He had his offices located behind the inn, what was the name of that inn, the name eludes me now but I am sure I will remember before I finish my story. Alongside his office was a small cottage where he lived with his wife and children, a nice family, just shame about what he did as a job, but I would grow to like the man and have great respect for him. Next door to the cottage was his offices and from there, he had a clear view of the small harbour and from his desk, he could see the comings and goings, noting in his big red book the names of the vessels entering and leaving the harbour and of course, what cargo they were carrying. As you left his office and turned the corner, there, cut into the side of the valley was the Revenue Bonded stores, where all of the seized goods would be taken and stored, ready to be sold at public auction or to be destroyed at a later date. As the years would pass, this is a place I would come to know well, as I can admit now having received my pardon to have broken into the stores to recover goods that was legally mine and no one else's and that's all I took, only items belonging to me. I am not a thief but an honourable man who believes in free trade for all and not just for the rich who can generally afford such luxuries. No harm was to become of the night watchman who was a man of older years and anyway, I knew him and his family so why would I harm him. He had no idea it was I that broke into the stores as I was in disguise, as you might say. Powder in my hair, my face covered such that no one could recognise me, and this applied to all my colleagues.

Chapter 9

So there it is Port Douglas, the place where it all started all those years ago and now being sixteen years of age, I would be allowed to sign on as an apprentice on one of the many vessels that traded from this port. So on my sixteenth birthday Captain Flanagan allowed me to sign on as an apprentice on the 'Charlotte' a sleek looking fishing boat. Like I said, in reality it was no more a fishing boat than I was a sailor. But, a fast open decked smugglers' vessel, capable in a good wind of travelling from the small fishing village of Port Douglas on the south coast of England over to Cherbourg in France, collect it's cargo which would of course be waiting for us, a few hundred kegs and bring them back in one night, landing them in some quiet little bay along the coast. It made a tidy profit for all those involved, and as I have said earlier, allowed those who could not afford such luxuries the taste of the high life, like a nice cup of tea.

My very first smuggling run came one evening on the 15th of June 1736, when Captain Flanagan announced that we were to go on a trip to France. What he omitted to tell me was the purpose of the trip. It was to bring back a cargo of wine and liquor (mainly brandy) along with a few yards of silk for the ladies and a few bags of tea. Tea was a very valuable commodity and could fetch a very good price when sold on the open market and the smugglers knew it. I suppose I should have realised this was no ordinary trip, as the time we set sail was in and around early evening. We never normally sailed at such times. We would normally sail out in the morning, such that we could get back to port before night fall, but this was a special trip which I was soon to find out about. We slipped out of Port Douglas very quietly, without drawing attention to ourselves, trying to making sure where possible, no one saw us leave and if anybody was to ask the captain where we were going, he always had the answer, that it was a training exercise for his new crew. Well I suppose you could say it was a training exercise, but not what many would think.

We set off just as the sun was setting, across the bay and that was one of the most beautiful sights I have ever seen. With the sun disappearing, what looked like, into the sea and the sky a mixture of the most beautiful colours and then as the sun went, the stars came out to guide us along. We slowly headed out to sea, leaving Port Douglas behind and as we left the harbour, we were met by a gentle swell and enough wind in our sails to take us on our journey towards Cherbourg at a reasonable speed. As we headed out to sea and into the English Channel, Captain Flanagan decided to tell us of our destination and also what we were to collect. There was an eerie silence among the crew as each of us thought long and hard on what we were about to undertake. Many of the crew already knew what they were about to do, as they had done this many many times before and of course, this was no surprise to them on where they were going. They knew of the rewards that would awaited them after a successful trip, but on the other hand, they also knew what was to await them if they were caught by the Revenue Cutter that patrolled these coastal waters, either a few months in jail if they could not afford the fine or even worse, being press ganged into His Majesty's Royal Navy, never to be seen or heard of again and a life of the cat of nine tails. The revenue men that roamed the coast were a special breed of men, hardened over many years of going out in all weathers and times of the day, to try and stop the smugglers (or Free Traders as we liked to be known) and capturing and impounding the illicit cargo, but worst of all, some of these revenue men were ex smugglers, persuaded to change sides on the promise of a full pardon for their crimes or just to stay out of gaol and pay off their fines and as such, knew what we would do to avoid capture.

To give the reader an idea of what and who our enemy were, let me explain. In this area of Port Douglas, there were four revenue officers, James Watts junior, Joshua Baites (John Baites' Father), Stuart Smith and William Barnes and one supervisor, a John Baites, who took over from James Watts and John Baites was a man of integrity and a man as I will explain later on in this story, would not turn to our side, unlike many of his officer whom we did manage to persuade to help us and turn a blind eye when needed, at a cost of course. They were a group of men whom roamed the area day or night, whatever the weather, just to try and stop us from landing a cargo, and I'll give them their due, they managed this on a few occasions. But I am glad to say, we managed to get the better of them many more times than they did stop us landing a cargo. It was a lonely and dangerous job, being a revenue officer, alone on horseback, riding along the many winding lanes and crossing through the surrounding forests, checking the ground for any signs of horses passing through and along the lanes, visiting the many small lonely bays that were dotted along the coast, just on the off chance they would catch us landing a cargo and along this stretch of coast, there is many places that we can land a cargo undisturbed, so they had their work cut out trying to find us. They would use the crossroads just outside of Port Douglas as a meeting place where they would stop and swap stories or observations, whilst smoking their clay pipes and then either ride off together or go on their separate ways, they may dismount and spend hours surveying the area looking for that tell-tale signs of the presence of any activity. But at the same time, keeping a watchful eye for anyone that might jump out and attack them which did happen a few times, as the local doctor would tell me on more than one occasion of how he treated another officer, after he was attacked whilst going about his work. I remember an incident where one of John's men, I cannot remember his name, but he was found the following morning badly beaten, his horse had been stolen and he was cut badly by a sharp blade across his face and hands. No one admitted to the act but let's be honest, who would, knowing the punishment would be harsh with two to three years' hard labour or even worse, the gallows. They all knew the dangers all too well, with stories being circulated around the officers, of an incident that happened a few years back when an officer further up the coast was woken one night by a group of men, who claimed to know of a landing taking place that night and as he came out of his house, he was set about and badly beaten, his limp body was taken away only to be thrown from the cliff top with his body being washed ashore the next day, ten miles further down the coast. No one could really be sure if he was already dead when he was thrown from the cliff top. The story goes that this was a punishment for a seizure earlier in the year, and for the attack and killing of a famous smuggler that was to frequent this area, that being a 'Jack Smith' whilst resisting arrest and trying to stop the Revenue officers seizing his goods. There were also other stories of officers being caught whilst trying to stop a landing, but not so brutal, that being tied up in the middle of a field of wheat, their horses set free with a note attached to their saddle, telling the reader where they might find the officers, and there they stayed till the following morning, after their horses found their way home and the alarm was raised by their families to find the missing officers. Something that was even stranger was that their family never even realised they had not come home that night till they heard the sound of the horse's hooves on the cobbles outside their cottage the following morning. Yet another embarrassing moment for them all, but no harm befelled these officers and an act I would impress on one or two officers later on in my story.

But looking back at my first run to France, this was not as eventful as I was led to believe. I had been told by my father that the life of a smuggler was full of adventure, swash buckling and evading and outwitting the revenue cutter, but as far as I could see, they were just stories, stories told to me by my father when I was a child, although in later life I was to experience a few close shaves with the Revenue Officers along with the local Dragoons. But as far as this trip was concerned, all that happened to me was to be shouted at by the captain for standing around day dreaming whilst spending hours just looking out to sea, checking for the presence of what we referred to as the enemy, the local revenue cutter, or even worse, one of the those many privateers, French or English, that roamed the area. The privateers would normally be armed and would not give up their prey easily or think secondly at opening fire with a volley of cannon.

We reached Cherbourg at around 11pm in the evening and pulled alongside the dock. Now waiting for us on the dock was the captain's contact, a man of distinction, well-dressed and sounds silly, but he did not look like the type of man that would get involved in such antics, but I would say he was a man of means. The captain left the ship and as he did so he turned looked back and shouted a few orders to Andrew, his second in command who he left in charge whilst he disappeared off to carry out whatever business needed to be done, but these orders when translated was to make sure the ship was fully loaded, secured and ready to sail by the time he returned, and god help you if it's not. Now Andrew took this very seriously and started shouting orders to the rest of us. If we were not ready when the captain returned, Andrew would more than likely lose part of his payment for the night's activities, so whilst the captain was away from the ship, we worked like dogs and loaded the valuable cargo of wine and brandy into the ship's hold, along with a few yards of silk for the ladies which having not seen silk close up before, looked beautiful and lastly, a few bags of tea to be sold on at great profit.

About two hours later Captain Flanagan returned with the gentleman, they turned to each other, exchanged a few words, shook hands and the gentleman turned and made his way off down the quay. I never found out who he was, but more than likely, he worked for the captain as his buyer and overseas contact. Captain Flanagan turned and boarded the 'Charlotte'. He stood on the deck, looking and taking in what was around him, he then turned and spoke to Andrew, asking if all was loaded and secure. Once confirmed and happy, he once more barked a few orders and we slipped our moorings and slowly and gently we left Cherbourg and headed out into the dark moonless night and made our way home, not for the port we left but a quiet secluded bay, approximately ten miles due east from our home port of Port Douglas, where a large group of men would be waiting to swarm over the ship like bees round a honey pot, and move the cargo away to be sold to an awaiting customer. Not sure who that would be but let's be honest I did not need to know, more than likely though, the cargo was to head up country to the black country and the industrial centres of the country where the cargo would be warmly welcomed.

The trip back was no more eventful than the trip over to Cherbourg. This time I was given an important task, or I was told how important it was, I was to be the lookout. I stood on the highest point on deck, given a spy glass and told to look out for any other vessel, namely a revenue cutter. I stood for hours, just looking through the spy glass out to sea and not spotting anything until we reached the coast and rising gracefully from out of the sea, I could see the welcoming outline of the English coast and the towering white cliffs of well, I don't know where, and at that point I shouted at the top of my voice "Land, land" only to be told, "Keep your voice down" as sound travels for miles at sea, especially on a night like this.

Captain Flanagan came over to me and took the spy glass and started to look towards the land, searching for a landmark which would identify where we were along the coast. I asked him what he was looking for, where he then explained to me that he was looking for three trees in the shape of a triangle on the hill top, and he went on to explain that certain smugglers and landowners would plant markers on hill tops, all along the coast and these markers helped the sailors, giving them a good idea of where, along the coast they had reached and most of all, directing them to the point where they were to land their cargo. But soon, the revenue officers would realize the significance of these strange markings on the hill tops and would go up and cut the trees down, removing the landmarks, but, the ever so resourceful the captain explained how they would be re-planted or some other form of marker placed on the hill tops. He shouted once more to the coxswain, to turn to port and head along the coast for about an hour. Handing back the spy glass, he instructed me to look out for a light on the cliff and to let him know when I found it, whereupon the captain retired to his cabin. As sure as his word, in about an hour, there on the cliff top I saw a green light. I called the captain who explained that this was a signal to say all was clear and to bring his ship into the small bay and with that, he returned the signal and turned, asking the coxswain to head into the bay. The entrance to the bay was narrow with the entrance lined with hidden submerged rocks. I was sent forward along with Josh, another apprentice and told to keep an eye out for any submerged rocks, whilst Andrew checked the water depth. With minimum sail up, we slowly moved into the bay to the muffled sound of Andrew's voice, as he shouted the depth along with 'to port' or 'to starboard'. I soon realized where we were. I knew this area well and I had played here when I was younger with my brothers swimming in the sea and spending a lot of time climbing up the cliffs, much to our parent's displeasure and being told on a number of occasions how dangerous the cliffs were. Never having seen the bay from this angle, it now seemed much bigger than I remembered. Being a sandy beach and no submerged hidden rocks, Captain Flanagan decided to beach his vessel. With it being low tide, it would not be long before high tide floated him off again, giving the waiting men on the beach plenty of time to unload their precious cargo. As we headed into the bay, I suddenly noticed men waiting on the beach. There must have been about a hundred or so and in front of them, there was one man smartly dressed. He had an air of authority about him and all he was doing was barking a few orders. I started looking among the men on the beach, knowing more than likely, my father would be one of the men on the beach, waiting to help unload our valuable cargo, we had just brought over from France. There I shouted to Josh, "There he is" and sure enough, coming towards the Charlotte, was my father. He was slightly surprised to see me standing on the deck of the Charlotte and greeted me with a look of worry. He headed straight over to Captain Flanagan and all I could see were hands being raised and words being spoken. Still to this day, I did not know what was said but all I do know is, the captain assured my father that no harm would come to his son. On the word of the smartly dressed gentleman, the men surged forward, along with my father and like a military operation ,they started to unload the ship. Within the hour, the ship's holds were empty and as you looked across the bay and heading inland, was a single file of men each carrying two to three tubs and then at the top of the cliff, I could see a row of carts and wagons all being loaded with the tubs we had just brought ashore from France and each cart or wagon had an armed outrider. When loaded, the order was given to move out and the procession suddenly left at great speed. The captain then explained to me that the procession of carts and wagons would not stop for anything, until it reached its destination which could be miles from here. After all was done, Father came over to me and spoke quietly and from his tone, I could see he was worried for my safety. I assured father all would be ok and the captain could be trusted, which of course my father already knew. Father then turned and left, wishing me luck and a safe return and asked me to please not mention to Mother of the events of tonight, as she would never understand.

We then cleared up, tied everything down, making all secure and then we just waited for the tide to come in. We did not have long to wait when we suddenly realized we were no longer sat on the beach, but once more afloat. We slowly moved back into the centre of the small bay and headed back through the small entrance of the bay and out to sea and made our way home to our waiting beds, and so ended my first experience of being a smuggler. I made a nice profit that night and from that night onwards, I knew in my heart what I really wanted to do. I daren't tell my mother, as she would not have approved and when she did find out what my future career was to be, you can just imagine the reaction I received. But my father, as always, understood which did not make it any easier for my mother to accept, all it did do was cause a rift between my parents, as Mother blamed my father for the career path I had chosen. Luckily though, the rift did not last long, once I made one or two promises to my mother on what I would and would not do. I stayed with Captain Flanagan for approximately four years and when I was twenty, left Captain

Flanagan to purchased my first vessel, The Valiant, a sleek little ship and an ideal smuggler's vessel, fast and manoeuvrable, just what was needed to outwit and out sail the old revenue cutters which were on loan from the British Navy and large old square sailed sailing ships. As we were no longer at war with France or Spain, these ships became surplus to requirement, so a new use was found for them and their crews. They would hunt down and stop the smugglers, which they did a very good job of, by blockading the channel which seriously jeopardised the activities of the smugglers. Many were caught but many also got away from the slower and much bigger ships. Those caught, like Peter Smith, a notorious local smuggler were taken to London and tried for their crimes at the Old Bailey. In Peter's case, for murder, murder of a revenue officer in the next county from us. He was tried and convicted, with a sentence of death without the presence of the clergy. The sentence was duly carried out the next day and his body gibbetted at the gates of the neighbouring village, as a warning to others.

Chapter 10

The year now was 1740, and I had just turned twenty and saved enough money over the last four to five years, to be able to purchase my first ship, The Valiant. She was a beauty, a 70 foot twin mast lugger, built in Scotland about 1720 which was the year I was born, so I had to have her. She was orignally used to carry general cargo and some not so general, fish, which had left an interesting odour, and may have been the reason I got her for the price I did. I paid the sum of £20 for her, which was the result of a lot of hard work and saving every penny I had, whilst working with the captain. Not that Captain Flanagan paid me much as an apprentice, I earnt most of the money to purchase The Valiant, smuggling. I could earn more in one night helping the smugglers than I could earn honestly in a week. Whenever I could, I would sign up for each trip and help the captain where I could and soon became a regular face among the crew and a trusted and worthy colleague, who could be relied on when needed. During those four years with the captain, there were times when a strong and steady head was really needed. I can remember one occasion, when we all came so close, in fact much too close, to being inmates at the local flee pit, referred to as the local gaol or even worse, joining His Royal Majesty's Navy. We were returning from France with a full hold of tobacco and liquor and we were met by a very persistent Revenue Cutter, whose captain had a fearful reputation for always capturing his prey, except on this occasion our luck was with us and his luck for once, had left him. Our vessel was much smaller and so much faster than his and we managed to out run him, but not without our pride taking a battering. He even had the cheek to fire his cannons across our bows as a warning to us, if we did not heave to and stop, showing us what he was capable of doing to us. But knowing we could out run him, we ignored his warnings. Not being satisfied at firing on us once, he had the cheek once more to fire a volley at us. By this time, we were well out of range of his cannons and the balls fell short of our bow, with an almighty splash, rising form the sea, shaking our little ship and sending spray high into the air and across our stern. But, on reflection, I would not like to think what would have happened if we had been hit. Captain Flanagan's vessel would have been match wood and we would have been sent to the bottom of the English Channel, along with The Charlotte. Captain Flanagan truly believed the revenue cutter was waiting for us but not expecting our reactions. He knew of our movements and also how the captain would react in such a situation. It was as though the captain of the Revenue Cutter was waiting for our captain. The Revenue Cutter was in the right place at the right time, with their cannons already primed and loaded and this was not by chance. But as luck would have it, we had a sharp eyed young lad on watch, me. I spotted the ship on the horizon, giving us enough time to be able to turn and start running before the captain of the revenue cutter realized what was going on. All I can say, is their captain must have been furious, as he and his crew would have lost out financially. If we had been seized they would have been entitled to a share of the spoils when the ship and cargo was sold at auction and as such, this made their efforts to capture a smuggling vessel much more aggressive.

When we were safe and we could relax, the captain reflected back on the last few hours and decided to head straight for Brandy Bay, named as such due to the amount of brandy landed in one night, ten years ago and where there would be waiting, a large gang of smugglers of a size I had never seen before, a green light was seen on the cliff top signalling all clear and safe to come into the bay, we edge around the headland and turned into the bay at all times looking out for the Revenue Cutter but luck was still with us and the Cutter was nowhere to be seen. Turning back to the beach, I turned the spy glass onto the beach and there must have been around two hundred to three hundred waiting men on the beach and in the centre, was a frenzied group of men, gathered round a pile of kegs while others could be seen carrying them away. At this point, I realized we were not the only ship landing that night. Sat just off the beach was another large lugger of around 70 feet also surrounded by men who were running around like ants, all with a purpose. Each man must have been carrying around two to three tubs and were taking them up to the waiting carts on the beach head. It was soon to be our turn to unload. We had been patiently waiting just off the beach, not that we liked to be hanging around. We must have been sat waiting for nearly an hour and the captain was starting to get agitated we were vulnerable and he did not like that he liked to come in land unload and be on our way home. Anyway, at last it was our turn. We beached The Charlotte and started to unload. A rope was thrown to the waiting men on the beach, they hauled the ship onto the beach (luckily it was still low tide), secured the rope and then like a swarm of bees round a honey pot, they boarded the captain's vessel and in the matter of an hour, the vessel was fully unloaded and ready to depart, back to sea and home. During the unloading of the vessel, a smartly dressed gentleman approached Captain Flanagan and they were seen quietly talking. You could see by the expression on the two men's faces what they were discussing, why the captain was late in landing his cargo, in which the captain started telling the tale of the waiting revenue cutter. The gentleman stepped back in shock with the look of terror on his face, raised voices could be heard clearly and I could just make out that he was worried we may have brought the revenue cutter down on them. But, as always, the captain assured him that we had evaded and lost the cutter long before heading into the bay to unload. They then parted company and the gentleman headed up the beach and mounted his horse and was seen riding at high speed off along to the head of the procession of carts. Captain Flanagan started talking to Andrew, making it clear that we were to leave straight away and head for our home port of Port Douglas.

Whilst the ships were being unloaded, I got talking to one of the men on the beach and it turns out, we were the third ship to land a cargo that night and that this evening would see the highest quantity of cargo being landed in this small bay in one night, than across the whole of last five years. I vowed that one day, I would beat this record and land an even larger cargo and true to my word, I did, but I put everything I owned on the line. I never did find out how much was landed that night but there must have been hundreds of kegs landed and I do not know how much tea. The procession of loaded carriages with an armed guard on each carriage could be seen for miles, moving away at high speed through the night and day, not stopping till they reached their final destination. The only reason they would stop would be to change horses and these would be tacked up ready to go as time would be of the essence and at these times, they would be very vulnerable. If you got in their way whilst whey moved through the countryside, that would be the end of you, as the tracks they would use would be just wide enough for the carts and the speed they would move, barely allowed time to move out of their way. I found out that the group of smugglers who whisked away the kegs into the night were associates of each of the three captains that landed that night and he was known to be the best in his trade. Over the years, he would become a very trusted friend and contact. His task was to ensure the cargo's safe removal from the shoreline and to later that week, deliver the cargos to their respective customers, who would be waiting to receive their goods. Now, this could be spread out across the country, and he was paid heavily for his actions. As for his reputation, well, this was unquestionable, dependable and trustworthy.

By the time we had unloaded, luckily for us, the tide had turned and was coming in and the Charlotte was once more afloat and free from the restraints of the beach. We released the securing ropes and when safely offshore, in the centre of the bay, the captain gave an order and the vessel hove too. Captain Flanagan gathered the crew together on deck, all seven of us, and carrying his horse whip, he started moving through the crew, looking at each one in turn and the look he gave each of us spread terror through each and every one of us. He then started shouting at all of us, asking if we had an informer aboard, a loose tongue and told us that one of the cures of a loose tongue was to cut it out. And if there was no informant, who knew of our whereabouts and our movements for this evening. This went on for about an hour, by which time we had an even bigger problem. We had not yet got back to Port Douglas and our families must have by now thought the worst, that we had been captured by the Revenue Cutter and on our way to the local gaol, or even worse, attacked and sent to the bottom of the English Channel. By now, we had been sat just off the coast for around an hour and the danger was, we might be caught and charged with hovering, which if you could not prove you were not hovering then the penalties could be quite severe. The first mate, Andrew, plucked up the courage and approached Captain Flanagan, taking him to one side and spoke to him quietly and with that the Captain turned back to us, barked a few orders and we raised the sails and headed home into Port Douglas, by which time Captain Flanagan had calmed down, realizing the informer may not be part of his crew and he was now sorry to have even thought that one of his crew would turn against him. He trusted each and every member of his crew with his life until proven wrong. We docked, I left the ship and ran all the way home and up the path to our front door. I carefully opened the front door at home and was met by mother with a barrage of questions, "What time do you call this?" and "I was worried sick, I thought the revenue cutter got you." This went on for about an hour, by which time my father had returned from work. Hearing I was back home, he just asked "Everything okay son?" To which I replied "Yes." After a few hours, Mother calmed down and life went back to normal, or as normal as could be, after that small episode. Now Father already knew what had happened that night, as word had already been passed to him to let him know that I was safe. He understood what needed to be done, but as for Mother, she would never accept or understand my career path.

As for the informer, there was a rumour going around the village that somebody had gone missing late that night in a very mysterious manner and some say, in a very violent manner, never to be seen or heard of again. Due to the circumstances, no one was prepared to ask any questions, except the captain was somewhat subdued for a few days and questions were being asked of what happened to his son in law, surely he was not the informer! The story goes that a person was forcibly removed from his bed in the middle of the night by around six men and taken, under force, to an awaiting lugger laying off the coast in Brandy Bay. The lugger apparently sailed for France and to an awaiting reception of around ten to twelve French men in a small secluded bay on the French coast, not far from Cherbourg. The story then goes on to tell of how this person was beaten to within an inch of his life then buried in the sand on the beach with his head just above the water line left all night and then he was dug up whilst still alive, only just and taken away never to be seen or heard of again. The story goes, he finally had his throat cut after sustaining much more brutality. It sounds like the saviour was having his throat cut with his final resting place the bottom of a dry well in northern France. So there endeth the first lesson for anyone who turns kings evidence and informs on their friends and the local smugglers. Each act against this man would not kill him but leave him just alive such that he would suffer more and more until he would beg his tormenters to put him out of his misery and finally they would, by cutting is throat, leaving him to die whilst still only just breathing. His by now, limb body, was thrown down one of the many dry wells in the area and to ensure he was dead, large rocks were thrown down the well on top of him. When he was found, his left arm had been severed from his body and the rocks thrown down on to him had crushed his skull. Not a pleasant way to die, but this is what happens to informers.

As for being an informer, not the best thing to do, inform on your friends and colleagues is it. An informer was thought as more of an enemy than even a Revenue Officer and the treatment of informers was much more brutal, as I was to find out when a colleague and friend of mine turned informer. He was taken out and brutally murdered. His body was found buried up to his neck at the water's edge in Barrow Bay, a common smugglers execution method. His death must have been a slow and painful one. He would have been helpless to try and break free, as when his body was recovered, he had been badly beaten and his hands had been tied behind his back so tightly the rope had cut deep into his wrist and he must have still been alive, only just though. He was buried up to his neck at the water's edge, half way between high and low water's edge and then left to drown as the tide came in and out. When they found him all that could be seen was the top of his head poking out from the sea. This was a grim warning to others, who decided to turn in his or her fellow smuggler and what would await them. No bag of sovereigns would be enough to help them then. It is now said that his soul still roams Barrow Bay late at night, and the sound of his screams as he drowned can be heard throughout the night. How true this is I do not know, as I have never heard these screams myself or even seen a ghostly figure prowling around the bay, but then I have never been down to Barrow Bay alone at night. Are these just stories to keep the unwanted visitors away, leaving the way clear for the smugglers to do their work in piece and undisturbed. Whatever the case, it does seem to have the desired effect. Who is going to stay around if there's a ghostly figure haunting the area?

Chapter II

The Valiant, was first registered in 1720 (the year in which I was born so I had to have her) in Fife, as a general cargo ship and then twenty years later, she was brought down south where I found her laid up awaiting to be sold at auction. I fell in love with her straight away. She is not the fastest vessel in the world but, clinker built from larch and oak and she was to be my first and as such, the most beautiful vessel afloat. Originally, she had been built to be used as a coastal ship in Scotland, taking supplies to the out-lying islands of Scotland until one day, she was charted to take a cargo of Scottish whisky from Glasgow in Scotland to London, only the cargo was not all that it was supposed to be and she was stopped on route, searched and seized by the Revenue Cutter as the ships manifesto did not match what she was carrying. She was carrying, instead of a full hold of whisky, a good selection of wine, tobacco and brandy, all in kegs marked whisky and when opened, the crew were surprised at what was found. The crew pleaded their innocence but to no effect. They were all arrested and ended up in the local gaol. After their trial, they finally ended up being transported to a waiting hulk in the bay, to be transported off to an awaiting naval ship, where they were enlisted into His Majesty's Navy, and the Valiant was finally put up for auction at a public sale and this is where I found her and eventually brought her for just £20. I must admit I did not consider at the time, how I was to bring her home to Port Douglas and how I would even find a crew that was willing to help me. But, as it so happened, I already told my father about the Valiant and he had decided to come with me to the auction, mainly I think, to keep an eye on me and check I was not buying trouble. So with his help and with his contacts, we gathered a crew of seven and took charge of the Valiant and went on board. It was a strange feeling stepping on board knowing that this, all this, was mine and I was her new captain.

The first thing we did was to check everything was ok and present. To our surprise, everything was there, nothing was missing. We found out, when she was seized by the Revenue Cutter, it happened so quickly that the old owners did not even have time to strip the ship of all her furniture, so lucky for us, she was fully original with all her rigging, sails etc. in place and surprisingly in very good condition. When we were all satisfied, she was all seaworthy and safe to leave port, we waited for high tide to cast off from the quay side. We headed slowly and carefully out to sea to bring her to a new home and a new era in her working life, proudly standing on the deck looking around and taking in my new purchase, realizing just how beautiful she really was. She handled like a dream and with my father alongside me, to share that moment, we entered Port Douglas, Valliant's new home and the feeling I got when we entered the harbour of Port Douglas for the first time with my mother, brothers and sisters waiting for us on the quay side, was immense pleasure and pride. A moment I will never forget was seeing my mother's face as we tied up alongside the quay in Port Douglas and then the whole family came on board to see what I had done and spent all my well earned money on. I thanked the crew we had gathered in London, paid the crew off and as agreed, paid for their tickets home on the London bound coach. Two of the crew though decided to stay in Port Douglas and asked if they could stay on and crew the Valiant, to which I agreed and we would become great friends over the years. What were their names? Ahh yes, Peter Finch and David Brown. Peter would, in the end, take over as captain of one of my future vessels and David Brown would become his second in command.

I re-registered the Valiant with her home port being Port Douglas and this was to be the start of a career at sea that was to last many, many years, and make me a very wealthy man in more ways than one and not just financially, it allowed me to enjoy life to the full. I was at home now and the sea was to become my mistress, who would take me away from my family and in particular, when I was to marry my wife. The sea was also to make me my fortune and as I have recalled a number of times, some made honestly and some from well, lets us say, not so honestly, but mainly in not so honest manor. I never did count up how many trips we made to France or other such destinations, but it must have been in the hundreds, but who's counting? As I am certainly not.

The first forage at sea was with my father at my side was on the 20th of August, 1740 and we had persuaded a local sheep farmer to trust us with his consignment of wool that needed to go up north to one of the great mills in Manchester. We were to deliver the wool to Liverpool and then see it loaded onto a barge to its final destination. Now being new to this, being a ship's master and owner, I did sell myself short, only just covering the cost with little profit. But, I did manage to pick up a cargo that needed to be brought down south and dropped it off in Plymouth. It was metal work for His Majesty's Navy. But time would tell and I was able to negotiate the contract to move the fleeces for all the farmers. Now having my father at my side, this would grow into a partnership that would last until he was an age when he could no longer follow me to sea and in reality, he became my conscious and would ensure that I did nothing that would endanger me and my crew from being killed, injured or captured by the authorities or for that matter, the many privateers that roamed these waters, legalised piracy through the government, but that's what a privateer was. We did on a number of occasions, come closer than I would have liked, stories which I will tell you later in this book. One of my many claims to fame and one that I am very proud of was that I did not kill any Revenue Officer, Injured a few and may be some seriously, but never killed one, although, there have been times when I wanted to. As for a fellow smuggler that turned Kings evidence to save their own neck, once more, I did not kill any but the lesson they learned was enough, such that they would not be able to do it again and certainly not enjoy the bag of gold sovereigns they received for their troubles. Best of all, no one and I mean no one, under my command got killed on any of my many trips. A few got injured when we clashed with the authorities and when this did occur,

I would look after them and ensure they were well looked after, ending up with a following of dedicated and reliable men with the understanding that I could rely on their help and support at any time and any place, and they too could rely on my support in times of need and trouble, and in certain circumstances and when needs must I would pay the doctor's fees if they were injured or their court fees and fines if they ended up in court before the judge who I always seemed to know, as they were all good customer of mine. Keeping my colleagues from the perils of the local gaol and in return, all I ask for was their loyalty which is not much to ask for such a generous gesture. Also, I paid the fines just in case they were tempted to tell all in return for their freedom and a bag of sovereigns. Although I must say, I had heard of one or two incidents involving one of my fellow smugglers which I found to be true and as such, we parted company after I pointed out the error of his ways. Yes I did organize a punishment or two but not as harsh as some would do, but they will not cross me again. Normally, a good beating would be enough to discourage any thought of double crossing me. On one occasion though, I did have to carry out one threat and we carried out a typical smugglers punishment and buried this person who shall remain nameless up to his neck at the water line in one of the many small bays along the coast. We left him there for about an hour as the tide came in lapping around his face and sometimes covering it. We did not leave him alone, we all sat up on the top of the cliff whilst eating and drinking and generally having a good laugh, but staying well out of sight, listening to his pleas to be released. Little did he know, we had no intention of letting him die, just leaving him there long enough so he learnt his lesson. That being, don't double cross me. When we thought he had learnt his lesson, we released him but not before asking him a simple question that he would not try and double cross me again, because if he did we would not let him go the next time. From that day on, he became one of my best and most trusted colleagues. I saw each fellow smuggler as a friend and as such, friends look after each other.

Not every trip to sea we made was for smuggling, most of the smuggling was done at night and if I am honest, we moved more cargo at night than plying an honest trade during the day. During the day, we moved whatever was needed, a cargo of gravel to London for example, in fact anything that was required of me up and down the coast and sometimes, much further afield. I could earn so much more plying such a dishonest trade than an honest trade and at the height of my career we would be using my little ships at least every two weeks for smuggling, where we would sail at night across to France or the Channel Islands and pick up a cargo or two, filling our ship's hold with whatever our financiers had purchased for us. At this stage in my career, we were not able to finance our own smuggling activities so we relied on those that could afford it and these people half the time we never ever found out who they were. We would always work through an intermediary, who would make contact and give us full instructions. The cargo would be tea, kegs of wine, liquor or tobacco. In fact, like I say, whatever the wealthy benefactors had purchased on that occasion. As time passed, I would gather a following and a very good reputation of somebody who could be relied on to complete whatever was asked of him and my wealth would keep growing, enabling me to start financing these trips myself and also, worst of all, taking all the risks myself. A lost cargo was an expense I did not want to bear and at that time in my life I could not really afford to lose. But at this moment in time, I had a wealthy benefactor who would finance my activities and it was them who would bear the losses. It only happened a couple of times, which was two too many. When it did happen, I would not be the most popular person in the village. Having this financier was in reality, very civilised with no risk to me except a lost cargo would mean no payment for me or my crew. But, there was still the risk of capture by the Revenue Cutters and the privateers. Like I said, I never knew who my benefactor was, but they must have had some money. In reality, I must have known who this illusive person was as I knew everybody in Port Douglas, along with all the gentry in the area and many were soon to be very good customers of mine. Somewhere along the line I would have met them and had something to do with them, but this didn't matter as if I did not know who they were I could not tell anybody, keeping them and their reputation safe. I had heard that many of the gentry and even people within the courts, like the magistrate, were heavily involved with the smuggling activities of the time, but due to their positions within society they must stay anonymous and their names must never be divulged, as this like I say, this would be their certain downfall.

I was soon to find the best places to land my cargo and also if needed the best places to sink a cargo laying just off the sea bed, ready to be collected later when the threat of being caught had gone. Not that I liked sinking a cargo, if the barrels were not sunk and hidden correctly, then the cargo could either be detected by a sharp eyed Revenue officer or if the weather turned bad before the kegs could be recovered, they could be lost, breaking free and ending up washed up on the beach, to be recovered by the authorities or even worse, picked up by the sea and smashed to pieces on the rocks. Either way, a lost cargo meant lost revenue, and I am sorry to say this did occurr to me a couple of times whilst being taught how to do it, an expensive lesson. Both times when we had not sunk the kegs correctly the line of 50-60kegs had floated to the surface and what bad luck we had, they floated to the surface just as the Revenue Cutter was passing by, they must have thought it was Christmas. The story goes that they could not believe their luck. Using grappling irons, they recovered the kegs and instantly seized them, taking them back to their bonded store. The second time was when there was an almighty storm and we could not get out soon enough to recover the kegs in time. We did try but it was too dangerous and they broke free from their restraints and many were washed ashore or even worse, smashed to pieces on the rocks and once more, when John Baites and his fellow officers did their rounds, the following morning, there they were just lying on the beach waiting for them. We recovered some ourselves but John Baites and his crew managed to recover about 30 kegs of the kegs which in reality, was about fifty percent of the amount of kegs we sank that week before. We managed to recover ourselves around 20 kegs with the rest being turned to fire wood as they smashed to pieces on the rocks along the coast. The smell of the brandy was noticeable along the coast that night which it would be with the quantity of kegs smashed on the rocks that night and it's a reminded us all to do our job properly the next time.

An expensive lesson in sinking a line of kegs correctly, there was defiantly an art to sinking a line of kegs correctly, not enough weights and the kegs will float to the surface and too much weight and the kegs will sink to the seabed and may get caught up in the sand and mud of the seabed making recovery extremely difficult. But either way this was a lesson learnt and like I said, an expensive one which we could ill afford to stand. But after a few more lessons from my father and ensuring all the future kegs, we brought were fully prepared to be sunk, all sealed to keep the sea water out and robes attached and even if we did not sink the cargo the robes would be used by the tub men to carry the kegs away, making good handles.

Chapter 12

It was on one of the many trips to France that I was to meet the girl of my dreams or should I say, this young lady, who as it turned out was to be become my future wife five years later, not that at this particular time I realized it or that it even crossed my mind but I will not forget that our first meeting. I can still remember that day as it was only yesterday in fact, this is one of the only things that I can remember that clearly. We set sail from Port Douglas late one evening. It was later in the evening than usual and our destination was to be the Port of Cherbourg where we had arranged through a mutual friend, a cargo of around 100 kegs of gin and wine, with a few bales of tobacco and a hundred pounds or so in weight of tea, all packed in bags that could be hidden in the waistcoats of the crew. If it was needed, we could move the tea away so easily as the crew left the ship undetected, but in this case, it would not be needed. We had an uneventful and slow trip over to Cherbourg taking much longer than usual with very little wind to fill our sails. In fact, it was a strange night and a worrying night, moonless and very earie, just the sort of time the revenue cutter would catch us. The whole trip I was looking over my shoulder thinking I was being watched and just waiting for the sound of cannon fire. We arrived at Cherbourg in the early hours of the morning, moored up along the quayside and went looking for our normal contact. We were first greeted by the French port authorities who noted our names and the ship's name, then asked of our cargo and where we would be going, which of course we lied about. Well we are not going to tell the truth are we. We bid our good nights and looked around for the person we were supposed to meet, but for some unknown reason, this time he was not here and in fact, nowhere to be seen, except waiting for us was a messenger boy, a small young lad that had stayed well out of the way whilst we were questioned by the port authorities. We had noticed this young lad earlier, staying back out of the way in the shadows watching us closely. When the authorities had left the young lad came forward introduced himself to us and then proceeded to convey to us instructions on what we were to do and where we were to go. Strange as it sounds it was quite clear. Within the instructions was where to find the cargo and who was to load it and where and what time we were to meet our contact or should I say, our well-dressed gentleman. We followed the young lad's instructions to letter and I must believe I was starting to worry if all this was a trap and we had unwittingly walked straight into it, still we gave it the benefit of the doubt. When loaded and fully secure I left the 'Valiant' leaving my father in command to watch over the boat along with our precious cargo whilst we went away to seek our contact who was actually an elderly gentleman a man of means and distinction, very well-spoken and very well-mannered. The instructions we had received had given an address in Cherbourg, due to the time available, we called a cab and gave the driver the address. We had no idea where we were going or what we were walking into. Was it a trap I kept asking myself. Strange as it sounds, my gut feeling told me not to worry, as all would be well. We arrived in about 30 minutes to a large house on the outskirts of Cherbourg; one thing I do remember was the large brass knocker on the very impressive black door, strange how you remember small facts even at my age. We knocked just the once and the door was answered by a man in a smart black suit I presume it was the butler as looking at the house which was very large and impressive. We introduced ourselves, in broken English he explained that we were expected and he showed us into what I must also assume was the drawing room, and told to wait for the master. Whilst we were waiting, I started to feel a little uncomfortable and a little out of place. Not being smartly dressed but in dirty working work cloths and after the trip over from England not smelling too good either. We did not have to wait long when our contact arrived. We had seen him many times before but he always came alone and unaccompanied. This time, accompanying him into the room was one of the most beautiful young women

I had ever seen, not that I had seen many in my trade. Women that worked at sea had muscles bigger than me. Although around Port Douglas, there were some very beautiful women but none with such smooth and silky skin as the one that stands before me. She was introduced to us as Charlotte, his daughter, in fact his only daughter, although he had a son who was away at present in Europe chasing a dream I believe. I was not good at guessing the age of the opposite sex but I would say, she was about twenty five years old but later, I was to find out she was around twenty two years old, two years younger than myself. Our eyes met and for the first time, I was speechless, yes me speechless, for the first time in my life. I tried to speak but nothing came out and I mumbled a few words of greeting and gently took her hand and kissed the back of it, not really knowing what to say to her. She smiled back at me with a small laugh. At that point, I was not even sure she understood me or spoke any words of English, but she knew alright and later, I was to find she spoke very good English. The old gentleman smiled at me and he knew what I was thinking. He took me to one side and we concluded our business. He then explained why he had not met me on the quay side so early in the morning. He had not been well and his daughter had told him to stay in the warm and not go down to a damp and cold quay as at his age, the damp weather was starting to play havoc with his joints. As for his daughter Charlotte, have you heard of love at first sight? Well that's how I felt each time I looked at her. I had butterflies in my stomach, something I have never felt before and I knew it was presumptuous of me that such a beautiful young girl from a very wealthy family would be interested in such a person like me, from a small English village and from a family that lived in a small cottage that would have fitted in her front garden, or more likely, in their front room. When the business was completed, we were duly offered breakfast which we gladly accepted as by now we were getting quite hungry so we were shown into what only could only be described as the breakfast room and a table laid out with more food than I had seen in a very long time. We did think of the rest of the crew and felt slightly guilty at tucking into such a feast whilst my father and the rest of the crew waited on board The Valiant, cold and hungry. Thinking of them I asked, trying not to be rude, if we could take some food for the rest of the crew back to the Valiant. Our gentleman called his butler in and asked him to speak to the cook to prepare a basket of food. Take it from me when we returned to The Valiant, it was gladly received. We stayed for around an hour, thanked him for his hospitality and then bid our goodbyes. By now, we were now running quite late so the old man very kindly called us a cab, and even paid the cabby, which we were very grateful for as we had little money. We headed back to the quay side as fast as we could to the waiting 'Valiant' and a very worried looking father and having been away for so long he thought we had walked into a trap. Their faces turned to the better when we gave them the basket of food, which they tucked into with smiling faces. Whilst they ate, I went on and explained to father what had happened and whom I had met. From that point on, each trip over to France, I would purposely seek Charlotte out and make my presence known to her. I visited her home on the pretence of seeing her father to discuss business but in reality, it was just to be around her. At first, she showed no interest in me but I persevered to the point where we became very good friends and she actually would ask her father when I would be visiting again. Let's be clear here, we were just good friends, no more and no less. Nevertheless, her father knew how I felt about Charlotte and most of all, he liked me. He liked me a lot, as I was to make him a great deal of money.

For the next five years, I spent plying my trade up and down the coast by day and by night smuggling. I took advantage of each trip to Cherbourg leaving the 'Valiant' with my father whilst I went off to meet Charlotte. Now father knew what I was doing and he approved of my actions. In fact, he encouraged me to pursue her. Trying to attract such a beautiful woman was no easy task. I was a lowly peasant in her eyes, living in a small house on the edge of the forest, whilst she was from a wealthy family and lived in a grand old house in a very good area of Cherbourg.

Father knew things were serious when I would change into my Sunday best, before leaving the ship to meet her and yes I even combed my hair and washed my face. I tried my best to look respectable before meeting her, which in the end actually worked when my approaches were returned. The time soon came when Charlotte would be waiting on the dockside, alongside her father and there she would be, smiling and waving to us, as I made for the dockside. I would make the Valiant secure before going ashore. At first, I would be greeted by taking her arm and kissed her hand, along with a smile, but in time, like I said, we grew to be great friends and I was soon to be met with a hug and a kiss on the cheek and then we would go back to her father's estate where we would just talk for hours or go for walk in her father's large estate. She even tried to get me to ride one of their many horses, something I declined to do, although as time passed, she would in the end persuade me to ride and if I do say so myself, I became quite an accomplished horseman. Whereas Charlotte was already a fine horse lady. When I realised Charlotte was the one for me in 1745, I plucked up enough courage to ask Charlotte to marry me, getting permission firstly from her father of course, who met the prospect of having a smuggler as a son in law rather interesting and not what he wanted for his daughter. He did make it clear he wanted her to marry someone who could have kept her in the manner to which she was accustomed but he could see we cared for each other and who was he to get between us. But many questions were asked about me and I sat for many an hour or two with my future father in law, explaining how I proposed to look after his one and only daughter. I explained to him in detail what my financial position was and where I proposed we would live together in England, and what I had in mind for the future with plans for my own shipping company. He was surprised and very pleased with what I told him. He then proceeded to tell me how he started out all those years ago and in reality, we were not much different. He came from a similar background to myself, with his parents being French peasants and he being a self-made man, gaining his wealth within the shipping industry and

I was soon to find out that his activities were less than legal, except his associates were much less forgiving than mine. We were soon to find out how he had upset them and had to leave France.

By now in the last five years I had made enough money to try and support Charlotte in the manner which her father wanted. In fact, by then my financial status was such that I had managed to buy a large house in England in the town of Port Douglas, more than big enough to start a large family of our own and as a bonus, leaving enough money for me to purchase my second ship, The Spruce, another large seventy foot twin mast lugger and so in 1746, Robert Bruce Smith Shipping Company was born. We started with two ships in the fleet and planned to expand to a third and maybe even a fourth and fifth vessel. The house I had decided to purchased was a fine old English house built in around 1720, the year I was born and best of all, and the main reason why I purchased the house, it was positioned ideally in Port Douglas with a full view across the town and the bay of Port Douglas. From here, I could see the comings and goings of my, by now, growing fleet of ships, along with being close to the only road in and out of Port Douglas, an ideal position to see and warn all of the impending arrival of the Dragoons or Revenue officers, as they galloped along the road to the Port or one of the many hidden bays in the hope of catching an unsuspecting smuggler plying his trade. However, as always I was one step ahead of them all as I had a system to warn my fellow smugglers of any impending danger. On the highest point of the house, I had a flagpole installed and when there was impending danger, I would (if I was home) go up onto the roof and raise the flag fully, letting all around know that danger was afoot. If I were not at home one of my fellow, compatriots would raise the flag for me. Warning at night was more difficult so a light would be hung from a point on the roof, normally a red light. If I was asked why a light was shining from the roof, I would simply answer with "to allow my captains to see their way into port of course, silly." The light would shine brightly and could be clearly seen from out at sea and I must say, a pleasing sight as you approached Port Douglas, knowing you were not far from your home and loved ones.

Chapter 13

The marriage of Charlotte and myself was one day I shall not forget, we were married in France in Cherbourg at The Sainte-Trinité basilica a Roman Catholic Church as Charlotte being Roman Catholic, on the 10–07–1747 at 10.00am in the morning. With the service lasting well into the afternoon, with the after celebrations held at, my now, father in laws home on the outskirts of Cherbourg. A celebration that was to be the social event of the year. Nothing was too much for his only daughter. Charlotte looked beautiful in her pure white laced dress with a long veil, carried by my nieces and nephews. My best man was my brother Sam, with the rest of the family all traveling over to France on the Valiant and the Spruce. My mother was not too happy at leaving her beloved country, even though it was for her son's wedding plus she hated being at sea . She would come aboard the Valiant when I was tied up on the quay side in Port Douglas, but every time I offered to take her out to sea on one of my, shall we say, more honest trips, the offer was always declined, much to my father's amusement, as he had never managed to get Mother onto the deck of any vessel, especially leaving the safety of land. My father got his best Sunday suit out and my mother wore her Sunday best dress. I have never been so proud of my parents, seeing father in a full suit is something I will never forget as he was always in his working cloths but mother well she always looked so beautiful whatever she wore. She took great care in her appearance and would always look at her best, even when she was doing the washing for her many clients.

Our next problem was the crossing over to France and getting mother to come aboard and leave Port Douglas. We made our way over to Cherbourg, two or three days before the wedding, thinking this would be easier than rushing on the day and you can never judge the weather. We packed our bags and made our way down to the Valiant and the Spruce. When we reached

the quay side, the crew in their wisdom had decided to deco-
rate 'The Valiant' and 'The Spruce' with bunting, what a sight
they were, we gathered up the crew thanked them. What a sight
it was, to see two working ships leaving the port decorated in
such a manner. We were on our way to Cherbourg and between
them, they all worked like dogs on the crossing whilst we just
sat around the deck in the Sunday afternoon sun and yes in our
Sunday best, doing nothing but enjoying the rest, whilst watching the crew run round the Valliant's deck. I was trying to tell
them what to do, until the captain pointed out that on this trip,
I was a passenger and he was the captain. Out of the corner of
my eye, I caught Father laughing to himself, to which he came
over to me and told me to just sit down and enjoy the voyage,
as I would not get much rest after I was married. How true his
words were. Lucky for us, the crossing was a calm one. It was
as though the sea knew what we were doing and gave us their
blessing with a calm and pleasant trip over to France, which was
lucky for Mother as I was sure she was going to be in a rather
sorry state, but she survived and actually, I think she enjoyed the
trip, not that she would ever admit it.

The plan was Charlotte and myself were to live in England,
in the house I had brought the year before. I had already taken
her around the house on one of her many trips to England before buying it, as I knew in my heart, she would be the one who
would share the house with me. It was a large country house, a
very distinctive house with a blue roof, white washed walls and
a large black door with a large brass knocker. In fact, not unalike
Charlotte's father's house in Cherbourg. It was situated on the
outskirts of Port Douglas. Charlotte had already seen the house
the year before and in fact, she was the one who persuaded me
to buy it and so I did, at a very good price of £1,500. I put a de-
posit of £700 down to secure the deal and paid the remainder
over the next five years with an interest of 5% per year until the
debt was cleared. The property came fully furnished apart from
some of those personal things only a woman's touch could add,
turning it into not just a home, but a home where we could live

and enjoy bringing up, hopefully, a large family, which, as time would tell was to prove to come true. Within the first five years of our marriage we were to have a family of six children, three daughters and three sons. On my side of the family, there is a history of large families and of twins, which as time would tell was to carry on into my family. We were blessed with two sets of twins, first to arrive was Elizabeth and Ruth our first born, born on 10-10-1748, followed by Roger Junior and Bruce, on the 28-03-1750 and then eighteen months later on 24-04-1751, John turned up only to be followed by Charlotte junior on 24-12-1752 at which point, we decided that the family was big enough, all healthy and wonderful children and all would grow up to make us very proud and thankful parents. Roger and Bruce in time would follow me into the family business whilst Elizabeth, Ruth and Charlotte would grow up and marry into wealthy families, whilst Charlottes farther in the end would have to flee France and come over to England to live with us.

We had a surprise one summer's day in 1760 when there was a knock on the front door and there standing on our doorstep carrying a large suitcase was Charlotte's father. He was looking a bit rejected and rather worried. We asked why he had not sent word of his visit and then he relayed the story of how he had to leave France rather quickly and there was no time to send word of his pending visit and more to the point, he was no longer welcome in his own country. He stayed with us for two years whilst he sold his house in France and wound up his business affairs, which I had to do as he was unable to go back to France. His past in the end had caught up with him. Like me, he was a self-made man and not everything he did was above board, even Charlotte, his daughter was unaware of his antics. It was a complete shock to her. He was persuaded to leave France or face the consequences by a group of less scrupulous men, which I later found out were his partners and you would not cross these men easily, or even at all. I did have a very good idea why he had to leave France so quickly although I never did ask what really happened, but let us just say never cross your partners and try to cut them out of the biggest deal especially when they too have heavily financed the deal itself. I must admit I was very careful how and who I did choose to do business with and who my partners in crime were. Although like I have said many times before we think of ourselves as 'free traders' and not criminals but you try and persuade the authorities otherwise, all we did was to make those few luxury items accessible to everyone and not just the privileged few.

The first few years of marriage was to be seen as what you might call, 'my careful years' where I would only ply an honest trade and let my crews use the ships at night for their own gains. I would finance the trips but take no part in them. I would only take a cut of the profits and also take the losses when a cargo was lost, not that this would please me and when it did happen, the men concerned would come to know of my displeasure. I dedicated my time to my wife and children, only going to sea on a trip that would bring me home at night so I did not have to travel far from home. But as the years went by, I became restless and yearned for the excitement of the chase, the outwitting of the revenue cutter and the revenue officers, in particular, my old adversary, John Baites. The sea was in my blood and I missed it. I was still making a nice profit and keeping Charlotte in the style she was accustomed to, but Charlotte knew something was wrong and she could see how I missed the sea. I was not depressed but I needed to be at the helm of one of my ships and not tucked away. Safe and sound was not for me. I needed that element of excitement. To try and bring some of that excitement back into my life, I decided once more, to expand my business portfolio and opened up another avenue to make money. I decided to become a wine merchant. Well, as a smuggler, it was another way of disposing of the goods, so on 25 June 1752, we opened 'Roger Bruce Wine Importers' Importers of fine wines. If only I knew then what I know now on how successful, this business would become and how good a business woman Charlotte would become, demanding the respect of the local businessmen and even me. I would bring in wine legally and then mix in some wine that I had smuggled into the country and as long as the figures matched on the manifesto then I was in the clear. Now I had many wine cellars dotted around the country, full of wine we had smuggled into the country. Now being an importer of fine wines, this was a perfect opportunity to clear the wine and make a good profit at the same time. So at night, we started to move the wine from its hiding places into the cellars of my new business venture and mixed it into the stocks we had imported legally. This also meant I could sell the wine cheaper than most others, as I was not paying the import tax on all of my stock, which at times would upset my fellow wine merchants as they could not understand how I was able to make a profit. They must have suspected all my stock of wine was not legally imported, but even this did not satisfy my craving to get back to sea so I had no choice but to go back to sea and my old tricks of an honest trade by day and smuggling by night. Charlotte was not at all happy at my new venture but she realized I needed to do it. I needed to get back to my old ways. So I left the running of the wine importers to Charlotte, who was to become a very competent business woman. I was able to leave the running of the business in her competent hands which took the pressure off me and allowed me to concentrate on my shipping company. She would expand the business and under her control, the business would grow to such an extent we became one of the leading wine merchants in the land, supplying wine to many of the gentry in the land and not just in this county. Charlotte was to become a much respected business woman. If only our competitors knew where most of our stock came from and if they did not, then they were fools. Our office for the wine merchants was next to the John Baites office which added that level of excitement. He knew what we were doing and could not stop it or even catch me. So above the entrance door, I had a sign put up 'Roger Bruce Wine Importers and Shipping Company'. This seemed to add to the excitement and aggravated John Baites as each time he passed our window, he would see me sat in my office and I would wish him good day and very begrudgingly, he would wish us a good day back, but he knew in his heart of hearts what was really going on and that aggravated him more. He could not or would not ever catch me, but not for the want of trying and for that I had to admire his dedication and perseverance.

My two sons, Roger and Bruce when they grew up, were to enter the family business, whilst Roger was no seaman, he was to join his mother and help with the import and export of wine and truly become an excellent businessman in his own right. My other son, Bruce, like me, loved the sea and was to become an apprentice on one of my two vessels, with the aim of learning the ropes and then in time, become master of the Spruce. He also had the blood of a smuggler in him and a good one at that, like father like son, or should I say like grandfather, like father like son. His grandfather used to tell Bruce stories of the smugglers that worked these coasts, in fact, they were the same stories he used to tell me when I was a child. I am sorry to say Charlotte, his mother, did not approve of me going smuggling, let alone the seed being planted in her son's mind of these great exploits of the smugglers, which I am afraid to say, were not as colourful or exciting as father would make out. However, by the time he grew up, smuggling as I knew it, became a dying trade, with the government realizing just how much revenue was being lost due to the smugglers, that they were to relax the taxation on much of the goods being imported illegally into the country. This would make smuggling a less profitable trade and as such a dying trade. As Bruce grew up, he would always want to join me on my trips to Cherbourg or the Channel Islands, and on the trips to Cherbourg before his grandfather had to leave France in such a hurry he would leave the ship and waiting on the dockside was his grandfather.

Now Bruce was about four years old when I went back to sea, not that Charlotte wanted me to. She wanted me to carry on with the Wine Merchants but as I explained, sea was in my blood and it was calling me back. I think she was more worried about me being caught smuggling, having seen what happens to other families after their husbands or partners had been caught and sentenced to a term in the local gaol or even worse to be impressed into His Majesty's Navy. The only comforting factor if I was caught was that I had the money to pay the fines. I think my wife was worried what it would do to the reputation of the business we were gradually building up.

By now, my name was appearing again and again within the revenue officers' log books and my reputation was starting to spread throughout the county and far beyond. A reputation one could be proud of, of a fair but not so honest seaman, one that could be trusted and relied on and most of all, one that has never and would never, harm or kill anybody, well not myself anyway, but I might well have given the orders, and yes I had many disagreements and yes we had our close meetings where a few times, I came close to actually being captured, much closer than I would have liked and yes some of the revenue officers would have reaped the benefits of my imports and export business. I recall one such incident when we appeared to be cornered by the authorities. My father and myself were making our way back to Port Douglas late one night, along the coast road. If I remember, we had been organizing the movement of about one hundred kegs of wine, all destined for my wine cellars when we were met by our friend John Baites and his fellow officers, with nowhere to go but over the cliff and into the sea below. It just so happened the area we had been caught in was by the entrance to a large cave at the base of the cliff, which lucky for us was a known landing place for the smugglers. Knowing the area well, we knew the sea was quite deep and safe to jump in. As a child, I had once or twice dived into the sea here because of dare when I was out with some of my friend's. So we turned looked at each other and just ran and leapt off the cliff into the sea below, having surfaced and checking for each other we swam over to the cave entrance and just waited, all we could here was the shouts of the officers on the cliff top who were looking for any signs of us. When the coast was clear and we could no longer here the officers on the cliff top we swam out of the cave entrance and onto the beach, wet through and laughing we then made our way home to a very frosty reception from my wife and my mother. I am not sure who I was afraid of more. We then both told the tale of how we had slipped the grasp of John Baites once more, only to be faced with a barrage of questions like "I hope they never recognised you?" Lucky for us it was a calm moonless night as things might have turned out much worse. I would not like to think what we would have done if it was a rough sea or even somewhere where we could not jump to safety were the sea was not deep enough. I was nearly always one-step ahead of the authorities and that was the key to my success of not being captured. Apart from a certain amount of luck and knowing my enemy and their weaknesses, all I had to do was leave a few barrels on the beach for the revenue officers to seize and they were happy. Although, once or twice someone new would take over and being new, he would have to try to prove himself, which proved to be very interesting times. Trying to find his weaknesses and his strong points and take it from me, each man has his weaknesses weather it's women, drink or money. I will always find out and take great advantage of it. Although on one occasion we had a revenue officer who I never did manage to compromise, that being John Baites, my friend and adversary. Whatever we did, he never did turn and change sides. He was a married man and we set a trap which involved another woman, but even that did not work. Whatever we did, we could not get him to turn a blind eye and in the end, he would become a major thorn in our side, but we did have many of his officers on our side, which was always useful when making sure we were always one-step ahead of him. Their task for a fair price was to keep us informed of his movements and plans and as I said, a few barrels would be left for them to seize and show they were doing their job.

As time went by the years seamed to sail past and my wealth just kept growing which enabled me to purchase yet another vessel. Smaller than the Valiant and the Spruce but still a nice clean and tidy Lugger. Once more, a vessel seized by the revenue cutter and put up for public auction the Bell brought at public auction in 1756. So now there were three ships in my small fleet, but the Spruce for some reason, was being watched and was being scrutinized more closely by the authorities. More than once, they came closer than I liked to being caught smuggling. So I decided to sell the Spruce and to replace her with a brand new ship, designed and built by my brother and best of all, to be named, Charlotte, after my wife, which my wife at the time, had no idea that she was to have one of our ships named after her and like my wife, she was beautiful.

My brother worked in the boatyard located on the mouth of the River Oxo just at the point the river emptied into the Bay of Douglas. It was only a small yard but he was very successful with their order books always full, which showed they were good at what they did. Un-be known to my brother thou the owner of the yard had decided to sell it and the price was right so I brought it and then gave it to my brother to run on the understanding he built me a new vessel. So now my business empire had grown once more and I was now the proud owner of a boatyard, which my brother had agreed to run for me. In return, he was to build me a new vessel that was to be fast, sleek and could out manoeuver and out run any revenue cutter in the fleet.

Therefore, I paid my brother a visit and we came up with a rough design. A two-mast shallow draft, sleek lugger, with lines that would be clean and tidy. The shallow draft was to be the most important feature, enabling her to enter much shallower water than most vessels especially the revenue cutters, giving me that edge over the revenue cutters, which would allow me to escape capture if I ever needed. I am sure one day, I will have too which as time would prove I did whilst being chased by a French privateer. We agreed the length seventy feet and a beam of about fifteen feet and a hold that would be capable of carrying about three hundred kegs of wine or whatever else I decided to carry. Fully loaded I would expect a speed of ten to fifteen Knots also I ask for a provision of an nine pounder cannon on the foredeck not that I really wanted to carry one but needs must when there was French and English privateers patrolling the English waters, legalized piracies that's what it is. 'Charlotte' took twelve months to build, starting the build late 1758, with his order books full I am afraid I had to wait, but what a vessel she was and well worth waiting for. The day came when she was ready to be launched. Charlotte came down to see the launch of her name sake. She was duly named and registered 'Charlotte' working out of Port Douglas and on 28 April 1760, she made her maiden voyage, taking a load of coal to St Ives in Cornwall, and by god, did she live up to her design. She was fast and handled like a dream. On my return we decided to sell the 'Spruce' and by chance, a gentleman from Scotland was down looking for a vessel to ply a trade between the Scottish islands and without too much ado he brought it and now the 'Spruce' for once is earning an honest trade unlike when I used her for a more dishonest trade. All the time I owned her, she was used for one thing, smuggling. How she never was caught and seized in that time, I shall never know. Maybe it was more luck than judgement or just good seamanship, being able to out run and out manoeuver the local revenue cutter that was a large and cumbersome vessel. Which was unable to turn into the wind like the 'Spruce' and then make a run for it? Although one advantage the revenue cutter did have was the number of cannons, which it did fire on us once or twice, lucky for, us their aim was poor or if their aim were good, I would not be telling you this story would I. The 'Spruce' would more than likely be firewood lying on the seabed along with her crew and cargo.

My small fleet now consisted of the 'Valiant' the 'Charlotte' and the 'Roger Bruce' a smaller vessel only 50' in length. I renamed her after my two sons, and with plans to expand my small fleet even further which in time would see me purchase another two to three vessels, all to be built by my brother and along the same design, as the 'Charlotte' and following the family tradition, would be named after my children.

Chapter 14

By now, I was 41 years old and spent most of my years at sea and most of which were smuggling contraband into the country at the dead of night onto some lonely desolate beach, and thinking back, I had the luck of the Irish, having evaded capture on more than one occasion. With spending most of my time at sea, my only regret was having missed out on my children's childhood, those years were the most important in their lives and I had missed them growing up. Coming home for just enough time to unload a cargo, go home have a bath get changed and then back to 'The Valiant' load the next cargo only to go back to sea, although I think and hope they understood. Well like, I say I hope they did. The only comfort was that each of my children along with my wife did not go without anything. Anything they wanted or needed, I would try and provide. All I wanted to do was ensure they missed out on nothing in life, to have a good education and the best start in life I could possibly give them, which hopefully, I achieved. We all have to make a few sacrifices in life and mine was to miss those early years of my children's lives. As I have already explained, the first few years of my marriage to Charlotte I did spend at home, but after that, I only came home when the voyage had finished. When I look back, I spent most of my life aboard the Spruce and the Valiant. The Spruce I used for smuggling whilst the other two vessels were used to ply an honest trade and after the sale of the Spruce, I would captain the Roger Bruce, another new ship that was soon to join my small fleet. The only time I would use all three vessels for smuggling is when one vessel was too small to bring in such a large cargo. Which so happened on 26 July 1762 when I decided to do one very very large run, as the quantity of kegs I was to bring in required the use of all three vessels, and it was supposedly my last act of smuggling, but alas, as always, it was to prove not to be. This run was to for fill a promise I had made to myself all those years ago, that I would beat the record made all those years earlier and land the biggest cargo of goods ever in the history of smuggling along the South Coast of England, and to go down in the history books. One point that must be made is that we must do this without being caught and nobody was to be injured or even worse captured.

Chapter 15

A new year and the start of a new adventure! It was 1762 and I was 42 years old, a time in my life when I started to take unnecessary risks. Was, I getting complacent, I asked myself. I think the answer to that is yes and the events that was to unfold over the year was due to me and nobody else. A year that was to see one of the biggest movements of contraband ever seen in on the South Coast of England in living memory. The idea was born the year before and now it was to become a reality, but resulting from that night, there was to be one problem and that being, my name would once more appear again and again within the Port Douglas letter book, bringing too much attention to me and my smuggling operation. Never would I be caught, and my name would once more be at the head of the list of suspects for the act that was to follow later in this year. Great rewards would be offered to anyone who could provide evidence leading to a conviction of anyone that took part that night and do you know the funny part of all this, this was supposed to be my last ever trip out as a smuggler. I was to become an honest businessman, so my wife believed anyway. Through the years, I have been asked if I would be interested in becoming the Mayor of Port Douglas, an honour which maybe one day, I would take up, but as you will see, it was once more a pipe dream that this would be my last trip and let's be honest, that was never really going to happen, much to the disgust of my wife and children whom at some stage of their lives would also be involved in the illicit trade intentionally or by accident.

Against my better judgement, I decided to risk my entire fortune along with my complete fleet of three ships. I must have been mad to put my wife and family through such an ordeal. The plan was to bring into the country 12,000 gallons of wine and liquor, involving all three ships and hundreds of men, all of which would stand to make a small fortune if the landing was successful. Each person involved knew what was to be expected of him. Men would be needed to unload the cargo from each vessel onto the waiting carts on the beach, whilst others would act as lookouts along the coast and inland, keeping a watchful eye for any revenue officer, especially John Baites, the local Supervisor who knew what I got up to, but never was able to catch me. I decide to have a network of lookouts dotted all around the area from Port Douglas down to the beach were the landing was to take place, such that we would have good warning of any impending danger. If any danger were approaching, then the lookouts would signal each other until the last man would signal the men on the beach. This would enable everyone to move off without making a sound. Melting back into the blackness of the night as quietly as they had arrived and evade capture. Then there would be the men who would transport the cargo away inland to a good hiding places yet to be decided. There was so much to plan and decide on, and all so much that could go wrong.

To aid with keeping the whole plan a secret and to stop any carless talk, I had my own methods. With such a financial outlay, I intended to involve as many people as possible, and by financing the landing this way, I limited my exposure to the possible losses and also, doing it this way, I ensured nobody would talk. Why would they talk if they stood to lose their share of the profits? I even managed to involve one of the local judges, as you never know when a friend in high places would be needed. A loose tongue would mean the certain loose of such a large cargo, and like I said who is going to talk knowing they could lose their investment, but even so most of my fortune was still to be invested in this supposedly final act of smuggling, as the cost of such an operation was rising well above my means.

Most of the wine brought into the country that night would end up in many of my wine cellars throughout the South coast. When ready, it would be mixed in with my existing stock, whilst the remaining cargo would be sold throughout the county and more than likely, taken up to the black country to a good client who already had his own clients, waiting to receive their valuable cargo, knowing what profits could be made and as such, eager to receive such a lucrative cargo.

The planning was meticulous and took many an hour to organize with secret meetings going on late into the night, with visits to France to purchase the cargo and then no mean task to find a safe place to store it. When we brought it home, I needed a person I could trust to oversee the removal of the goods from the beach head and off to a safe place. If anybody did step out of line, a special treat would await them and no bag of gold coins would be a saviour for them. With so much at stake, I decided to purchase the goods myself and made six or seven trips to France that year, just to set up the deals and purchase the goods, placing them in storage ready for that great day. The problem to solve was who was going to move the cargo down to the waiting ships. This task had to be treated with care and respect and most importantly, discretion with so much at stake. With so much being moved at the same time we did not want to bring attention to ourselves, as you never know who is watching you and reporting to the revenue officers in England. Now in my time of going back and forth to France, making these purchases, I had made a few less desirable contacts, all who knew who I was and who I was married to and in turn, knew who my father in law was. As time passed, it soon became apparent, these were the men my father in law had fallen out with, in rather a big way. Nevertheless, they held me no grudge and as such, I decided to employ them to look after what I had bought and when ready they were to transport the goods down to the waiting ships at a point were ever we decided to dock. All my transactions were carried out in the strictest of secrecy and trying not to bring attention to myself, although I did have the cover of being a wine merchant but even so the quantities I was purchasing was far beyond what I would normally buy and the merchants I was buying from knew that all too well. But luckily, for us, nobody spoke out of line or informed the authorities what I was doing. My cover was that the price was right and I was going to store the goods in a warehouse in France, which in reality was not so far from the truth.

My concern was the men that I had employed to look after the goods, like I said, bore me no grudge but they did my father in law and my concern was that they may use me to get to him. Although there were many questions asked about him too which there was many questions back on what he had done to have so many men looking for him, I never did find out.

One of the biggest problems that needed to be resolved was how we were to move such a massive cargo without drawing attention to myself. A procession of wagons and men on horseback that more than likely would be stretching for well over a mile, racing through the countryside at night at high speed was to be no easy task, especially without being detected. So for this, I turned to an old friend of mine a George Smith, a person of great reputation and a person who knew all the tricks of the trade of moving such a large quantity of goods in the dead of night, without drawing attention to themselves. He would employ all of the local farmers on route who would move their livestock along the lanes after the procession had passed by ensuring any traces of the passing wagons and horses had been obliterated. The farmers would leave their barns open and haystacks well stocked to allow him if needed to hide the kegs away from the prying eyes of the authorities. To help cut the noise down from the fast moving horses and wagons he would heavily grease the wagons axels and wrap all of the horse's feet with felt and sacking when going over the cobbles, and of course for all of this he would charge a small fee for all of his services. I was sure it would be quite a large fee. Looking at it though, he was taking a very large risk of moving such a large consignment at night without being detected or worse, being stopped. The details of how he was to do this and where he was to store the cargo was down to him. I do remember one morning, George and myself meeting at my house in Port Douglas were we went through the details of how he was to achieve his part of the job, when George started to relay to me how he was full of tricks and he told me of a trick he played on a local farmer. One night, he decided to move all the hay ricks in this farmer's field, then stayed close by to watch the reaction of the farmer the following morning. When the farmer came up to the field, he found all the hayricks had been moved and also grown in size. He told me of how the farmer stood in the field for an hour or so, scratching his head and had a look on his face of total bewilderment till he heard the sound of laughter and then watched George approach him from one corner of the field. The penny finally dropped and the farmer realized what was going on and how he was the centre of a very good practical joke. The two men then embraced each other and whilst still laughing they retired into the farm house for some breakfast.

The plan was slowly now coming together the last point to consider was 'when', when would we actually sail and when would I risk my entire reputation and fortune on such a reckless act. My wife Charlotte, by now, was hardly talking to me, actually she was not taking to me at all and I had been banished to the back room of the house to sleep and things were not good between us. As for the children, they soon realized what was going on and that I was to go on a great adventure, an adventure which could be my last if caught. Nobody but the crew of each ship and a few key persons knew totally what was about to happen. Even some of the people who had invested in the purchase of the cargo did not know the total extent of what had been planned and if they did, they might not have risked their money on such a reckless act. They were only interested in one thing, making a profit and not in the details of how they were to make it.

It was soon decided when this great run was to take place and a plan was hatched on how we would hide the real landing place by creating a very large and clever diversion. What we did was wait until we knew John Baites the revenue officers would be in the local Inn and we paid some men from the next village to go into the Inn in a slightly intoxicated state. After a few more drinks, they started to get louder and louder and then started to boast about what they had heard the night before in The Bell in Stroud and of a plan by a well know local smuggler to land the largest cargo of wine and brandy ever know in living history, thousands of gallons of wine and liquor along with a few tons of tea and a few rolls of silk. We too were in the Inn that night and looked casually across towards the revenue men and lifted our glasses to them they smiled back and in return lifted their glasses back. At the right moment we decided to leave, we got up staggering towards the door, I accidently bumped into one of the officers who in turn smiled and pushed me away. I apologised and made for the door. I stopped at the door turned back and shouted a thank you to the landlady who responded with her normal response "go home to your wife and children, you are in enough trouble as it is and you should know better a married man like you." As I left, I casually looked back to the group of revenue men who by now, were busy in writing something down. With luck, the bait had been taken and the trap was set. We were ready to go and the day had been set was the 26 July 1762. Remember John Baites, officers three or four were in my pocket and as such, on my payroll, so it was up to them to convince their boss what was going on, and where the diversion was to take place, which was now set to be Brandy Bay. We had told each one of them what we were planning and were the diversion would take place and their job was to ensure their boss John Baites knew this fact. If all went well and nobody got hurt, then each of them would be greatly rewarded, but if they turned Kings Evidence, they knew what would be awaiting them, as well as a great many people whose money was invested, would be looking for them. Remember the seeds had been planted that night in the local Inn when our drunken friends had very loose tongues, which normally would have been met by a severe punishment from our fellow smugglers. Something that really surprised me greatly was how quick word got round the village of this great landing at Brandy Bay and how it was to be the biggest in the south. I could not have asked for any more. As I carried on with walking through Port Douglas with a little smile on my face as I bid good day to John Baites as I entered my office knowing that soon I was to get the better of him.

One further matter needed to be arranged and that was to keep the revenue officers busy whilst we carried on undetected ten miles further down the coast landing this great cargo. I sat down with my Father and between us, we hatched this most ingenious plan. The location of the diversion was already set and that was to be Brandy Bay and here on the beach, we would stage a fake landing of around one hundred kegs, which would be full of seawater giving them weight, and authenticity, well no point in wasting good wine is there. So the night before I arranged for about a hundred or so kegs to be taken down to Brandy bay, filled with sea water and then hidden away just in land in the undergrowth ready to be taken down to the beach later that night and then to be left on the beach as though they had just been landed. We would also lay tracks in the sand as though a boat had beached and then unloaded their cargo earlier that evening. We would then leave the men on the beach to clear the kegs away and load them onto waiting carriages/carts ready to be moved off but mainly, to stay there until the revenue officers turned up, keeping them as busy as they could and for as long as they could, without being injured or god forbid killed. If something had gone wrong, I would never have forgiven myself for putting good men in such danger. But that was the key keep the officers as busy as they could and out of our hair enabling us to work in peace and undisturbed for as long as we could, and then at the last moment they would disappear and melt back into the night as though they had never been there. There escape route was well planned and practiced taking into account everything we could think of.

The time soon came round for us all to leave and prepare for our little adventure. We all gathered down by the quay in one of my many wine cellars and well out of sight of the Revenue Officers. After I had addressed the men, trying to instill in them, that no one was to be a hero and get themselves killed or injured, we split into two halves, one half after dark went down to Brandy Bay as planned, getting ready to move the kegs down onto the beach. Then, when finished they were to sit down on the beach and just wait for the revenue officers to arrive whilst the second half went to a small bay just around from Port Douglas, a very secluded spot where nobody ever goes. Now to keep everyone away from the area. the old stories of a ghostly figure roaming the area were made up and circulated around the village, the ghost headless of course. We told these over the last year and just to back the stories up I decided to walk through the undergrowth and along the beach, face whitened and hair whitened with powder and to add to the deception I would add a few moans and groans. I did on a few occasion disturb the odd courting couples who would leave screaming the gentlemen with their trousers down around their ankles frightened half to death. The stories soon got round of this ghostly figure that roamed the area moaning and groaning like a drunken old sailor, but it worked; nobody from then on would set foot in the area at night except myself of course who knew the stories were total rubbish and having spent so much time in the area, I knew every inch of the area like the back of my hand. Well I had to make it my business to know the area, as I needed to move around safely in the pitch black of a moonless night whilst landing such a valuable cargo.

One great advantage to this area was that the carts and wagons could make their way right down to the waters' edge whilst staying well hidden within the undergrowth. To prove the point beforehand we had gone down with a cart, parked up and then made our way up onto the cliff top checking as we went, nothing could be seen of the cart, I smiled to myself and turned to father exclaimed perfect and I made the point that nothing could be left unchecked or stone unturned. As I said, one of the main points for choosing such a place was the access to the beach, this allowed the wagons to meet the ships directly. With little distance for the tub men to move the tubs from the beached ships up to the waiting carts whilst at the same time staying well hidden in the natural shape of the valley and amongst the undergrowth. Speed would be our greatest friend here we could not want for more. We also chose this bay as it was big enough to run the three large ships onto the sand at low tide side by side, unload and then wait for high tide and with luck just float off again. Being sand, we would not damage the bottom of the boats, but still had to be careful not to become stuck in the sand. With the tidal rise and fall, this area should have been no problem. The tidal drop within this area was around twenty feet and at low tide, there was more than enough beach to land three ships. But, when the tide did turn, we would not have long before the bay would disappear once more to be claimed back by the sea, leaving just a rocky outcrop at the base of the cliff face.

The men working the beaches had now left, making their way down to their respective areas. It was now time for us to leave and set sail for Cherbourg and the start of a great adventure. We had stripped all three vessels of all unnecessary items trying to reduce the weight as much as possible but mainly to make space for the cargo we were about to pick up. We left Port Douglas early evening under the watchful eye of John Baites and of course after asking many questions on where we were going and what we were doing. After leaving Port Douglas and we were in open water, I signalled the other two vessels turned and made for the French coast and Cherbourg where our precious cargo awaited us.

I had already sent over my older brother Sam to Cherbourg a few days earlier, his job was to ensure the cargo was ready and waiting for us on the quayside, a quick turnaround was essential to allow us to be back in England at low tide. We would have just enough time to berth, load the three vessels and make our way home, but yet again I was once more in great trouble with my brother's wife and especially with my mother for involving Sam in this little adventure of mine. Therefore, I had to make one promise that he would not sail back with us. Never in Sam's lifetime had he been involved in smuggling and if I am honest, I had deliberately avoided involving him at his wife's request of course, and if there was any trouble, Sam would not really be prepared for such events. The last thing I would have wanted would have been for him to panic, start running and injure himself in some way.

Sam lead a life defined by his wife, he just did as he was told and lead a life lacking in any excitement at all and I was soon to realize just how much he envied my life style and wanted a life of excitement and if I am honest a life away from his wife. Now Sam over the years had begged me to take him on just one of my trips to France and in the end, I gave in and decided to use him on this expedition. So, I sent him to France with very strict instructions on what he should and should not do. However, I had to make a promise to his wife and most of all, my mother, who, if I am honest, I was more afraid of than his wife, who herself could be a very formidable opponent. The deal I made was I was to leave him on the dockside, pay for a passage home for him the next day thus ensuring that he was well out of the way and most of all safe from any danger. I would never hear the end of it if he was carried off and impressed into His Majesty's Navy or worse still, injured or god for sakes, killed. He did not know this and will never know what I had agreed with his beloved. Like I have said, his wife was a lot stronger, at ensuring he did, as he was told and even I would not venture to upset her or even dare to cross her. She was quite a formidable woman and certainly did not agree with my choice of career as she told me on more than one occasion.

As always the sail over to Cherbourg was uneventful and if I am honest, a little boring but luckily, we had a good head wind, which ensured we reached Cherbourg in good time but at the same time, we kept our wits about us and we all kept a good lookout for that elusive Revenue Cutters. However, as always, the Revenue Cutter was not the only danger that faced us as we crossed the channel. There were French and English privateers, yet another danger to keep a good lookout for, as they too would seize your ship and cargo. If you were caught by the French you would end up being taken to France, thrown into a stinking rotten French gaol and your ship and cargo sold to the highest bidder. All this was a form of governmental piracy and all above board and there was nothing you could do about it. Whilst a portion of the revenue raised would then go to the captain and crew of the ship that caught you. So, you can see the incentive to become a privateer, was led by the only thing that excites most men, money and what profit can be made. In a way, this is what drove me to become a smuggler, profit, along with the excitement and the danger. But if I am honest, mainly the profit I could easily make in one night and in one year, well this is why I am so wealthy.

We reached the French coast in good time and headed into the small port of Cherbourg and there waiting for us alongside the quay was my brother and a small group of men from my memory I think there was about ten or was it twelve I cannot remember not that it really matters now it may have been more. All I could remember was Sam had done his job well. I had given Sam strict instructions to be waiting for us quayside and to arrange a few reliable men whom we could trust to assist with the loading of the vessels and at the same time that could be trusted and to keep their mouths shut. If they did not then they knew what I would do, have their tongue cut out so they could never talk again. As we tied up Sam jumped aboard and came over to explain what he had arranged and where the cargo was being stored. At the right signal from Sam, the cargo started to appear from nowhere and the group of men along with the crews of the three ships started to load the three vessels, speed was of the essence and no time could be lost with idyll chitchat. I must admit I was impressed with Sam's, as promised he had everything under control and where the cargo appeared from well was just amazing it juts appeared. All three captains knew what was expected of them and ensured their own vessel was loaded correctly and evenly. Each member of the crew knew what to do and like ants they were running over the decks tying down the cargo as fast as it was loaded, making sure it was secure. As the last thing we needed if we encountered a storm was the cargo to break loose, as that would surely send us to the bottom of the channel. Sure enough as fast as we arrived, we soon found we were ready to leave. As promised, I found a small French fishing boat and it were agreed with its captain to bring my brother back to England the next day well after we had landed our precious cargo. This ensured Sam would be safe and well out of the hands of any revenue officer, especially the one John Baits who was rather a ruthless officer who took his work very seriously. Whatever we did like, I have said before we could never get him to turn a blind eye towards any of our activities. We did try on many occasions with many different methods we even tried to compromise him with a woman, a woman of the night who frequented the local Inn I believe. She had no scruples and helped us out on many occasions, but even that failed and he would not turn and change sides. He never did find out who was behind the efforts to try and get him to change sides.

Now to ensure Sam did not suspect anything when we were ready to leave I sent Sam ashore on the pretence of paying the men who helped us. Whilst he was ashore and completing our business we quietly cast off leaving him ashore in France and headed back to England a much happier person. Knowing what was in our holds would make us a very good profit. Sam, however, was furious at being left behind. He understood he was to sail back with me and to assist with the unloading. However, he was left in France to come home the next day. As we slipped out of Cherbourg, all we could see was Sam on the quayside waving his arms and shouting at us. Luckily, I could not hear what he was saying but I bet I was no longer in his good books. The only problem was, as we left the commotion on the quayside, we had drawn the attention of the authorities and all I could see through my spyglass was Sam explaining to this person on the quayside he'd been left behind, to which I just laughed.

We slipped out of Cherbourg as quietly and unobtrusively as we had arrived or at least we tried to, trying not to draw to much attention to ourselves and certainly not letting anybody know where we were going, but Sam had other ideas; well we did leave him behind on the quayside. We cleared Cherbourg and then turned and headed for the English coast and to the hundred or so men waiting on the beach whose job it will be to unload our precious cargo. As we started back to England, I started to wonder how the diversion was going. Hope of all hopes I prayed that John Baites the Revenue Officers had taken the bait and was heading at full speed towards Brandy Bay and those waiting kegs filled with sea water and not to that small bay about ten miles to the West were the real landing was going to take place. What I would give to see the face of John Baits as he opened one of those kegs they had just seized only to find it full of seawater. I know this sounds a bit childish but how pleased I was going to be able to get one over him 'a red faced revenue officer what more could I want'. I knew very well, if all went well that night and we landed the cargo then I would be a target, and sure enough, I was to be proven right. John Baites was out to get his own back and he would try every method in the book to achieve this. Luckily for me, I am always one-step ahead of him. Maybe it was the revenue officers on my payroll, who kept me well informed of his movements and his plans. As a reward, the two officers would be kept well with the bonuses they would earn if the information I received was worth it.

As part of the deal to keep the officers on my side, we would also supply them with the kegs of wine and liquor for them to take to their supervisor John Baites as seized goods, which showed they were doing their job. Not that they were doing their job. It was I, I was providing the goods for them to seize in return all they had to do was keep me well informed on John's movements and if they did not or they told me incorrect information then John would find out just how reliable his men really were. Yes, it was bribery, once they accepted my first payment they were in reality mine to do with how I pleased. The power over them was quite satisfying; in reality, they were just greedy men who had no loyalty or respect for their trade, and we had no respect for them either.

We seemed to be sailing for hours, well it seemed hours but in fact it was only about six to seven hours, I could not sleep how could I sleep with so much at stake and my mind was racing with different thoughts, I kept thinking what could go wrong. I kept going over and over the plan in my mind and playing out each part of the night's activities in my mind thinking what could go wrong. Would George be waiting for us? Will we be caught? Then I reassured myself that all would be ok which as you will see is nearer the truth. Then I started to question myself again, was everybody ready to accept such a large cargo? Had the bate been taken for the well planned diversion set up in Brandy Bay, but as always I should have known better and have had trust in everybody involved. We needed to keep a good lookout for anything and I mean anything so I placed two crewmembers on each vessel as lookouts and told them to report anything they saw to their respective captains nothing but nothing should be ignored, any doubt tell your captain. They were all told it does not matter what you think you might have seen or heard just report it, better to be safe than sorry. I could not understand, we saw nothing at all no other vessel not even a rowing boat, but then who would be out at sea at the dead of night in a rowing boat, only a mad man would venture out in the dead of night in a rowing boat and try to cross the channel, well apart from us. Anyway, we made good time and we would soon be seeing the white cliffs of England and what a pleasing sight that was to us all. Soon out of the mist rose the pure white cliffs of the South Coast of England, the word started to spread throughout the crew after sighting the coast of England and home. I turned to the crew and told them to keep the noise down. I took the spyglass and started to run my eye over the coast looking for that familiar landmark trying to see where we had made land. We had navigated our way over the channel directly to the area we needed to be and there in front of us on the highest point along the coast was the marker I had planted all those years ago on the top of Granton Hill, a pattern of six trees which if you knew what they meant would tell you directly where you were on the South Coast. I could not have wanted for better. We had managed to navigate our way across the channel and sighted land right where we wanted, what more could I ask for. I congratulated my captain for such good seamanship. I instructed our captain to head slightly east and try to keep out to sea as much as possible whilst I signalled the men on land. I instructed the cabin boy to signal the other ships and their captains to follow us into the bay when signalled. Looking carefully, for what felt like hours, at last I saw the signal, a blue light being returned. A red one would mean danger and to stay at sea, but no, it was blue, the signal to head inland and into the small bay. We had timed our landing perfectly, such that it was low tide which is what we wanted anyway. Being low tide enabled us to drive the vessels onto the sandy beach safely.

We had a small window between low and high tide in which to unload and then re-float the vessels, which then allowed us to move off the beach quickly and easily, and then head back out to sea. As we approached the shoreline, we saw what appeared to be stars in the night sky, but we soon realized they were not stars as they were moving. I trained my spyglass onto the shoreline. What I saw was a long procession of carts and wagons, making their way down to the beach. This transport would take the precious cargo we were carrying away. I thought for a moment, if we can see them who else can see them. I called over to the captain and pointed out that this was not part of the plan. The beach was supposed to be in total darkness with the only light showing being the signal for us to come ashore, a blue light. Looking closer through the spyglass I saw men were waiting on the beach. It looked like hundreds of them, all waiting to board these three vessels like soldier ants running all over the place, each one knowing what was required of them. We sailed in as close as possible then one by one; men jumped ashore from each of the vessels and grabbing the rope, pulled the three vessels ashore, allowing the unloading to start. The speed that the unloading was done was incredible and with such clockwork accuracy. These men had done this before and it showed. At this point we were at our most vulnerable, I posted lookouts on each ship with instructions on what to do, that being not to shout out but to find one of the three captains or me but to do it quietly and most of all do not panic.

Whilst all this was going on, Brandy Bay was turning into a very interesting place to be; with the bait having being taken well and truly and the whole of the local forces against smuggling were heading towards what John Baites thought, was to be the biggest catch of the year, and lead him to a promotion. He also, unbeknown to us, enlisted the help of the Revenue Cutter. All these forces were heading towards Brandy Bay. Oh how I would have liked to see his face when he realized he had been made a fool of, but best of all, little did he know, only a few miles away the real landing was taking place and we were offloading unhindered and undisturbed. We fooled them but we didn't want to get complacent, we had not yet unloaded our precious cargo and even worse, we had not moved the cargo away from the beach itself into a safe hiding place. Not knowing the revenue cutter had been called on was probably a good thing, as we must have only just missed him as we passed by Brandy Bay, on our way to our landing place ten miles further down the coast. The most worrying thing was we could not see him, but we were soon to hear him, as he fired his cannons inland and onto the beach.

To complete this part of the tale we now were only a few feet away from the water's edge and the three vessels had run ashore, close enough to ensure a quick unloading. The carts, wagons and horses were right down to the water's edge by now and only a few feet from the vessels and still on firm ground, well hidden from the surrounding cliff tops. All of which had been planned out and we had even rehearsed how we were to do it just the other day. By now I had left the Valiant and was looking around among the men for George. There he was up amongst rocks talking to one of his Officers as he liked to call them giving out instructions on what he was to do. I walked over to him and asked him to make sure all of these fires were extinguished. I do not want to bring attention to ourselves if we had not already brought enough attention to ourselves. I then proceeded to tell him we could see the lights for miles as we approached the coast. By now, the time was 2am and we were in full flight of unloading the three ships. Hundreds of men came over, forming a line with men onboard each of the vessels. For speed, we had decided to unload the three vessels at the same time, something we would not normally do. The process of unloading went like clockwork with men on board handing down a keg to the first man in the queue who in turn passed the kegs down the line to the waiting transport. Each wagon would pull forward be loaded, when loaded the wagon would move away only to have its place taken by yet another, this carried on until each of the wagons were fully loaded and all three vessels were empty. This seemed just too easy but I was not going to question the methods and means by which the unloading took place. The tide was now turning and gradually the three vessels started to lift off the sand and were once more afloat, free from the restraints of the beach. Now fully unloaded and the tide was on the turn we suddenly realized they were in danger of floating off, shouting a few orders more lines were thrown out and the three vessels were secured once more. We did not have long before the tide would fully turn and we would be on our way back to Port Douglas.

Within the hour the job was done, the ships were unloaded, all the wagons and carts were fully loaded with their riders and outriders in position and all armed prepared for what might lay ahead. These men had all been ordered to rest by George whilst everybody else worked hard loading their carts but their time would soon come as the night was young and what lay ahead for them would be a very gruelling one as there will be no resting until the job was done. Which may be a few hours away yet. George called his men all together and then told each and all where they were going along with where they would be stopping to change horses for fresh ones. When he had finished talking, he bid them goodbye wishing them a safe journey and then came over to me, we had a few words were I wished him good luck and gods speed. We bid him goodbye, he mounted his horse turned to us and tipped his hat in a gesture of goodbye and then galloped off at high speed to the front of the procession. What a sight it was, the procession must have stretched for over a mile or more with armed guards front and back of each wagon, outriders carrying a keg or two were also armed. The order was given to move out, gradually the procession started to move, after about 30 minutes, the last wagon moved off and the speed was soon picked up. The wagon train would now not stop until it reached its destination or to change horses with the last stop being the hiding place for me and my fellow investor's fortune.

All I could see was the burning light of the procession as it moved off into the distance. I then suddenly realised we were alone, just the crews of the now three empty vessels and all of the hundreds of men used to unload and move the cargo, had disappeared into the blackness of the night as easily and quietly as they had arrived, quietly and confidently just disappeared, how strange. There was an eerie silence, one minute the beach was teaming with men running around all doing their own little thing and now there was just us and the sound of the sea, lapping up the beach and slapping against the wooden ships' side. I then had a slight panic, thinking how will I get these three great ships off the beach, forgetting that the tide had turned and we were empty, so much much lighter. My thoughts returned rather quickly when I suddenly realized my feet were getting very wet and the sea was cold which made my feet cold. I turned round to see all three vessels now fully a float and no longer resting on a sandy beach which was a blessing, as we needed to head home. We all boarded released our tethers and carefully using oars moved the vessels back out into the bay. Relieved that this part of the night was now over and we had done it. We had successfully landed the largest amount of contraband this area had ever seen in living history. Our names would go down in history. I sat back on the deck of the Valiant, just thinking this was just too easy, had I been too clever and had the diversion on the beach at Brandy Bay really worked? Or were the authorities just waiting for us, ready to leap out of the darkness. What will they find, nothing, we had landed the cargo, moved it away and all that was left was three empty little ships in the bay. All they could charge us with would be hovering. Then it hit me again we had done it, we had actually successfully landed the largest amount of contraband this area had ever seen in living history. I started to laugh louder and louder and with a big beaming smile on my face, I turned to the captain and asked him to take us all home. We raised our sails, signalled the other two ships and then turned for home with my thoughts turning to that procession racing through the night, and how were they going to hide such a quantity, which if I am honest was not my problem but George's who was a master at such things.

May be he's going to use the local church to hide some of the kegs and let's hope the local church congregation when they prey don't look up into the roof rafters and see what's there, as this was a prime location to hid the kegs the roof space within in the local church. Thinking back, I remember about five years previous, the roof in one local church collapsed under the weight of all the kegs hidden in the roof space during one unfortunate service. It collapsed during the sermon I believe. I cannot remember what the sermon was about but I am sure it was thought to be a message from God, luckily no one was injured. A few of the congregation were knocked out though, but nothing too serious.

But back to us. As we headed back out to sea and home, reality kicked in when we started to hear the sound of cannon fire. It must have been around ten to fifteen miles away, it was very faint but we soon realized what it was and where the sound was coming form. This sent a shiver down my spine, was John McDougal in trouble and was he under attack from what we were soon to realize was the Revenue cutter. The Oak, was sat just off the beach in Brandy Bay. What we did not know at the time was they were only firing powder shots as a warning. We also had an even bigger problem. On our way home, we would pass by Brandy Bay. The only hope was that, as we turned, the headland into 'Port Douglas', the Revenue Cutter would be far enough in shore and would be so busy firing on the beach that they would not notice us slip past and into Port Douglas. But, my thoughts were still with John and his men or should I say, my men, sat in the middle of the beach under fire from The Oak's cannons. I just hoped and prayed they were okay and they had left the beach well before the firing had started. I was soon to find out they had not.

Chapter 16

It appeared that John Baites was so easily led and moreover so more gullible than we first thought, but never in a month of Sundays did we think he would involve the Dragoons and as we were soon to find out, the local Revenue Cutter. The Oak had also been involved that night which confirmed what we had heard and saw on the way back home last night. We had hooked John into our plan well and truly, in fact, much better than we could have even imagined and the best part, he did not even know that he had helped us that night. God I wish I could have told him the truth. It would have been worth it, just to see his face. Now as I mentioned earlier, the plan was to carry out a diversion. That being at Brandy Bay and sure enough, around midnight, a light was spotted coming across the heath towards Brandy Bay. Our lookout a young lad counted around 20 to 30 men, most of them in uniform, which meant they had brought out the dragoons from the local garrison. Following closely behind them was a line of wagons and carts. Maybe they were expecting a large seizure and maybe they expected trouble and trouble they would certainly get. I left in charge at Brandy Bay yet another one of my highly and most trusted colleagues a John McDougal and as the name indicated of Scottish origin and a very hard man to understand, especially when he was drunk. But the main thing was he could be trusted and he was a man of his word. As planned, he arrived on the beach with his men around 11am, moved all of the kegs onto the beach, as though they had just been landed. Then made marks in the sand as though a small boat had beached and unloaded the kegs. Hidden up in the undergrowth was around twenty carts ready to take them away, enough to move around 50–60 kegs.

We also placed a lookout on the headland near the mouth of Brandy Bay and sure enough our worst nightmare occurred. Spotted heading towards the bay in full sail was the Revenue

Cutter, the Oak, an old navel square rigger and its captain was an old naval officer on loan, along with his ship from His Majesty's Navy. This was something we had not bargained on or even considered. They would have been outgunned and certainly out manned and if a battle did happen, then my men stood no chance, and more than likely if the cutter opened fire with its cannons, they would be cut down like wheat at harvest.

By now the men on the beach had also heard of the approaching men from Port Douglas and the signal could be clearly seen from our lookout on the headland, notifying them of the impending danger approaching from the sea would side and if John McDougal had seen the signal, surely the approaching authorities would have seen it. When John realised what and who was bearing down on them, all hell broke out on the beach with John shouting orders to his men to take cover as quickly as they could, but where could they go. They could not hide in the undergrowth on the beach as they would be caught straight away by the approaching forces from behind them and they could not enter the sea as firstly, they had no boat and if they did, they would be blown out of the water by the Revenue Cutter. It appeared they were trapped on the beach and all they could do was use the kegs on the beach as their protection. Now John by now could see the Naval ship The Oak enter the bay heaved to and clearly see the gun ports open along the side of the ship and then without any warning, she opened fire, a full broadside. One by one a flash appeared from each cannon. John's heart stopped and he waited for the woosh of the cannon ball, followed by the explosion and then the screams of pain and suffering that would surely follow, and the worst part was the beach turning red with their blood, but none came, no whoosh and certainly, no explosion as the canon ball found its target. The naval vessel was just firing gunpowder. This was a warning and a warning that needed to be heeded.

I wondered if things could get any worse, but yes, they could. From the undergrowth, the young lad appeared and he started to convey to John what and who was approaching and from what direction. John's thoughts now turned to the safety of the young lad and gave an order that the young lad was to be taken home and away from this mess and to safety. As he gave the order, he looked up in time to hear yet another volley of explosions and once more along the side of the Naval vessel appeared a series of flashes the young lad by now was becoming very frightened, John tried his best to calm him down but without success. The lad by now was really frightened and starting to cry. John had enough to worry about without having to calm the lad down, but as luck would have it, one of the men on the beach, knowing the lad's parents and the lad well, took him in hand, leaving John to concentrate on trying to escape this horrific ordeal which was much worse than he or I had ever expected. Mr Baites this time meant business and intended to either stop the landing, or if he could capture whoever was behind it.

John McDougal's attention once more turned to the naval vessel, now anchored in the bay. A third volley came from the ship and by now the smell of gunpowder was thick in the air but luckily, for us no cannon balls fell onto the beach. John realized if he did not do something soon there could be no one left alive on the beach and John by now finds himself and his men pinned down on the beach under attack with nowhere to go. In our favour, Brandy Bay was very well known to all the smugglers. They could and have, moved around the area in the pitch black of night and still known where they were and even though they were now pinned down on the beach, they had planned an escape route from such an ordeal. Even though this would be a miracle if they escaped without anybody being injured. Luckily they did escape. John and myself had rehearsed these escape routes and that night was no exception. They would need every ounce of luck and good fortune. Except what we had not bargained for was such a response from John Baites. John Baites was determined to get his man that night and had used everything at his disposal.

John McDougal thinking fast, ordered his men to take cover among the kegs; they were no match for the firepower of the cannon or musket rifles of the naval ship or John Baites and his merry little followers. Swords and bludgeons were the only defence the smugglers had and they would do little against the men who attacked them. If they tried to fight their way out, they would be just cut down in minutes. John gave out instructions that there was to be no heroes. He did not want the beach to turn red with their blood or for that matter anybody's blood. Their job was to keep the revenue officers as busy as possible and for as long as possible, whilst the real landing took place ten miles further down the coast.

It was now nearing 1am in the morning and John Baites and his men were nearing the beach. John tried to be clever and outwit the smugglers. He decided to split his force into three and send a man to the headland to signal the revenue cutter that the attack was about to start and to send a force from the seaward side cutting off any escape route for the smugglers not they could have done anyway with no boat, I suppose they could have swum away. However, what John Baites had never bargained on was the ingenuity of the smugglers and John McDougal, their leader.

John Baites approached the beach and when he was about 200 yards off the beach as planned, he split his forces into three leaving a small group of men about 200 yards off the beach, hiding within the undergrowth ready to catch any of the smugglers trying to escape across the heathland. The remaining men, he split into two smaller groups, sending them to each end of the beach where they would spread out across the sand and approach the centre of the beach hoping to trap the smugglers on the beach with nowhere to go or hide. They could not escape seaward side as there would be a boat approaching from the cutter, loaded with armed marines. Where would the smugglers go thought John, right into my trap he thought and the promotion he had been promised would be his.

What John Baites had not taken into account was we knew all about his little plan apart from the revenue cutter that was of great surprise. I would have words with my friend in John Baites' office. That was something rather important they should have told us about. We had been prepared, with an escape route well planned and well-rehearsed, although at one stage John and his men were pinned down on the beach and their escape route had been cut off by the approaching forces. To our advantage though, he had spread his forces to thinly leave a few gaps for John and his men to slip out and away from the beach, which meant when John Baites reached the centre of the beach and the kegs of sea-water, no one but no one would be there waiting for them. John and his men left lots of signs of them being there, but nothing was left that could be traced back to us and with some luck, we were long gone and on our way home, leaving a very red faced officer on the beach surrounded by his men, something I would have given anything to see.

John McDougal gathered his men together and told some to start leaving as planned, our escape route out having slightly changed, due to approaching forces. The small group headed off towards the end of the beach, which was only around three hundred yards away staying under cover and well out of the sight of the small group of officers now moving closer to the centre of the beach and now the small group of smugglers. Having reached the end of the beach, they headed out along the headland till they reached a small cave which was only accessible at low tide which to the uninitiated, was just a small opening in the cliff face but to those that knew, this was the route to their freedom and escaping John Baites and his officers. This was the cave I got trapped in all those years ago when I was only ten years old only to find my father sitting round a fire with his compatriots. This particular cave was common knowledge between the smugglers and was used many many times to escape the Revenue men. The small group of men entered the cave one at a time keeping their eyes open for anything unexpected. When everybody was in the cave, they made their way to the back of the cave and entered the large manmade cavern. The cave was used mainly for hiding any cargo that had been landed and could not be taken away that night. The cavern at the rear of the cave had been made much bigger as a result of some of the stone being needed to build many of the large grand houses within the area. Now the cave was disused and forgotten, except by the smugglers that now use it for less honest reasons. The cave must have gone inland for nearly a mile, which was just as well as the exit to the cave, came out in the middle of the heathland and well away from any of the officers that may be hidden, waiting to catch any of the fleeing smugglers. By now it was nearly 2am in the morning and been a moonless night it was pitch black and one by one the men emerged into the darkness and the safety of the heathland and the road that would take them home safely and to a warm fire and a warm bed.

Going back to the beach and the small group of smugglers that were left, it was time for John McDougal and the remaining smugglers to leave. John could be now just make out the approaching forces from each end of the beach and could make out a small boat heading towards them from the Revenue Cutter. It's was by now between 2 and 2.30 in the morning and his job was done they had kept the Revenue Officers and Dragoons busy whilst the real landing took place further down the coast. Gathering the remaining men up and ensuring all was present, John gave the order to leave the beach. Leading the way they headed off into the darkness leaving the kegs of seawater to the approaching John Baites. They followed the same route as the men earlier; reaching the cave they entered one by one and made their way through the cave and home to safety, as the last man left the cave which was John he ensured the entrance was well hidden and could not be seen, unless of course you knew it was there.

John Baites by now had reached the centre of a very deserted beach, standing in the centre of the beach surrounded by about one hundred kegs of what he thought was wine or liquor he surveyed the area but the beach was deserted nobody but his own officers were on the beach. He turned to his fellow officers and with a bewildered look and a slightly angry tone to his voice asked them "Where is everybody? There should be men here? Where are they?" he asked repeatedly. He could clearly see from by the footprints in the sand that there must have been around fifty to sixty men on the beach and from the look of them they were fresh footprints, but there was nobody to be seen. How had they missed them? How had they got passed us? Questions he kept asking himself and to this day, he still has no answers, and they never ever did find the cave that allowed John Mc Dougal and his men to escape the events of that night. If only he had followed the footprints in the sand that night, he might have found them but he was so engrossed in trying to capture them that he did not give it any thought. Anyway we did our best to ensure that we did not leave any trace of where we going and more to the point after John Baites and his men had moved around the beach and among the kegs he could not tell whose footprints were whose.

John Baites turned his attention to the kegs on the beach and started to mark each one with a white cross, which signified they had been seized, and now the property of the crown. As he did so, a smile appeared on his face. Surveying the scene in front of him, he realized the size of the seizure and what this would mean towards his pending promotion. His thoughts of the men that had escaped him seemed that night to disappear, as he soon realized the size of the seizure and he had the evidence but little did he realize what was in the kegs.

John McDougal had played his part well in the diversion, but curiosity got the better of him and instead of heading home after leaving the beach he turned to his mate Bill and told him he was heading back to the headland to see what happens. All he wanted was to see was John Baites reaction when he found out what really was in the kegs. Bill not wanting to leave John on his own reluctantly accompanied John back to the headland where they watched the events of the night and what John and Bill saw that night will stay with him for a long time and he would be able to tell his children what happened and the part that he played that night. A tale that no doubt will be told again and again of how they made a fool of the great John Baites the local Revenue Officer something that I am sure John will be able to re-tell and impress the local ladies with.

They found a good spot well out of sight and with a good view across the beach. Making themselves comfortable they could hear all that was being said and they could clearly hear John Baites barking orders to his men to spread out and try and find the smugglers little did they know they were long gone by now and they would find no one on the beach. However, if they had looked up onto the cliff tops they may well have seen John McDougal and friend looking down on them laughing at their misfortune. All they could hear and see was men moving through the heathland just off the beach looking for anything or anyone that may be left and then reporting back to John Baites·that there was no one to be found, nothing and no signs of anyone having been here. John Baites voice rose a few octaves and we could tell by now he was getting really upset and annoyed, turning to the kegs he barked some orders to get the wagons and start loading them and get them back to the bonded store. Wagons started to arrive and then there was a flurry of activity as the men started to load the kegs onto the wagons ready to be taken away. By now, the Revenue Cutter was getting ready to leave their job done. As for the local detachment of Dragoons their Captain barked a few orders and in an orderly manner the men formed a line in twos and started to march back home to the barracks leaving John Baites and his men on the beach in total darkness, on their own and at 3am in the morning. John and his men felt a little uneasy at being left alone, there was only five of them left on the beach and lurking in the darkness could be hidden out of sight, an army of smugglers just waiting for that right moment to jump out and kill them all. But no we had no intention of killing or harming anybody, anyway John McDougal and his men were nowhere to be seen, more than likely most were now back at home in bed.

At this point John McDougal could not believe their luck, they had made John Baites look a right idiot, not only in front of his own men but in front of the captain of the Revenue Cutter and in front of the detachment of the Dragoons. We had out manoeuvred once more our greatest enemy and got away with landing the biggest cargo ever seen on the South Coast in living history, and only ten miles further down the coast, and best of all John Baites knew nothing of it. When he does learn of it, it will be too late for him to do anything. The cargo will have long gone into hiding or even sold on to its new owner, making all those that took part a very nice profit.

All of a sudden, there was a commotion on the beach and John's attention was brought back to the beach when they realized one of the kegs had rolled off the back of one of the wagons and been smashed open on one of the hidden rocks on the beach, but what was inside? Wine, liquor or seawater yep seawater. John Baites ordered more of the kegs to be opened and one by one the kegs were opened and in each one was found seawater they all contained seawater. John Baites just turned into a mad man, he went over to one of his men and took the axe he was carrying and started to smash open the remaining kegs and in each one was the same 'seawater', this went on for about thirty minutes the sight was something I would have paid dearly to see. John Baites by now had realized what had happened and that he had been made to look an even bigger fool, an idiot and in front of all his men. I could have not wanted for more.

John Baites still standing on the beach had by now had realized what had happened, with the look of surprise on his face he realized that this was a decoy and somewhere along the coast a real landing was taking place, he was angry, angry that he had been tricked and deceived. Where the hell was the real landing taking place, had it already happened and yes it had happened and yes the cargo had been landed that night and by now was well on its way to safety. His thoughts then turned to what was he going to tell his supervisors that he had been tricked and fooled into seizing around 100 kegs of salt water whilst somewhere else without any hindrance or interruption the real landing had taken place. He had called out the Dragoons and even the Revenue Cutter for what about one hundred kegs of seawater. Instead of looking forward to promotion, would he still have a job, which as it so happened he did, but no promotion ever came his way. The worst thing was he lost face with his supervisors and never again was he trusted without his actions being constantly questioned and reviewed. Now John Baites would have been the laughing stock of the organization and of Port Douglas as word was soon to get round on how he had been made to look such a fool and such an idiot.

John and Bill sat up on the headland and by now were smiling away to themselves as they bid their farewells and started heading home with a good spring in their step knowing they had done a very good job that evening.

John Baites called his men together on the beach telling them to leave the kegs where they were and to gather their things up and head back to Port Douglas where he would have to face his supervisor and explain the night's events, how he had called out the troop of Dragoons and also involved the Revenue Cutter to seize about one hundred kegs of seawater. This was a report he was not looking forward to writing. It would appear in the local revenue book in due course, with the real landing when the true extents of the landing became known. In due course, it also appeared in the local paper and even made the headlines on how the Revenue Officer was fooled in seizing one hundred kegs of seawater. He never got over this and it haunted him for a very very long time. It was even mentioned at his funeral.

It was now about 4am in the morning and I had just got home to my bed. I started to reflect on what we had done and I conveyed the evening's events to my wife who congratulated me, but was more excited about me coming home safely. We also reflected on the amount of profit that we were about to make on such a large amount of wine, liquor and other valuable commodities. Yes profit, the only thing that drives men and in this case, women, to take risks that maybe you would not normally do.

Chapter 17

That night's activities were to be the subject of many a tall tale of how one man 'me' with a group of unorganized and dishevelled men fooled and tricked the great John Baites the local revenue officer. That night's events were entered in the Revenue Book along with the true landing place. But the extent of the real landing was never to be found out, so there were many details left out in the revenue cutters report. John Baites was soon to hear of the great wagon train winding its way across the countryside that evening and then of the great landing in a bay ten to fifteen miles down the coast where three ships had beached and landed, all at the same time unloading hundreds of kegs and getting away with it.

A list was gathered of suspects, of those who were thought to be involved and in particular the ringleaders. Who were they and guess what my name appeared at the top of the list, although no evidence existed which linked me to the events of that night. John deep down knew who was responsible, and the hunt was now on to prove it, that I was the man fully responsible for that night's events and for making him look such an idiot in front of all his men and worse of all his superiors. A reward of £100 was posted for any information leading to the arrest and conviction of any of the men that took part that night. But like I have said many times, who is going to turn Kings Evidence, turning in their friends and anyway, many of the village had money invested in the deal and they all knew if they turned Kings evidence they would not live long enough to enjoy the money and the threat of what would happen to them was more than enough to deter them from turning kings evidence. The reward was soon to rise to £150 and then up again to £200, a lot of money and enough to tempt anybody. It was good to know I was worth such a great reward.

My thoughts turned to the procession of wagons hurrying through the night and I decided to pay George a visit the following week as I had not heard from him since the night of the landing. I also decide not to accompany my fellow seafarers for a while and to lie low for a short while and try not to bring attention to myself and to concentrate on the running of the wine business along with my wife Charlotte, which by now was growing into a flourishing business thanks mainly to Charlotte. Charlotte did not approve of my attention to the business, but when I explained my reasons why, she soon accepted them and between us, we made plans for the mixing of the smuggled wine with the legally imported wine. I also instructed my fellow seafarers to lie low as well and only to carry a legal cargo for a while, which of course I was to organize. Now we had also quite a few bushels of tobacco and few well nearly 100 yards of silk. The tobacco was no problem that would end up at the local tobacco and snuff factory as it always did. The only thing we needed to do was too slowly deliver the tobacco in small quantities as to deliver the lot in one go would bring to much attention to us. As for the silk, this would end up in London to an awaiting client, a dressmaker I believe, to the rich and famous if only they knew where the silk that make up their dresses came from. The liquor, Brandy or Gin would end up in the midlands and the Black Country. Messengers were sent to each client with instructions of how and where they could get their goods along with how they were to be paid for. When all was sorted, a messenger would need to go to George and pass on the full instructions of how he was to disperse the cargo and where it was to be sent. After careful consideration and a long discussion with Charlotte, I decided to deliver the message to George myself. Curiosity had got the better of me, I needed to know where the cargo was being stored. Anyway, I wanted to see all that I had risked my life and my friends' lives for, so it had better be worth it. To be honest I was more interested on how he had got on travelling through the night with such a large procession of horses and carts without being disturbed, but George had many friends to call on in times like this.

Now George lived around twenty to thirty miles away from Port Douglas along the London road. I sent word to George of my impending visit and that I would be around on the following Saturday morning. Knowing how long this would take to get there, I left nice and early on the Saturday morning, bid Charlotte a goodbye and headed on horseback out along the London Road. Now I knew how desperate John Baites was to catch me and I knew he was watching every move I made and even I suspected he was watching the house. May be now he was following me thinking I may lead him to the illicit goods, as if I would. I followed the London Road for around an hour, when I had this feeling I was being watched. Suddenly to my left, there was the sound of breaking twigs coming from the forest, my heart jumped a beat and a few beads of sweat appeared on my forehead, then out of the undergrowth ran a dear and ran across in front of me. A sigh of relief came over me and I carried on with my journey but still keeping a watchful eye for any unsuspecting person. I did stop a few times, looking back down the trail, thinking that I was being followed.

Thinking to myself, if anybody was following me, they would not be far behind me so I decided to hold back and check, finding a small hollow to hide in just off the Road, which by chance was a smuggler's hole. I bedded down and just waited, I did not have to wait long when in the distance there he was John Baites the revenue officer. Keeping my head down but at the same time keeping John well in my sights he passed me by not realizing that I was only feet from him, watching him as he rode passed. When John had disappeared off down the road and round the corner and out of sight, I left my hiding place mounted my horse and started following him but keeping my distance and staying well out of sight. Knowing the forest well I knew of another track that led through the forest but on a parallel path to the main road and looking at the state of the path very rarely used. Doing this I could keep John well within my sights, I could see him but he could not see me. I had been riding now for quite a while and I had no choice but to re-join the main track through the forest, as I had to find a marker, a marker, which indicated the point I need to turn off to find George and where he lived. It was not long after re-joining the main track that I came across a marker, a large pile of rocks very purposefully placed and this was the point I needed to leave the main road. I rode down this narrow looking track which after about ten minutes, which opened out into a very well kept drive way. I carried on riding for about five minutes and there through the trees came into view was a rather large house or should I say mansion. Which made me stop and think 'was I in the right place or had I taken a wrong turning not thinking that George was that wealthy or even that he had a title and owned such a place.

As I drew closer to the house there outside the house was a horse and carriage with George just getting out, seeing me he jumped down and came over to greet me. He actually seemed rather pleased to see me. This was his home. How I had misjudged him. The house itself was rather grand with a large flight of steps that reached down from the front door and each side of the steps was two large ornate pillars, which reached up and held the canopy above. I was soon to find out that George was a Lord, a Lord that was involved heavily with the likes of me. He turned to his groom who was tending the horses and carriage and told him to take my horse, I dismounted passed the groom the rains and headed off with George into the rather large and palatial house. I turned back to look across the grounds from the front of the house. There was nothing out of place, the lawns were beautifully tended and in the centre of the main lawn was the most beautiful fountain with a large statue in its centre, spouting water into the surrounding pond and the pond itself was filled with the most colourful fish I had ever seen. We entered the house and his butler approached us. George addressed him as James and asked him to show me into drawing room. George turned back to me and told me he would be with me in a minute, he just wanted to get changed and freshen up. Leaving me, he went upstairs only to re-appear in about ten minutes through another door across the other side of the room, which at first glance just looked almost like any other wall in the room. George could see the surprise on my face and he explained in his line of work he needed many methods of escape from whoever might come his way and as such had built a few hidden passages and escape routes with hid a way's throughout the house. He explained he could move around the house without anyone seeing or hearing him and he could leave the house through a hidden tunnel in the cellars coming out somewhere in the local area, not that he was going to tell me were the tunnel came out. But there were many stories of tunnels leading up to the local church and also beyond to the Inn within the village of Barn's about two to three miles down the road, maybe they are true and they all start somewhere here, still who knows and for that matter who cares. George discovered these tunnels when he was a lad and used them extensively when he wanted to leave the house without being noticed. He was soon to discover they were in reality servant's tunnels used by the servants to move around the grounds of the great house such that their masters were not disturbed by the lower classes. The fact that they could not survive without us lower classes as they put it is another matter. George thou was, to have these tunnels extended and made bigger to allow the free movement of goods and men without being disturbed.

We settled down to discuss that evening's activities and how things had gone and more importantly, where the cargo was stored. George went onto explain how he like me hated John Baites and like me would do anything, he could to get one over on him and make him look a fool. He and I were more alike than I realized, like me, he was an adventurer and liked the thrill of the chase and evading capture the game of cat and mouse. George went onto explain how he had three of the four revenue officers under John Baites in his pocket which surprised me as I too was paying them for information and assistance as and when required, like that night. This is how my men had escaped John Baites they had been paid to let my men go but it looked like they had been paid twice, once by me and once by George. No wonder they were so eager to help. Most of all they aided in keeping John Baites away from the true landing place. When I told, George they were also in my pocket this brought a smile to his face. Therefore, these men must be making a small fortune and are making fools of us. George promised to sort this small matter out and we came to an agreement that only one of us would pay these men and we would join our forces against the common enemy John Baites.

George rose and made his way over to the fireplace and pulled the servants cord, with that James suddenly appeared and came into the room, George turned to him and very politely asked him to get cook to make some tea and send up some of her rather good cake. With that, James left the room only to return a little later with a large silver tray on it a large pot of tea and as requested a tray of rather good looking cakes. We sat back down, drank our tea, and ate the cake and I must admit George was right it was good cake. George could see I was enjoying it and he told me how his cook was famous in the area for her cakes and had won prizes at the local village fate. I looked across at George and just asked was this some of the tea we imported that night? Looking back his reply did not surprise me; yes, I hope you do not mind I took a couple of pounds for myself. Without thinking, I replied with 'No I don't mind as long as it cannot be traced back to us and really I think you earned it, but make sure no one knew where it came from. Which surprised George rather, I am very careful I mixed it in myself with tea we already have in the house; I did this personally ensuring no one suspected the origin of the tea.

George proceeded to tell me how he got on that night and most of all where the cargo was being stored. George told me how he travelled through the night without meeting anybody or any trouble finding him. He explained how he used the local farmers to hide his tracks by allowing them to move their livestock along the tracks he had just passed along even though it was at night. Like me, he could not understand how easy it was, but who is complaining we had managed between us to land the biggest cargo ever on the South Coast in living memory. The only thing we could think was that the revenue officers on our payroll had done a great job in keeping the formidable John Baites well away from the bay. A bonus had to be paid to these friends of ours which I agreed I would do.

On finishing our tea and cake, George decided to show me were the cargo was stored. On questioning him, it turned out that there was a very large cellar very well hidden on his estate and his estate was many thousands of acres so it would be like looking for a needle in haystack. The complete cargo was stored there which did worry me a little, to know the complete cargo was being stored in the same place. He explained that he had organised the local farmers to ensure the haystacks were well stocked and the barns were left open, just in case they would be needed to store a keg or two.

George pulled the servants cord once more and instantly James re-entered the room. George asked him to get the groom to prepare his horse as he was going for a ride across the estate and to bring it round the front of the house, along with my friend's horse. I rose and walked over to the window talking to George as I gazed out over the front of the house. George then explained this was his country estate and had been in his family now for about two hundred years and that he also had a London residence, which he uses only now and then spending most of his time here at his country estate. We carried on talking as James came back into the room and informed his master that the horses were ready and out the front of the house. We thanked James and headed out to the horses. As we left the house by the front door, I thanked George for the tea and cake and I told him it made a change to stop for a moment, as my life is a permanent merry go round where I seemed never to have time to just get off and rest a while.

We mounted our horses and at a gentle walk we left along the main driveway turning off and headed out onto his estate, we carried on at a walking pace for around thirty minutes until we came across a rather dense wooded area and George stopped and dismounted. We tied our horses to one of the trees and we headed off into the wooded area we walked for around ten minutes when we came across a clearing and there to one side of the clearing was a set of steps leading downwards to a door a rather plain door nothing interesting or memorable. What a strange place to find a set of steps in the middle of nowhere, in the middle of a forest. We made our way down the steps and George took a key from his pocket opened the door and there laid out in front of me was the cargo that had caused me so much heart ache and worry for the last few months. I then realized and it finally hit me, seeing all of the kegs laid out in front of me like that. We had done it, we had landed one of the biggest cargos ever and best of all, fooled and made John Baites look a right idiot in front of many important people. He will not cause us much trouble now for many a month or two or that's what we thought.

George lit a lantern and hung it in the centre of the cellar and the light shone throughout the cellar and we just sat there on one of the kegs looking at what we had done. We must have sat there for I do not really know how long. George asked me how I wanted the cargo moved on from here brought me back to reality. I started to explain were and I how wanted the cargo moved, all of the wine was to be moved gradually into my own cellars across the South Coast and I would notify him when and where it was to be moved. The liquor 'Brandy and Gin was to be moved straight away to the Black Country and an awaiting customer, he would be advised when and where to take it. The tobacco was to go to the local tobacco and snuff factory and that could be moved whenever he wanted to, as the client was waiting for it but in small quantities and not as the customer requested, too much in his cellars and that could bring attention to us which we could do well without. I went onto explain how the current owner was a good customer of mine but also that he was an impetuous man and did not consider the implications of what would happen to him if he was caught with smuggled goods, goods that did not match his manifest.

We turned and left the cellar ensuring it was locked and the entrance hidden. George then told me the cellar had been there for a hundreds of years and was in fact, the only remaining evidence of the original country estate, which was destroyed by a fire and demolished about a hundred years earlier and as such, was a good place to hide away anything you wanted to lose.

We headed back to the house, reaching the driveway I bid my farewells, we parted company and I headed back down the driveway to the London Road, and George headed back up to his country estate. On reaching the London Road, I turned and headed back to Port Douglas and my waiting wife and children.

As I rode home, I started to think about John Baites and his obsession with trying to find out who was behind the actions of that night and what he would do next. As the year progressed, I soon found out.

Chapter 18

For the remaining part of the 1762, we decided to lie low and I concentrated on the legitimate side of my business. I used all three of my vessels to move cargo up and down the coast with the odd trip over to France taking a cargo of wool and leather, all above board of course. Well we say legitimate, apart from the few yards of silk I was asked to bring over from France for a friend whose daughter was getting married and needed to have a wedding dress made for her, which I did not charge him for. Call it my wedding present to the lovely couple. The few pounds of tea for myself of course all of which had to be smuggled into the country, which was not that difficult really. The tea was packed into special tunics we had made with compartments sewn in them, to hide a few packets of tea and once loaded, you just walked off the ship and walked home with the tea hidden on yourself. As for the silk that was a little more tricky. I needed a quick and easy way of getting the silk off the ship before the searchers came on-board. For that, I employed the services of a young lady from the Bell, who would turn up when we had docked. She would go in to my cabin take her dress off and then wrap the silk around her body and then just put her dress back on and yes she did look a bit fatter but nobody noticed. Then she too would just walk off the ship and head back to my house where she would take her dress off again and unwind the silk from around her body, easy really, when you know how.

It was strange how everybody in the village came to me when their daughters were getting married. Do not forget we were still wine merchants, which Charlotte ran, and gradually, over time, we moved at night more and more of the smuggled kegs, into our wine cellars. Then of course started to sell the wine much cheaper than anyone else but still making a very nice level of profit and at the same time upsetting our competitors, who could not understand how we made any profit. Nevertheless, we had made enough money for me now to make two new purchases. One being a fourth vessel which like the 'Charlotte' I asked my brother to build and was to be named the 'Elizabeth Ruth'. She was to be launched the following year, around December of 1763 and I also decided to purchase yet another business, I decided to go into the tobacco and snuff industry. This was just another way to dispose of the tobacco I imported into the country more easily. You see each time I purchased a business or a property there would always be a reason, with the Tobacco factory this would assist me with my import and export business and the disposal of goods effectively.

I had heard through the grape vine that the local tobacco and snuff factory was to be placed up for sale so I approached the owner made him an offer he could not refuse which he duly accepted and so within the week I had added once more to my business empire. Not sure who was to run the business thou and if I am honest I had not really given it much thought. Therefore, I decided to ask the current owner if he would run it for me for the time being, until a more permanent arrangement could be made. I am pleased to say, he refused my generous offer so I once more turned to my eldest brother and offered him the chance to run the business which I am very pleased to say he accepted. So Sam became my partner or should I say my partner in crime, much to his excitement and to the anger of his wife who just thought I was going to lead her Dear husband astray which I had no intention of doing. Do I look that stupid to upset his wife who probably would knock me out with one punch? Sam's wife was built like one of my crew and had muscles where ladies should not, and I was sure she would fare well aboard the Charlotte as a deckhand, and give any of my crew a good run for their money.

In the meantime, the hunt was still on to find any information that would bring to justice those who were responsible for that nights landing, and I must say I was very pleased to see the how much they valued my head. The final reward was raised to £200 for any information that would result in the capture of anyone involved in that night's activities. Although I was not named on the poster, it was obvious who it was aimed at, and how little they knew of just how much my involvement was in that night's activities. Nobody come forward that year or for that matter any year as there was so many people involved with so much money invested in the deal who's going to put all that at risk. So John once more, was beaten into submission and in reality, he never really recovered from the embarrassment and humiliation of that night and if I am honest, I started to feel sorry for him. It was like he was a broken man with no purpose in life. We had taken this man and ruined him, which was nothing to be proud of, but many did celebrate.

Over the remaining part of 1762 and all through the following year of 1763, we gradually moved all the wine into our cellars mixing them into our general stock. The tobacco ended up into what soon was to become my tobacco and snuff factory and all of the liquor, brandy and gin, ended up being moved under the watchful eye of George up country to Birmingham and the Black Country. The tea was split up, some went to my own cellars and some ended up in George's cellars as part payment for his work that night, the remaining was sold on. In all a tidy profit was made by all with my share, being used to expand my growing business empire and a small amount was used to purchase a small gift for my wife Charlotte. A piece offering, as Charlotte was still not really talking to me. I Knew how to get back into her good books, I bought her a foal not just any foal but a stallion of great breading and knowing how she loved to rid every morning before breakfast I thought this would bring her round to me and forgive me. Therefore, I arranged the foal to be delivered one Sunday morning early and when she saw the foal, she smiled and turned to me and kissed me on the cheek. I knew that at that point, she had forgiven me. Charlotte named him George I thought a strange name for a horse but hey it was her horse. She cared for that horse, nurtured it when it was ill she never left his side to the point they were inseparable. I never forgot the day that horse died you would think her world had ended but me being me, bought her another horse once more not just any horse but one of Georges off springs one that he had fathered two years before, so George lived on.

Getting back to John Baites and his efforts to find the culprits, which I could not believe how the hunt for the culprits of that night had become an obsession with John Baites. The way he had handled the situation that night had already heavily damaged his prospects and his rise through the ranks of the revenue office and most of all he knew it. He was now destined to end his days in Port Douglas, as a supervisor and any chance of promotions were lost. He was now on borrowed time in the eyes of his supervisors and unless he found some evidence or even better, someone who was responsible for that night activities he was more than likely going to lose his job. Not only had he lost face with his superiors but also, he had brought the office of revenue group into disrepute.

He tried many different methods to get people to talk, threats, money with rewards that kept rising, which was good to see I was worth so much. The strange thing was he knew all along who had done it, but could never prove it, and on one occasion when we met in the street just outside the local school he actually told me as much. John openly asked me how I had done it and then went on to congratulate me on such a well-planned and executed job. Of course I thanked him for the complement but told him I knew nothing about what he was talking about and that I was no more than a man that owned a few ships plying and honest day's work, and at all times trying my hardest to keep a straight face.

By the end of 1763, John Baites started to give up trying to find the culprits so making up his report and completed the two entries in the great revenue letter book. One for the landing at Brandy Bay, which he of course attended and by chance, he learnt of the location of the true landing. So an entry appeared in the book with many gaps, which he stood no chance of filling in, and to this day there was only speculation on how much was landed that night, but I knew the answer to that question.

Therefore, from that point onwards John Baites even though he officially had closed the investigation would not leave me alone and increased his attention to my every move. John Baites became my shadow; wherever I went, he would appear. So I decided for the next few months, which in the end actually turned into around two years to leave the smuggling to someone else. Except I did keep my hand in by financing the odd trip or two, but not actually taking the risks of going out at night smuggling.

As for John, he was soon too got bored again and in the end left me alone to get on with my life although it did take a few months. In that time I had decided to stay in my warm bed at night with my dear wife who I must admit was rather relived, I was at home, even thou I was getting under her feet and interfering with the wine importers. I still needed to keep my head down thou. Being the financier I still was able to make a small profit, and that kept me involved to some degree and the excitement and the thrill was still there even if slightly subdued, most of all I still felt I was part of the gang. I must admit I did not make as much profit as I would have liked and a lost cargo would fall totally to me. A financial loss I could ill afford at present and the client was normally waiting to receive his goods which if it was lost at sea he got nothing as well.

1763 to 1764, I lost a tidy profit and my men knew it, as they were not paid for their troubles. During that time, also tragedy was to be fall Port Douglas not only was one crew not paid but the captain and his crew of that ship lost their lives to the sea. It was not in of my ships but a very good friend, which did not make the loss any easier, or the fact they were on my business and working for me at the time.

The year 1763 passed by and 1764 came and like I said I stayed at home until late 1764 when I decided to travel over to the Channel Islands in my new ship the 'Elizabeth Ruth'. She was less than a year old and named after my daughters and the sister ship to the Charlotte', another beautiful and fast ship. Her cargo this trip was gravel destined for a client building a large country house and on our return journey; we were to bring back two hundred kegs of wine for our cellars, which by new was starting to run low. We needed to re-stock our cellars with some legally imported wine, which would allow us to mix in the smuggled wine without being detected. Whilst in the Channel Islands my job was also to meet my agent on the island and get them to purchase around three hundred kegs of wine and around fifty kegs of Brandy and a few pound of tea. The tea was for me and the wine was to replenish my gradually emptying wine cellars, not my main cellars but those which nobody knows about and yes this particular purchase was to be smuggled into the country later this year. I had the tea packed in waterproof kegs. In fact, all of the kegs were prepared that way, just in case we needed to sink the cargo on route home as when it came to landing the cargo, the local revenue officers have had a few successful seizures lately and also have had successes in stopping a few ships from landing their goods. This was why I had the kegs prepared for sinking. I paid the merchant for the goods leaving full instructions on where the cargo was to be taken and at what time. Along with the name of the vessel in which the cargo was to be transported back to England in. With that I left and headed back to the 'Elizabeth Ruth' by now she was fully loaded and ready to make her way home, how happy I was to be back at sea although only this time as a passenger. We edged our way out of St Helens in Jersey and made for Port Douglas and home. With the wind in her sails, she pitched over to one side as she picked up speed and then she started moaning and groaning with the hull creaking, groaning as she was put under strain as she made her way through the sea. It was as though The Elizabeth Ruth was talking to us and letting me know she too was pleased to have me on-board and making her way with ease through the waves. Leaving all of the crew and captain on deck, I bid them goodnight and made my way to my cabin and my bed where I slept the rest of the way home, I soon realized I was now getting to an age where maybe I should leave this job to the younger generation.

Once home I made contact with an old friend of mine John McDougal yes the same who helped me make such a fool of the one John Baites on that night in 1762. Now John was going to collect the goods I had purchased in the Channel Islands and bring it home, via some quite little bay along this rugged coast. So I gave him his instructions on where to go and what to do and then without further ado I bid him good-bye and left him to it. Knowing I could fully trust him, but how was I to know that this would end up in tragedy and even worse loss of life. So many friends were to die that night. In the May of 1764, John made his way to the Channel Islands, picked up the cargo and brought it back to England, except that particular night the weather turned badly, starting off with just enough wind to take John over to the Channel Islands but on the way back the weather was to change and changed for the worse. The weather changed so quickly, with the wind wiping the sea into a boiling mass with twenty to thirty foot waves which were breaking across their decks and smashing into the side of the vessel. How the hell they made their way home, I will never know. Any respecting sailor would have turned back and made for shelter till the storm had passed, but not John. I found out he even tried to land the cargo, he must have been mad to try in such bad weather and not only endangering his vessel but also his crew and where he was to land the cargo was so close to the rocks, even I would not have attempted such a thing. I am afraid to say John McDougal was the sort of person to take such risks with himself and his crew and not to say his ship, this night his luck had ran out. Only the month before, a vessel trying do the same and land their cargo had its bottom ripped out as it was thrown onto the submerged rocks and then left high and dry stranded on the rocks. It was not long before the sea ripped the vessel to pieces as the boiling sea kept on smashing onto the sides of the vessel turning it into matchwood in no time, a lost vessel and a lost cargo. It was pure luck the vessel was close enough to the coast that a line could be got to the crew and they managed to escape with their lives and only minor injuries.

But getting back to John McDougal, John McDougal soon realized he had no hope at all of landing the cargo safely so the next best thing was to go into the centre of the bay and as safely as possible try and sink the cargo and collect it a few days later.

The sea was so rough that he was not able to even sink the cargo and he and his crew were to meet a similar fate as that poor vessel the month before. Except John McDougal and his crew were to lose their lives and his vessel was to be thrown onto the rocks only to be smashed to pieces and turned into firewood. Apparently, as the story goes from somebody who was watching from the cliff tops and saw what happened that night. He was also the one to raise the alarm. John McDougal was attempting to sink the cargo which in this weather was no easy task when a large wave hit the side of his vessel forcing the vessel over onto her side and at this point, he lost control and we believe the cargo in the hold moved, causing the vessel to lurch further over to one side. With the ship being constantly battered by the sea, it capsized throwing the crew and John into the boiling sea. More than likely, the crew was tangled up within the rigging and was smothered by the sails and drowned. It was not long then before the vessel was then driven onto the rocks splitting the vessel open and spilling its cargo into the sea, where many of the kegs along with the vessel were smashed to pieces. Some of the kegs did however get washed up onto the beach where they were picked up by the locals or even worse by the revenue officers who of course would seize them, taking them back to their bonded store. Apparently, there was a strong aroma of brandy coming up from the base of the cliff and then spreading out across the bay.

The bodies of the crew were never recovered but claimed by the sea and I lost a cargo, which I must admit was nowhere near as bad as the families of the lost crewmembers, who now had to fend for themselves without their husbands or love ones. I did what I could do to help as they were out on my business. I paid for their funerals, and as for my old friend John McDougal, I made a promise to ensure that his family were well catered for. I had a cottage on my estate. It was an old cottage but could be made into a nice little home for the family so I instructed that the cottage be made habitable and then moved them in. Ensuring that at least they had a roof over their head and that was not the end of it. She needed an income so speaking to my brother who ran the tobacco factory for me I made a job for her. She now had the means to look after her family. I also made sure that the remaining crews' families were also looked after and cared for.

Knowing this would draw attention to me, I decided to take whatever came my way and sure enough questions were being asked why I was being so generous and charitable but I could not let anybody suffer to the degree these families would do without their men folk being able to support them. Let's not forget they would not have been at sea if it was not for me financing this particular run.

Incidents like this bring it home to everybody how powerful the sea can be and also so unforgiving. The church services brought this to our attention over the next few weeks and at least one part of the service would go back to this fact.

After the events of that month in 1764, I drew together the captains of my small fleet now four ships with a fifth in mind, and gave out instructions that they were not to go to sea in such weather and if caught out, then to make for cover whatever they might be carrying.

Chapter 19

So where do we go from here, the story of my life was to go through yet more pain, pain of a family under pressure, the pain of a parent's worst nightmare, the loss of a child and not any child our child our son John. 1765 started with one of the worst storms this country had seen in living history, even worse than that fateful night in 1764 when John McDougal and his crew lost their lives to the sea. The south coast and around Port Douglas was continually battered day after day and night after night, by the wind and the sea. Great areas of the cliff would just disappear and collapse into the sea. Areas of the valley side outside Port Douglas would just slide into the valley bottom. What a strange sight that was to see great trees moving down the hill as though they were alive, only to crash into the base of the valley and into the River Oxo, were the great branches would just snap off the trunk and then be washed away down the swollen River Oxo and out to sea. The ground was by now so water logged it turned fluid, blocking the only road in and out of Port Douglas. We were temporarily cut off from the outside world, unless you left via the coastal path, but that was far too dangerous during the storm. The cliffs were high and shear faced, some of the highest in the area and as such the wind and rain would wipe up the cliff face and over the top of the cliff, surprising the unprepared walker and if you were not careful, you stood more chance of being blown from the cliff top, or even worse, the ground collapsing from under your feet. Whichever way, you would find yourself at the bottom of the cliff, more than likely dead.

This part of the coast is also littered with small hard to access coves and beaches all of which are very dangerous when the weather turns and as always a number of lives would be lost including our son John who would be taken from us so young and so innocent by the sea. A cruel and vicious act, which we were never to get over. Nobody gets over the loss of a child; as parents, you do not expect to have to bury one of your children. There were three lives lost that month of February from the village and for visitors to the area the crew of four French luggers were to lose their lives. From the village, my son was one of the three and as for the other two men, who they were I do not know, they had moved here the month before looking for work on the ships. Being new to the area, they did not know their way around. They did not know where to go and not to go. They had gone down onto one of the smaller beaches in the area and managed to get themselves cut off from the path that lead to safety by the approaching sea, as the tide turned, their way out had been cut off by the incoming tide. What they were doing on the beach in such conditions, no one will ever know or will ever find out. The only thing we do know is they lost their lives to the sea, as their bodies were washed ashore the next day. Both covered in blood and badly disfigured after being constantly thrown on the rocks by the sea as the waves broke on the beach and against the cliff face. Let's just hope their end was quick and they did not suffer the pain of being battered on the rocks. The lower parts of Port Douglas ended up being flooded as the sea surged forward on the high tide, backing up the River 'Oxo which then bursts its banks as it could not cope with the amount of water surging down the river from the hill side.

Port Douglas was lucky not to face the perils and the pain of the neighbouring village who suffered worse than just flooding. Half the village was washed away as a great tidal wave came crashing through the village late one night, turning the gentle stream that flowed into the bay into a raging fast flowing river that covered the whole of the valley floor. No warning came, apart from the rumble of the tidal wave as it came thundering through the valley bottom, bringing boulders the size of a small house tumbling through the village. Just like skittles, knocking the houses down as they crumbled under the flow of water and the large boulders smashing into walls of the cottages only then to be washed away along with their occupants. With many still in their bed. That night thirty men, women and children lost their lives. Their bodies were never recovered, only to be taken by the sea. The fishermen lost many of their boats that night as they too were smashed on the rocks as they were ripped from their moorings. Some managed to recover some of their belongings but not many. It was strange how the water came so fast that the villages did not even have time to leave their homes and reach higher ground and safety. When the waters subsided, there was nothing left but rubble and empty shells were once stood a white washed cottage. We did our best to help that night; it was a time when everybody pulled together. It did not matter who you were, enemies came together putting their differences aside just to help each other. We gathered up search parties to look for survivors, we found none. When the water subsided, the true damage could be seen, homes washed away roads and bridges gone. There was not much left that could be identified as a town. There were families trying to find their loved ones but they had gone and also trying their best to salvage their personnel belongings and all you could hear was the crying and wailing of the towns occupants. This is something that will stay with me until my dying day. Over the next few months, we helped to re-build the village and tried to bring an element of normality back to the village. Four of the cottages in the village that were destroyed that night happened to belong to me just another part of my business so as always I took the lead and without any questions or arguments I had them re-built and handed back to my tenants and of course whilst they were re-built I found somewhere for them to live. It took about three years to completely re-build the village and try and forget the terror of that fateful night, but those that died that night will be remembered forever, as each year on that night a party is held, where each person's name is read out and celebrated in song and dance and of course, lots of wine and ale which I seemed to end up donating a few kegs towards.

During that month of February in 1765, no vessel dared to venture out from the safety of the small harbour at Port Douglas, if they had, they may never have come back. The storm went on for days and days and we would pray every Sunday at church to god for the rain to stop. The rain just lashed down continuously it was relentless and without mercy, the roads turned to mud the surrounding heathland were flooded and we could not move anything and if we did try, the carts just sank into the mud where they would stay, but worse of all my cellars were running now low and we could not re-fill them.

During February, we heard of four French luggers in bound from France that founded as they tried to find shelter whilst making for the nearest port. However, before they could reach safety they were dashed without mercy onto the rocks with total loss of life, forty-two men that night loss their lives. The only winners in times like this would have been the beachcombers, who after a good storm would go looking to see what had been washed up on the beach but not this time. Sometimes the villagers would be lucky and after a ship had founded and the cargo had spilled into the sea, items of value may well end up on the beach only to be collected and taken away by the villagers. All they found in this occasion washed up on the beach was the forty-two bodies of the four French Luggers crew, along with the remains of the four ships. They were brought to the village, identified where possible and then given a Christian burial in the local church. Turn out at times like this was high, as all knew that their loved ones may well die in foreign waters and they all wished that their loved ones would be treated with the same respect. Word would be sent to the French authorities of the loss and were the sailors were buried and any personal possessions would be returned to the sailor's families. A corner of the local church was dedicated for occasions like this and sadly was filling up with graves of lost seamen local and from afar. I did my part and contributed towards the cost of burial and the tending of the graves. Somehow, each week fresh flowers would appear on these graves and no one really knew who put them there.

Along this part of the coast we also had the less scrupulous villagers who would sometimes draw the unsuspecting mariner ashore, who thinking they were somewhere where they were not. By shining a false light, they would think they were coming into harbour or they might just get confused on where they are. Only to find themselves being drawn onto the rocks or to run aground on a sand bank and find themselves marooned, ending up at the mercy of a gang of ruthless men. They would then be boarded and strip them bare of anything valuable. As for the crew, they would meet their maker in some horrific way. I once was asked to take part in such an act to which I refused, how could I treat a fellow mariner in such a way.

Chapter 20

It was during one of these storms in 1765 we lost our youngest son, John. He was by now fourteen and an adventurer, he took after his father. Why he did what he did we will never know and we will never find out. Late one Sunday afternoon he decided to meet up with his friends and go down to Brandy Bay and watch the storm and the large waves breaking onto the beach. From what we could gather, after talking to his friends, John decided to go down onto the beach itself and was last seen running up and down the sandy beach trying to avoid the waves as they smashed onto the beach. When a large wave which must have been about fifteen feet high suddenly and without any warning, came crashing down onto the beach and then John was gone, nowhere to be seen. The sea had taken him and swept him out to sea to his death. The sea had taken him claiming yet another life, a young life that had not even had the chance to live, to see and experience anything and everything life could throw at him. Except this life was more precious to me and my wife than anything and the loss was to hit both of us very hard, as it would anyone, being your own flesh and blood.

Charlotte for a while was to blame me for our loss, it was me that always took John down to the harbour were he would help load the ships and like me when I was his age he would sit on the harbour wall watching all if the ships entering and leaving the little harbour. How many times did I have to tell him that the sea is a dangerous and an unforgiving place where a small mistake could cost a life, and this was to be proved true. John's friends came running back to the house screaming and crying and all we could hear from them was that 'John had gone' 'John had gone'. We calmed them down and then asked what had happened. They explained what they had been doing and what John was doing on the beach. I could not believe what I was hearing, as we had only this morning forbidden John to go anywhere near the beach at the present time. Of all people, I knew what the dangers were and how powerful the sea can be. I without thinking ran from the house and started to gather a search party up. Charlotte stayed at home to explain to John's brothers and sisters what had happened. I called on many of my old friends who without any hesitation put their coat on and joined in the search

We gathered on the cliff top and there standing next to us at the back ready to join in the search was John Baites and his officers I did not know what to say to him, he was the last person in the world who I would expect to join in the search. He was my adversary he was always trying to catch me out and place me behind bars. He made his way through the crowd to me; he could see the surprise on my face along with many of my friends. We stood facing each other not knowing who was to speak first. As much as I was surprised to see him I was grateful for the help, every little bit of help wherever and whoever that might be from was gratefully received. Now John took me to one side and very quietly told me *'let's put our differences aside for tonight and find your son ok'* a side of him I never thought or could ever see. A side of compassion and of a man of principal that he was able to put his differences aside, however deep they might be. From that day, I saw John Baites in a different light. Still being very wary of him thou as he could still but me in the local gaol for a very long time, maybe he is not such a bad person.

By now, it was late and the rain was hammering down and visibility was limited but never the less John was lost out in this somewhere and we had to find him. If I was really honest though, after being told how he was taken away by the sea, in realty, I knew what the outcome would be. Me of all people knew this. I looked out across the bay and heading towards us across the sand was my two eldest sons coming in search of their little brother. I told them in full what had happened and what needed to be done. We split the group up into two and moved off along the edge of Brandy Bay, searching everywhere shouting at the tops of their voices for John, just hoping to hear a reply and trying to be heard above the sound of the waves crashing down onto the beach along with the rain which by now was hammering down, but there came no reply. All we could hear was the sound of the waves breaking onto the beach and being careful ourselves that we too would not be carried away by the sea. We carried on searching all through the night and found nothing then at about 6am when the storm had subsided and the tide had gone out we were then able to reach along the base of the cliff safely. Looking across the bay I noticed a close friend of mine George, I did not know he was here but word of my loose had reached him and so he had come to help in the search for John. But what was he doing he was rummaging around in the rock pools when he stooped down and appeared to be gathering up a package or a bundle or something which I was at the time not really fully sure what it was. As he approached me I noticed all of the men, they had removed their caps and then my heart dropped and I realized what he was carrying it was John. They had found him, my world had stopped, and it was as I had feared the sea had taken John from us, and delivered him to our lord.

By now everybody on the beach had heard that John had been found. They had gathered around me and as George approached me, the crowd opened up like the parting of the sea allowing George through. He walked up to me and there laying in his arms was the limp body of John, lifeless and looking so innocent, for god sake he was only just a child. George passed him over to me and I carried John back through the streets of the village of Port Douglas with the whole village following behind, caps in hand out of respect, to our home and to his waiting mother; who on seeing her son in my arms, collapsed screaming and sobbing. John was buried the following week in the family grave, next to his grandparents within the local church, a short life but a full and happy one. I stood in front of the church congregation and said a few words as a parent would do. His brothers and uncles carried his small wooden coffin into the church whilst I followed trying my best to comfort Charlotte and the rest of the family. The small coffin was placed in front of the whole congregation and covered in flowers along with his favourite toy, which was to be placed inside the coffin in his arms. I was surprised on how many attended his funeral to pay their respects, John's school was given the day off so his friends could attend, all came and paid their respect and it was here I found out how loved John was throughout the village, and how he would walk around the village singing and being a happy little soul. Stopping to talk to anybody who wanted to listen to him, no wonder he was always the last one home from school each day. Charlotte took a long time to get over John's death and I do not think in reality she ever did get over his death and the way he was taken from us at such an early age. I would find her at least once a week at his graveside talking to him and telling him what had happened during the day whilst tending his grave. I would leave her alone with her thoughts and sit on the wooden bench on the other side of the churchyard watching her and waiting for her, and then we would walk home arm in arm whilst I comforted her. I must admit I would now and then visit the grave and spend time just thinking what might have been, like I said, you never get over losing a child, and you don't expect you to outlive your children. The only thing that helped us as parents was to try and keep busy, Charlotte with the wine importers and me with the shipping company and my next endeavour. Although we did do one thing every year on John's birthday and that was to make that one day in the year a special day when all of the family would be together to remember John and think what could have been. We would all go down to Brandy bay and celebrate his life; Brandy Bay was to become a special place for our family were we felt close to John.

The loss of John that year at such an early time in his life hit the family very hard, but we still had our other children to consider. By now, they were of the age where they should start to think about what they wanted to do in their adult lives. Elizabeth and Ruth our first born and our first twins were now 17 years old and blooming into two of the most beautiful young daughters and starting to gather the attention of many of the local young lads which as a father I did not approve of. My two sons Roger

and Bruce were now 15 going on 16 years old and then there was
the baby of the family Charlotte 13 years old and like most children she hated been called the baby of the family, and of course
even though John was no longer with us he would have been 14
this year. His brothers and sisters missed him dearly and much
much more than we realized. I think it affected his younger sister Charlotte more than all of us and as her parents we soon realized when her teacher called one evening to see how she was,
as she has not been to school for the last few days. It was at this
point we found out she was skipping school and when she did go
to school she was miss behaving and being very disruptive which
was just not like Charlotte in fact she was just the opposite the
model child. I bid her teacher goodbye and then tried to talk to
Charlotte but she just burst into tears and ran off to her room.
My wife told me to leave it and she would try and talk to her, but
I could not leave it, it upset me to see Charlotte in such a state
so I decided to follow her one day to what I thought was school.
I know it was wrong of me but we were worried about her, she
had become withdrawn and irritable and just not the Charlotte
we knew and loved. As we suspected she did not go to school but
headed towards Brandy Bay, when I caught up with her I found
her on the beach sobbing her eyes out just looking out to sea. She
was surprised to see me and tried her best to hide the fact she had
been crying. I sat down beside her and put my arms around her
comforting her. She was at last grieving for her brother, which is
what she needed to do. I then asked her what she was doing here
and why she was not at school to which she replied that she wanted to be close to John her brother and this is where she feels safe
with John watching over her. I told her how I understood how
she felt, that we should really be getting back home, and just for
today she could have the day off from school. I would explain to
her teacher. With that, Charlotte buried her head into my jacket
and started sobbing again, to which I just let her get on with it.
Telling her to let it all out, which I thought, was the best thing
for her. We sat for what seemed around a couple of hours both
just staring out to sea hardly speaking just thinking when we sud-

denly realized the tide was coming in and if we did not move quickly we would get very wet. Turning to Charlotte I jumped up and smiled and shouted this is John's doing he is trying to get us soaking wet, laughing Charlotte jumped up and turning to me smiled exclaiming yep that's John's doing alright. The ever practical joker was John. We turned and headed home arm in arm to her smiling. Charlotte was at last starting grieve for her brother and it was doing her good. I know I am just a man but I think I understand and this was all that was needed. She had to let all of the grief out, but she will never be totally the same and she will never forget her brother which neither will we, as the family will never be the same. There is a great empty space in our hearts which can never be filled. We had been away from home now nearly all morning and Charlotte my wife was getting worried something had happened and came looking for us and it just so happened, we met her as we walked along the lane towards the village. Arm in arm with Charlotte in the middle and her mother and father each side, we sang and skipped along. I told Charlotte what had happened and that everything should now be ok and Charlotte would not be going to school today, she was going to spend the day with us. Her mother looked at me with surprise but agreed and the rest of the day, we spent together at home. Charlotte just for this one day was allowed to do whatever she wanted, whatever made her happy. She needed to grieve for the loss of her dear brother.

Chapter 21

It was now approaching my 45th birthday and Charlotte was also approaching her 46th birthday and let's be honest life was comfortable for us. We had a growing family business my Shipping Company with now four vessels, a growing fine wine import business and of course the Tobacco and snuff factory not to mention a growing property portfolio which by now had been extended to a number of good status properties along with many of the cottages in Port Douglas and the neighbouring villages. But something was missing I craved the excitement of the life of a smuggler, the smell of the sea. After the death of John, I became very restless and just financing the trips was ok but not enough. Where the excitement was the thrill of the playing cat and mouse with the authorities, but of course my wife, did not approve or understand what I was going through? She just saw how we were very comfortable off and why would you want to jeopardise this to go back to smuggling a few kegs into the country, which I must admit I had no answer for although, maybe the death of john had something to do with it, maybe I had something to prove to myself, maybe John's death affected me more that I realized.

After John's death, I became restless and not able settle and I know I should have been with Charlotte she was suffering as much if not more than I was but I could not bear to be in the house. So in the March of 1765, I decided to pay some old friends a visit and between us we planned around nine trips throughout the remaining part of 1765 and they would range from trips to France the Channel Islands and a few trips further afield where we ended up along the coast in the Netherlands, meeting a small ship laying off the coast where we would purchase some tea. So in late March of 1765 I purchased a very old Seventy foot lugger. She must have been about forty or so years old, financed by all six of us. We each owned $1/6^{th}$ of the ship. I had never been a part owner in a ship before. This was all new to me. Normally I brought each ship outright myself but we did it anyway and we renamed her 'The Imagination' strange name I know but that was the majority decision. She came from up north, we heard or should I say I heard of this ship for sale through my many contacts and we found out the vessel had been laid up in a yard in Newcastle now for a number of years, it was cheap, if you saw the state of her well you can understand why she was cheap. The price not so much the state of her drew my curiosity, as we only needed this vessel for the nine trips and after that, she would be disposed of. So up north we went with my brother (the ship builder) and the five other owners to check the vessel out only to end up purchasing her. Why did we buy her, well she was cheap and more to the point this vessel would not be known by the local revenue cutter on the South Coast and as such would not draw attention to us? Who would suspect what we doing and then immediately after we had completed the ninth run we would sell her, and of course at the same time try and make a profit on the sale. Looking at her as we sailed home, It would be a lucky year if we even made the nine trips in her or for that matter if she lasted that long and does not sink, I thought to myself. Looking at the state of her it is lucky we did not pay very much for her so if she was seized we would not lose much and if she sank well our loses also would not be too bad, apart from if we were carrying any cargo at the time. Anyway, the state of her she was not worth much. So the first run was to take place in April with that in mind I sent my brother Sam over to France with instructions on what he was to buy and who he was to buy from. So early one morning in April Sam said his goodbyes to his wife and children and made his way to Port Douglas where he met me on the dock side and boarded 'The Valiant' and got ready to set sail for France. The plan was for us to sail over to France, pick up a legitimate cargo of wine and bring it back to England. As a wine importer I had to be seen to bring in some wine legitimately, not everything in my cellars was illegal you know. Sam my brother came with us and his job would be to purchase enough cargo for nine trips and to arrange storage for about seven to eight months. By now Sam had helped me out on more than one occasion and was getting good at searching out a good deal whilst running the tobacco factory which he was also doing rather well and turning a good profit. On one of his many meetings in France, Sam came across a Dutch man who had a consignment of tea he wished to dispose of and Sam being a clever businessman that he was managed to pick up the cargo at a very good price in fact an extremely good price. Sam also came across a few other items, which were not on the list to purchase. Which I was soon to find out these were personnel items which he had financed himself like for example a few yards of very expensive silk which I found out was to be used to make a wedding dress for his daughter. I must admit Sam did have good taste, after knowing what he wanted it for I added the consignment to my list and told him I would pay for it as my wedding present to his daughter my niece. When all the deals were struck and the cargo moved to a secure store word was sent to me and we went over once again to France in the Valiant to collect Sam bringing him safely home to his wife and family. Although, he did do something that was to put us in in jeopardy and if caught we would all, including the crew, have been heading to spend some time at His Majesty's pleasure. Much to his wife's joy. By now, she had started to accept me and what I was doing for Sam; he was a changed person, he was a man with a purpose and a man knowing what he now wanted to do.

The silk was to come back with us on the return trip and I did wonder how my brother was to get the silk back without being caught and thinking about it, I too along with the whole crew would be in trouble. Could this be the point my luck would run out but I was soon to find out and I must admit a very clever and ingenious method was to be used to smuggle the silk ashore. I did point out to my brother next time to consult me before using one of my ships to smuggle goods in to the country and how it was a very reckless thing to do to put himself and the whole crew of 'The Valiant' in such a position but he assured me all would be all right. We did not speak much on the trip across the channel and yes I was annoyed and more upset at being put in such a position. Although I did have something up my sleeve just in case, anything was to go wrong. Now in my cabin was a secret hiding place just big enough to hide the silk, if there was a problem then this is where we would hide the silk. But in reality, this was where the silk would stay throughout the crossing. So taking the silk from my brother, I locked the silk away until we reached port and we were ready to smuggling the silk a shore. When we reached Port Douglas there, waiting on the dockside was Sam's wife and when I looked at her, she must have put on about two stone. I looked across at Sam and asked what the hell had she been eating and I was soon to find out. She came aboard and Sam whisked her off into my cabin and I followed wondering what the hell was going on. As I walked in she was undressing and the reason she was so fat it was padding. Sam removed the padding and then started to wind the silk around his wife's waist, when finished he secured it and then she put her dress back on and as casually as she came aboard she left the ship cools as ever. I for once was speechless and very impressed with the ingenuity of my brother and with what just had happened. As she left the ship she waved her husband goodbye and smiled at the Revenue Officer who by chance was just coming aboard to check our manifesto and cargo. Not realizing what had just happened right in front of him, little did my brother know I had used the same method on a number of occasions to smuggle in a few yards of silk, but I did not realize my brother and his wife had it in them to do the same and take such a risk.

So all was arranged. The cargo for the next nine runs was purchased and stored safely. The first three runs went off without any problems and the wine was delivered by my old friend George to my wine cellars along the coast and the tea ended up in my cellars in Port Douglas and also in Georges cellar in his house near Barns and as usual any liquor made its way up to the black country. Apart from one keg of brandy, one of the local gentry had taken a liking to a keg of brandy every now and then, which I delivered personally to him each time. The fourth trip was another story; it turned into a bit of a fiasco. We picked up the goods as planned in the Channel Islands and started to make our way back to England. That part went well and with no untold problems, but we knew all was not well soon after leaving the Channel Islands when one of the crewmembers noticed we were being followed. Orders were given to the crew to run up more sail to try to get some speed up and make some distance between the two vessels. Now the Imagination was an old and slow vessel, and had not really been well cared for through its hard life and as such was not being used to being pushed to its limits. As we got faster through the water she started to creek and grown under the new stresses and strains being placed on her hull and her rigging. We just waited for the crash and sound of splintering wood as she tore herself apart. I sent one of the crew below to check the hull for any leaks and to make sure the cargo was secure. He came back up to report the cargo was secure but we were taking on water, asking how much, about ½" to an ¾" this was not good, not good at all. In the middle of the English Channel, being pursued by an unknown vessel and now, taking on water, we were in trouble real trouble. The worst part was the perusing vessel was starting to catch up with us and she was a much bigger vessel than us, a large square rigger, and she had much more sail up than us. At this rate, she will soon be up on us. My main concern now was to try to find the leak in the hull and stop any more seawater entering the ship, no easy task. I decided to go down into the hold and look for the source myself. I climbed down into the hold and found myself paddling in an inch or so of water. This was not good, at this rate the pursuing vessel could be our savour. It did not take long to find the problem as just above the water line on the port side of the ship I could see water running down the inside of the hull. On trips like this, I always made sure a carpenter or somebody that could carry out repairs of this type was on board. Going back on deck, I called over Brian Smith a deck hand who as it so happens was a good carpenter. I explained the problem and sent him down in the hold to carry out temporary repairs. Then instructing the crew to try and bucket out some of the water now lying in our hold. My main concern was if we lurched over to one side then the water moving would cause us to capsize.

Leaving the crew to sort out our problems below deck my concerns returned to our pursuer. I grabbed hold of the spyglass, trained it on the ship, and from the main mast was flying a French Flag my god I now knew who was chasing us and fear ran through me. French Privateers were pursuing us. Trying not to panic or show any fear on my face, the last thing the crew wanted to see was their captain panicking or even worse afraid. I needed to stay calm, composed and relaxed not an easy thing knowing they will be heavily armed and relentless on their pursuit. I turned the spyglass towards the English Coast to try to see if I could identify where we were approaching the English Coast. By now, I was really panicking inside and sweat was starting to pour from off me. I kept asking myself where were we, and for god's sake where are they. There they were, there on the hilltop, in the distance, and there came my point of reference, three trees in a particular pattern. I then knew exactly where we were along the coast. I knew we would now be safe. We had kept our distance from the approaching French Privateer and being smaller we were more manoeuvrable than our pursuers. I took the helm and headed inland and into the shallower waters. I gathered the crew and between us, all we hatched a plan to shake off our pursuers and at the same time trap them leaving them high and dry. Being a much smaller vessel we could easily enter much shallower water than they could and this is what we intended to rely on, using our size as an advantage; let's just hope they do not use their superior fire power and fire their canons on us. Handing the helm back I took the spyglass and trained it back on our pursuer.

Now I had two problems to deal with the hold filling with seawater and a French Privateer trying its best to capture us. This is what I lived for, the adrenalin pumping round my body, the excitement and the thrill. Knowing in the end we would win, yes, it is all a game at the end of the day, and I was always the winner.

I knew these waters like the back of my hand and as such, this would be to our advantage and hopefully our savour. I ordered the helmsman to turn to starboard and head for a small town on the coast called Church Street. Then we allowed our pursuers to close the gap a dangerous move I know, he was armed with cannons and we were armed with nothing, if they caught up with us we would lose the ship and the cargo only to be taken back to France not what we wanted, and not what I intend to happen.

The plan was to run, taking our pursuers across the great sand spit off Church Street that guarded the entrance to the harbour. A moving sand spit that moved with the tide. So knowing the area and the tidal movements was to be a godsend and our savour. Our pursuers were getting closer and closer by now and I could feel them breathing down my neck as we passed the headland just off Church Street. I spotted the town to my left and so sent forward our youngest member of the crew and told him to start taking soundings. We soon realised it was also high tide and that's just what I needed, so when our pursuers ran aground at high tide they would get stuck on the sand spit with no way of getting off. I needed to find the point, which we could safely cross the sand with enough water below us such we did not run aground but at the same point knowing our pursuers would. Over there shouts one of the crew, who also knew what I was looking for. Hard to starboard I shouted and with that, we turned and started to travel along the edge of the sand spit and sure enough, our pursuers followed us. Well they did for a short time when there was an almighty crash and scrapping sound as they ran straight at speed onto the spit and there they stayed. We could hear orders being shouted and many raised French voices. We just turned back and cheered. To conclude this little tail, we then carried on to yes Brandy Bay where we landed our cargo safely and then made for Port Douglas where we tied up along the quayside, and made our way home. Our French friends I am afraid to say stayed well and truly stuck on the sand bank. The French ship stayed there on the sand bank being continually battered by the sea until one stormy night in December 1765 when the ship finally broke up.

The ship became an attraction were people would come from afar just to see this French Privateers ship sat on the sand spit. I never thought we could have charged a penny. To all those that wanted a trip out to the ship, a missed opportunity I think. The crew of the French Privateer were taken into custody, taken to London and eventually they were sent back to France, a few weeks later. The news headlines read 'French Privateer run aground On English Sand Spit whilst in pursuit of an English ship' when we read this we just chuckled to ourselves knowing it was us they were chasing. Shame we could not claim the success of that day but if we did then we would be admitting our guilt.

As for 'The Imagination' the first thing we did after that trip was to take her out of the water and get her hull repaired. My brother did the repairs the best he could but he warned me that she did not have much life left in her and that her hull was in a very bad state. So, she was patched up, returned to the water, and off we went again.

After the repairs to 'The Imaginations' hull and through the remaining part of the year we carried on and did a further five runs. All once more successful and each one went off without any problems. In January 1766 as promised we sold the 'Imagination' but for scrap as by now she was no use to anybody especially after we had finished with her. She was not in the best shape when we purchased her and after we had taken her tired hull to its limits and in fact beyond her limits to the point her hull was starting to come apart and let water in again, this time beyond the point of repair. She had actually started to give up with her hull starting to take on water faster and faster in fact much more than we could remove. It was on our last trip I actually thought she would sink before we reached our home country. As for her rigging and furniture this was by now very old and tired and full of rot to the point a refit would cost more than we could sell her for, and the worse part of it she was now very well known to the authorities. As my old friend, John Baites was starting to look for her and tipping off the captain of the revenue cutter when we left Port Douglas. In the end I paid off my partner's share of the

'Imagination' and I gave her to my brother who stripped her of all worthy parts and then had her hull broken up using what he could, but mostly she ended up on the fire keeping him warm in the winter months. At least she was used for something useful.

That year was also a good year for entries in the Revenue letter book we had I think between eight to nine entries and best of all John Baites still could not catch me, although he did try his best and I must admit I was starting to admire his determination and his dedication. Which made me even more determined to ensure he never actually caught me.

Chapter 22

Like I have already said the year of 1766 and started with the sale of 'Imagination' or should I say the disposal of the 'Imagination' she was beyond repair and owned me nothing as we did not spend a penny on her in the time I owned her. Well that is not strictly true we did have her hull repaired, but my brother took pity on us and charged me I think it was one keg of Brandy and I think it was two kegs of a fine red wine. The Imagination served us well and had just reached the end of her natural working life, but it was such a shame she ended up the way she did, being broken up and ending her life on the scrap heap or on the fires of many of the homes throughout the village keeping us warm at night although. At least she ended her life in a useful way. I always find that a sad moment to see a good ship ending up being broken up, a ship is a living breathing entity that needs to be nurtured and cared for bit like a good woman really, although a good woman would never be sent to the scrap heap.

This year was to carry onto be one of best and most exciting years of my life apart from the year I married Charlotte of course and how could I ever forget that day, the events of that day have stayed with me throughout our married life.

Now something I have not really felt in the last few years was the rush of blood through my body and the excitement of not knowing what was lying ahead and best of all the game of cat and mouse. I had now bought yet another vessel 'The Bell' and I was to be her captain, and this was to be the year that I and my fellow smugglers, one being my son, which made the events of the year even worse was so nearly to become a guest of His Majesty in the nearby gaol, a fate we did not want to even consider as many that ended up in gaol, left broken men. Men that spent all their time in the open air either out sea fishing or working the local trade routes whilst others who could not see themselves going to sea would spend their time in the surrounding fields tending their flock or their crops. These men would in the end see themselves gradually going mad incarcerated in a cell that was no bigger than six foot by four foot and away from the outside world. Many of these men spent the largest part of their lives in the outdoors and to be locked up like this is not natural for them. Their only savour if they were lucky, would be the man of god who would visit the gaol every Sunday and try and make life better by preaching the word of god. Attendance to the Sunday service was compulsory as the governor of the gaol was a strong churchgoer and believed every soul could be saved from the devil's way. To show this a program of rehabilitation was developed and a report of inspection of the gaol was published in the local paper which showed that many of the men who entered the gaol were illiterate and non-believers of god and by the time they left, sixty percent could read and write, whilst twenty percent would learn more than when they entered the gaol whilst the remaining twenty percent were far beyond help and left no better off. But many left believed to be on the road to being saved from the path of the devil. Well until they got home and they had a knock on the front door to help with a vessel landing a cargo that night. Money at the end of the day is a good incentive, as a Tubman they could earn more money in one evening than in a week in the fields.

This year was also to prove to be the year that my old friend John Baites would come as close as he ever would to catching me in the act of smuggling or in this case receiving tobacco that had been smuggled into the country. Although there would be many more opportunities presented to him throughout the years before I eventually would retire, obtain my pardon and finally hanging up my sea boots.

I pick up the story not long after the disposal of The 'Imagination' and the purchase of yet another vessel the 'Bell' now my fifth vessel in my small fleet. This too was another old 70 foot lugger although the 'Bell' was a much drier vessel than the 'Imagination' and much newer and having just gone through a full refit at my brother's yard. Purchased from my brother who had just finished the refit on her and had added many interesting features at the request of its previous owner, The Bell was for all intense and purposes a true smuggling vessel, she had been modified to such an extent with so many good hiding places and rails being fitted along each side of the ship to allow the sinking of a cargo at sea whilst on the move. The previous owner of 'The Bell' during its refit suddenly In one night lost two of his ships at sea on a stormy night or well he tells us it was stormy night, but there is another story of a French Privateer who caught up with them one night and opened fire on them de-masting them and giving the crew time to abandon ship and make their escape. The French then supposedly boarded them in full view of the crew, took their cargo and finally opening fire on them using the two ships for target practice, finally sinking them both, but they lost their cargo that night which plunged the owner into a very bad financial state in fact it bankrupted him. He ended up owing money to many of his creditors and as he had not paid for his cargo, he found he could not pay and for that matter he had no way of paying my brother for the work being done on the 'Bell' as a result a bargain was struck and my brother seized 'The Bell' as full payment knowing he already had a buyer for her 'me'. A better result for him than ending up in debtor's prison. The said gentleman struck the deal and gave my brother the vessel and I was to reap the benefit of this gentleman's misfortune or was I, unbeknown to me 'The Bell' was very well known to the revenue officers so much that that in the first few weeks whilst on legitimate business carrying gravel from Wales to Port Douglas we had been stopped by the Revenue Cutter searched and warned that if caught smuggling we would be treated with no mercy. Luckily for us our cargo matched our manifest each time and luckily the interesting features that my brother had added to the vessel was so well done nothing was found of our extra cargo. We had silk for the ladies and tea for the gentry well hidden away. 'The Bell' was shall we say had many hidden compartments that to the untrained eye no one could see or would even suspect they were there. One good feature we had was the double deck a, perfect hiding place for the right cargo in this case tobacco and a few yards of good silk.

Whenever we would leave and return to Port we would soon realize that something was wrong by the amount of time the searchers would take checking the vessel and our cargo against the ships manifest, the weigher's would check and recheck everything as it was unloaded. As for the Tides-man, sometimes we would have two come aboard both taking notes and watching every member of the crew, whilst the Tidewaiters carried out their checks and as we would leave port we would be questioned and cross questioned on our destination in fact much more than we would normally get with my other ships. Worst of all, as time passed, these similar checks started to be carried out on the rest of the fleet which was starting to cause me some serious grief in time and energy, in trying to put them off the scent and most of all was starting to restrict my smuggling operations, which in turn would cut my potential of making a good profit and this was not good

I had had enough of all this so I decided to do some checking of my own and asked around and through my many contacts within the service, they were soon to inform me of who the previous owner was and what the vessel had been used for. After checking the records, we found that 'The Bell' was very well known to the revenue officers with many entries within the local Revenue letter book and like me had never been caught but had been implicated on many occasions on many different landings throughout the last five to ten years. I did ask myself how the hell did I not know of this vessel. I knew every single smuggling vessel within the area and The Bell was not one that had worked this area. As for her captain and owner, this too did not ring any bells. Further checks were to prove this vessel was very well known within the West Country and had been moved into the area due to the fact it was so well known that it could no longer go to sea without being stopped. Finding this out did not impress me at all, all I wanted was a vessel totally unknown to the revenue officers here or anywhere, not one that was so well known to them that each time I went to sea I would be followed or shadowed. Having someone watch every move that I made which is what was happening. So what do I do, I decided to carry on using 'The Bell' but not for smuggling, I transferred the captain from 'The Valiant' on to 'The Bell' and I carried on using my best friend 'The Valiant' but not for long as tragedy would soon bring the end to my old friend. But strange as it might sound the act of being caught or should I say, nearly caught, was not whilst at sea or landing a cargo but as simple as receiving a cargo of tobacco at my tobacco factory from an old friend 'George White' or what I thought was a friend but was soon to be shown as a turn coat somebody that had sold his soul to the devil for a bag of silver. But time would also tell that the bag of silver was to be no good to a dead man. His demise would be one of fear and his end would not be by my hand or even by my request but by the hand of a friend who was also to face the prospect of spending a few days in the local gaol and to eventually meet with a gruesome end.

My problems all started one morning in the month of May in the year of our lord 1766, our tobacco stock sheds where low and bad luck had befallen my normal supplier. Two weeks previous, John Baites had been out searching along the coast when he saw a light, a light signalling a vessel just lying off the coast and was being made ready to head into shore and into a small and secluded bay. Now waiting ashore was a small group of well-armed and determined men getting ready to greet this small vessel unload it and send it once more on its way. These were men you did not want to meet on a dark night, men that would without fear or worry slit your throat if they thought you might be a threat and it was these types that were to give smuggling such a bad name. But this time I am afraid to say they would not be going home to their loved ones but heading off to the local gaol and there they would stay until they could face the magistrate the following month. Having been faced with a troop of heavily armed dragoons, and being outnumbered and out gunned they decided to surrender and fight another day rather than to be carried off in a wooden box, leaving their families to suffer and more than likely end up in the poor house.

Luck was with John Baites that night for once, as at around 11.30pm he was to stumble across this landing as he was going about his normal business. Now he would normally ride alone around the area never a safe thing to do and so if he could he would try to meet up with at least one of his officers. Once a month he would meet up with his four officers and by chance this was the night they had arranged to meet up. So around midnight John could be found at the cross roads into Port Douglas atop his horse waiting for his fellow officers. Now the reason why they met each month was that John had to check their diaries and sign them off, but with the events of the night meant that this would have to wait. Having met up with his officers around midnight John started to tell his officers what he had witnessed earlier that evening and that they should head back to the bay and try to catch them landing the cargo red handed or at least stop the landing. It did not take long to reach the small bay and sure enough down on the beach was the group of men John had seen earlier in the evening and there moored just off the beach was a small open lugger with men standing around her knee deep in the sea, unloading her whilst others took the goods and carried them off to a waiting cart. After a short discussion John decide to watch from a safe distance and just see what happened and what else he could learn. So bedding down in the wet undergrowth high on the cliff top they waited watching the men on the beach below unloading their cargo totally unaware of being watched from afar. John and his men from their position could see right down into the bay and being such a quiet night they could also hear everything that was being said. That night John Baites was to learn a lot about the area and along with who was who and who was doing what and the worse thing was that he also learnt of some of our hiding places which was to cause a bit of a problem and a headache. A loose tongue can cause us problems which is another story for another day. After a short time, John Baites hearing enough turned to his fellow officers and instructed one of them to proceed back to Port Douglas as fast as they could and notify the local Dragoons and request their assistance. There were defiantly too many men on the beach for just the five officers to handle, so they would need help. So making for his horse he rode back to the barracks as fast as he could all the way back to the to Port Douglas and the small garrison which was cited on the quay side next to the Inn, which was to prove to be the wrong place. As the officers spent most of their time sat in the inn getting drunk. His first stop was the garrison to raise the alarm but as he thought, the commanding officer was not in the garrison but next door in the Inn, which the Sargent on duty gladly pointed out and there they were slightly worse for wear. Entering the Inn, he found the Garrison commander propping up the bar with a lady of the night draped all over him. He requested the commanding officer for assistance in the apprehension of a group of smugglers landing cargo in one of the small bays along the coast. The commanding officer waved his arms around uncontrollably and made some comment to the lady who just turned and left him shouting back to him some not so pleasant comment. Not sue what it was but let's say it was no very nice or for that matter lady like. So the commander left the Inn retuning to the barracks, he started barking orders to his Sargent and within in a few minutes there was about twenty dragoons neatly lined up on the parade ground, arms in hand and ready to move out. Well we say parade ground in reality it was the quay side, and the dragoons had to be careful or else they may well have fallen into the harbour, as has happened one evening. The Officer barked more orders and his men started to move out and guided by the revenue officer the dragoons made their way to the small bay just outside Port Douglas and there waiting on the cliff top was John Baites and the remaining three revenue officers. After about ten minutes and a discussion between John Baites and the Officer, who by the way stank of booze and could hardly stand up. A discussion on how we would capture the smugglers was made. They left the relative safety of the cliff top and started making their way down onto the small beach keeping well out of sight, as surprise was the main weapon in capturing the men and their cargo, who were now all on the beach preparing to load the cargo onto the waiting carts and leave. Now John Baites and his men approached the smugglers on the beach who by chance were going about their business totally unaware of the approaching danger. At the last moment, John and his men surprised the smugglers and closed in on them preparing to arrest them and seize the cargo. The smugglers by this point had finished unloading the vessel and were standing around a large pile of wine and spirits kegs along with my ten hogshead of tobacco the tobacco which was to find its way into my tobacco sheds and was to cause me so much pain, financial as well as physical. Taking the smugglers by total surprise who found themselves surrounded, cut off from their weapons which were lying close by on the beach. Realising they were outnumbered, out gunned and with no were to go they gave up without even a fight, which surprised John. Knowing the men and their reputation, he was expecting a fight and one that many would have involved injuries. The small vessel which was still just lying off the beach was by now fully unloaded and was no longer resting on the sand but just starting to float and being prepared by the crew to leave the shore line and head back out to sea. The crew realizing what was going on the beach right in front of them tried desperately to get their little vessel back out to sea before it was seized but John and his men soon realized what was going on and seeing the prize that lay before them they soon started to grapple with the ropes which held her to the shore and seized her along with her cargo which by now was sat on the beach. This would go down as a night to remember and a night that would be seen as a very profitable one to all those involved with the seizure. The men were rounded up, hands bound and arrested and taken away to the local gaol. The goods were loaded onto wagons and taken back to the bonded store whilst the ship itself was seized, boarded and taken back to Port Douglas where it was impounded ready for disposal. A profitable night was had but not for me, and that hurt more than anything.

The worst part is I financed this trip and as such the wine and tobacco was destined for my cellar yes my cellars and I lost a large sum of money that night along with the crew and all of the support men who would not be paid. As for the ships master who now had lost his vessel and this means his lively hood had gone, no ship would mean no income for himself and his family. As it was his dear wife and family were now in serious trouble how are they going to pay their rent and how more to the point how are they going to feed themselves, no income or husband or father for his children. Talking to Charlotte, something needed to be done and quick.

The seized goods were taken back to Port Douglas and placed in the bonded store on the dockside, only soon to be auctioned off at a public auction with the proceeds being split between those who seized the goods and the crown. The vessel seized that night would be sold either at auction or depending on the state of it, may be passed over and used by the revenue men or if not just broken up whichever way it would not be returned to its original owner. Anyway, what good would it be to its original owner he sitting in the local gaol awaiting trial and being caught red handed he will be spending time at His Majesty's pleasure. Which is where he and his crew presently are residing, and where he is likely to stay until the magistrate returned to Port Douglas in the next month or two. God help him if he faces the present magistrate I do not rate his chances of getting off with a short sentence. The only thing in his favour was that he gave up without a struggle; we will have to wait and see what happens, as time will only tell. Those that gave up without a struggle or resisting arrest or injuring a revenue officer going about their duty would be treated fairly but those that did injured a revenue officer would fair not so well as their sentence could be much worse, death without the presence of a clergy.

Chapter 23

By now my small business empire had grown and grown into very profitable set up, no longer was I just a wine merchant and a ship owner, I was also now the owner of the local tobacco factory and the owner of a shipyard. Small as it might be but one of the best on the South coast of England and in great demand, with their order books full for the next two to three years, thanks to my brother and his hard work. I had also invested much of my fortune in property through the years around Port Douglas and surrounding area such that many of the locals were tenants of mine. I owned a number of farms in the area, which always came in handy when needing a good hiding place. As such, I find myself being quiet an influence within the town and from nothing, I had achieved all this. Hard work and faith was all that was needed, along with a good wife of course and a family whom had devoted much of their time in building up the business. Although most people knew were my fortune really came from and that did include my old friend John Baites which riled him even more, knowing what he knew and that he could do nothing about it, he had nothing on me at all. Nothing that could link me to any smuggling activities, well nothing that would stand up in a court of law anyway. Each time we met, he would just stare over at me and all I would do is nod my head in recognition. If I was out in the local Inn the 'Bell' I would just raise my glass to him and you could see his expression change and the anger rising in his facial expressions and sometimes I would do it all the more just to see what reaction I might get. Charlotte would warn me off from doing such things on the pretext that I should never upset him as he might one day get the upper hand and find a way of getting to me. He never did find a way.

My age is getting to me now, and my memory is going and I do seem to ramble on sometimes. Getting back to the story of the how John Baites seized my goods that night and what was to be done with the captain's wife whose husband was now languishing in the local gaol. Using my influence and good nature, I wanted to help as much as I could so I discussed the matter with my wife Charlotte and she knew in her heart of hearts what I was to do.

I needed to help Captain Turner, he was carrying a cargo destined for my cellars and as such, I felt rather responsible. As for the men on the beach, it was partly their fault that we lost the goods so they could fend for themselves in court, let that be their punishment. They had also spoken out of turn whilst working the beach. Now John Baites knew names and places within the local smuggling community, hiding places, which were no longer safe and worse still names of important people who would help the smugglers. Who then find a knock on the door and John Baites and his men standing on their doorstep, with a request to search their homes? For the next few Weeks's many of my friends found themselves under the watchful eye of John Baites.

However, let us get back to the problem in hand, what we are to do with the family of Captain Turner. After a long discussion with Charlotte, we came up with a solution, so I paid Captain Turner a visit in the local gaol and informed of my intentions. Those being as the owner of the cottage he lived in I would allow his family to stay in the cottage rent-free for the duration of his stay in the local gaol. I would ensure that his family would not go without food along with anything else they might need. Finally, when his trial came up the following month I would pay his fine allowing him to go free and tend his family. In return he would work for me and only me on one of my ships as the master and do as I ask. This does not include any revenge attacks etc. on anyone who caught and incarcerated him.

All I needed now was to find him was a ship and I had already had one in mind 'The Valiant'. Up to now I was the master and I was the one at sea so much that Charlotte was once more getting more and more upset each time I left, and each time I left I would tell her this is my last trip, but alas I never kept my word.

Charlotte thou kept pointing out I was getting to old to keep going to sea in all weathers and if I am honest, my bones were telling me the same thing. Therefore, with that organised and all agreed I decided to drop round to his family and inform them of the arrangement. Knocking on the front door of the cottage I was greeted by whom I presumed was his wife. The look of terror on her face sent a shiver down my spine. She knew who I was and she started beg me not to throw her and her family onto the street as she had no way to pay the rent. I took her hand and told her that I had no intention of such an act and why would I do that. Therefore, without any further to do I started putting her mind at rest, I informed her of my intentions and my visit to her husband in the local gaol the day before and what we had agreed. She burst into tears and it was a pleasure to see her face turn form a look of terror to that of happiness and relief, the tears were of joy and not of sadness. Without thinking, she gave me a hug and thanked me so much for my generosity. I told her that food would be delivered weekly to her from the great house that being my house and when her husband was released not to worry about the money owing on the rent etc. that it had been sorted with her husband and an arrangement had been struck. Knowing my reputation of being a local smuggler, she stepped back from me looking rather worried. I could tell something was wrong, especially when she turned back to me and asked me what the arrangement was. To which I explained that he was to be the master of one of my older ships 'The Valiant' an older ship in my fleet and one that was his to work and look after. She looked me straight in the eyes asking me if it would involve smuggling. 'No, he's not use to me that way' I replied 'he is known to John Baites and as such would be under suspicion.

She thanked me and I just pointed out that I had gained a new contract to be worked and that 'I need somebody I could rely on to work the coal route bringing coal etc. into Port Douglas from Wales and 'The Valiant' is ideal for that, and so is your husband. The pay is good and it will ensure he is kept safe and well out of harm's way' well for the time being anyway.

His wife started crying again, but this time with joy, joy in the knowledge that she would soon be reunited with her husband, and their children would soon see their father again. For once, she would not have to worry how she was going to make ends meet; she thanked me again and told me I was the families Guardian Angel. My last words as I left to her that day was a warning that if her husband was ever tempted back to his old ways she was to send word and I would ensure he stayed on the right path and away from the troubles that smuggling may bring. If only she'd knew what I did, or maybe she did, and realized how much influence I had within the smuggling world and one word from me and nobody would offer work to her husband or should I say anything that was illegal and broke the law.

I left the cottage feeling good with a warm feeling inside and headed back home with a skip in my step to Charlotte. On reaching home I told her what I had done to which she smiled and told me that's why she married me and loved me so much and would always love you. You have the capability of thinking of others and you do not put money and profit ahead of others unlike many others in this town, who just think of themselves and nobody else and how to make a great profit at the expense of others. You have a heart and a soul and are a much better person than they all will be combined.

As good as my word and my bond I looked after the family ensuring they were well cared for and when the magistrate arrived the following month I found out as it so happened he was a very good friend of mine, well he would be he was a client of mine and I had organised it. The magistrate that arrived that day was not the normal magistrate. The normal magistrate had been taken ill and was on bed rest. Well he would after being slipped something in his food that caused him a mild case of sickness, which insured he was unable to attend the court that month. He was a bit of a tyrant and a right bugger, he was a man that not many people liked and god help you if you ended up in front of him. He had been known to send children as young as ten to spend time in the plantations for just stealing a loaf of bread, for god sake they were hungry and had no money, I would have gladly brought them the loaf. To ensure he could not attend that month cost me ten shillings, just to persuade his cook to lace his food with an herb from the garden, not a poisons one, just one that brought on a feeling of sickness and meant he would be taken to his bed for a few days. She was more afraid of being caught and then thrown out for such an act or even worse, being deported to the plantations, which would never happen. So with him out of the way, off to court I went and spoke up for all those who were caught that night, many were sent down that day. One or two who unbeknown to me decided to strike out at the officers whilst doing their duty, which was not the best thing to do. Lucky for them they did not injure any of the officers. The magistrate as good as he was had no choice but to send them down for a longer sentence, between one to two years' hard labour, whilst many of the others got a short sentence of between six to twelve months along with a small fine. The ships master Captain Turner was so lucky he was fined £10, his vessel was seized, not to be returned to him and if he could not pay then his sentence would be six months in the gaol.

It was strange really why so many of the sentences that day were so lenient and John Baites who also attended the trials could not understand. Well I knew the answer to that one very well, I knew the judge and like most of the gentry in the area he was a fine customer of mine, one of the best. I suspect his cellars was full with the amount he would buy from me, mainly wine along with a few kegs of brandy. What would happen if that ever got out that his cellars where full with goods that had been smuggled into the country. That would be the end of his career not that he really cared, he was retired now and only attends the court these days when the regular magistrate is unable to attend. Picking my moment, I had a quick word in his ear and a promise of a good price on his next order this was all that was needed to ensure he did as I requested and he also knew the damage I could cause if I wanted to not that I needed to add that threat into the conversation.

After the trial I paid the Captain's fine and he was released into my custody and we left the court room and headed home. Now on the way home we just so happened pass the local Inn on the quay side and we decided to pop in for the one or two just to celebrate you understand his release back into the outside world except he was feeling guilty in the fact he was free whilst his men resided at His Majesty's pleasure. So giving it great thought, I told him I would think about what could be done. The celebrations went on late into the night and into the early hours of the morning, we were merry no let's be honest we were very merry by the time we left the inn. We were not even sure what the time was as we wended our way home through the streets of Port Douglas but we were happy as was sang at the tops of our voices as we walked through the village and waking all as we passed by. Take it from us we were not popular the next day, many reminded us of what we did, and that we woke everybody in the village last night. When we got home the front door was locked and bolted from the inside I did try and wake somebody but no lights appeared and nobody opened the door so we ended up sleeping in the shed at the bottom of the garden along with the chickens and horses. We woke in the morning or was it late morning not really sure curled up together in a pile of hay with the chickens and my children standing looking over us laughing and Charlotte, my wife, holding a bucket of cold water and was just getting ready to throw over us, which she actually did do in the end especially when we could not explain what was going on and why we were asleep drunk in the shed. I will tell you what the cold water woke us quite quickly. I bid my friend goodbye, he headed back to his wife to more than likely another such frosty greeting, and I headed indoors for some breakfast. By God it took a while to be forgiven for that night's activities but Charlotte came round in the end although I was band from the Inn for many a month and when I did manage to go in I was turned out by the landlady and sent home with a flee in my ear. I never thought I was that bad that night to be barred from my local drinking hole, but later I was to hear that I was not, it was Charlotte, she had gone in and asked the landlady and Elizabeth Smith to make sure I was no longer welcome in her Inn. I must say she was a force to be reckoned with my wife, that is not the landlady.

Two or three weeks passed and my thoughts started to turned to the public auction, when was it due. I kept checking and double checking the local paper for the notification, and then one evening there on the back page as bold as punch and right in the middle of the page was what I had been waiting for the notification of the sale by public Auction of a rather large quantity of goods. Looking down the list and the quantity of items to be publicly auctioned, I would say they would be emptying the local custom house, the advert read.

On the 28 April 1767 by the order of the Honourable Commissioners of his Majesty at 11am in the forenoon will be exposed to public sale at the Custom House Port Douglas (at a price not less than the duty)

- 1300 Gallons of Brandy
- 250 Gallons of Geneva (Gin)
- 250 Gallons of Wine (French)
- 1 Silver Waist Band
- 2 Pair Bracelets
- 2 Silk Handkerchiefs
- 18 Staves, above 36 and not exceeding 50" in Length
- 5 Pieces – Quantity 79 Feet Fir Timber
- 11 Pair Kid Gloves
- 2 Pairs Silk Stockings.
- 2 Linen Sheets
- 7Ibs Verdigris
- 3 Pieces of Rope
- 8 Glass Tumblers
- 3 Fancy Boxes

Also the sloop Juliana admeasuring 40' 48–94 tons with all her tackle, apparel and furniture.

Looking down the list, I noticed that there was no ten hogshead of tobacco so where is it. I double-checked and checked again, it was missed off the auction list. Maybe it will be auctioned off later in the year. Having checked with a good friend of mine in the Revenue office it was not missed off the list, it was never on the list. The tobacco had disappeared and was nowhere to be found. The wine, brandy and gin was there but where was the rest of the cargo, and at the bottom of the list was the Juliana, my old friend's vessel, being auctioned off. This was very strange. Normally if it was any good, it would be used by the customs service or if it was no good and rotten it would be broken up for scrap and anything useful on board auctioned off. I should know with the amount of vessels offered to my brother before being broken up.

The day came for the auction and now I intended to retrieve what was truly mine the wine, brandy and gin and as such, I intended to get it for a very good price. I did think of mounting a raid on the store and retrieve what was rightfully mine but that was much too dangerous and more than likely they would be waiting for me and then that would be the end of me and for that matter my freedom. The word had been circulated that nobody was to bid for the goods if they knew what was good themselves and if they did they would receive a visit from one of my many friends. The bidding started and as planned nobody placed a bid and the price started to drop and drop. At the right time and price I started the bidding off and being the only bid I would win the goods at the low price. But from nowhere a newcomer appeared somebody I had never seen before standing on the other side of the square he looked across at me smiled and started to bid against me. I was furious and without a second thought I indicated to my comrades, they soon encircled him and with a gently encouragement from a knife in his side he was persuaded to stop bidding and was slowly escorted from the area without bringing attention to himself or for that matter me. Having been persuaded to stop bidding he was taken off to one of the small cottages in Port Douglas. Now this cottage was empty, no furniture or anything was in the cottage except one chair which was placed in the middle of the room. He was ceremonial forced to sit down where his hands were tied and his mouth was gaged and there he stayed on his own guarded by a good friend of mine and he waited until my business was completed and for me to introduce myself.

Don't ask me why I also for some reason started bidding for the Juliana tell me why I did this and I will never know but within minutes I was now the proud owner of yet another vessel to add to my fleet. How do I tell Charlotte of the new addition? She is likely to go mad but still this new addition should earn me a tidy profit and anyway if not I can always sell her on, hopefully for more than I paid for her.

Having retrieved what was truly mine at a very good price I now had a good batch of legally purchased goods which I could place in my wine cellars without having to hide anything? And the price was still cheaper than I would normally pay. The only difference being I had paid for the goods twice, but still much lower than if I had imported the wine legally. But where was my ten Hogshead of tobacco my enquiries had shown that the tobacco was no longer in the bonded store, nothing but nothing leaves the bonded store without being recorded and there were no records to show where it had gone or even that it was ever in the bonded store in the first place, was John Baites turning to my side and feathering his own nest, making a penny or two on the side. But alas, he was not for turning. Shame, it would have been nice to have him on my side.

Having completed my business, I paid for the goods and gave instructions on where it was to be sent. I left to make my to introduction to the person who tried to outbid me and purchase what was truly already mine, by bidding against me driving the price up. I walked into the cottage and there he sat bound and gagged and sweating rather well I thought. He was a worried man and to be honest he had every right to be and it showed. I had the gag removed and started questioning him, I found out he was not from this area and had answered an advertisement for a man unmarried to work in Port Douglas and to work for the local revenue office as an assistant and office clerk with a cover note which stated that no one from Port Douglas should reply to the advert. It was obvious that they needed somebody that no one knew or recognized. After about an hour of question and trying to stop my friends from killing the poor man, which turned this poor man into a nervous wreck in fact he had tears in his eyes and started to beg for his life pleading for us not to harm him. Little did he know I had no intention at all of killing or harming the poor man for just bidding against me. If he had done something worse like turned kings evidence, then that would be something else and would need to dealt with in a different way. In the end after we had made our point I made him an offer which in the position he was in he could hardly refuse and being the clerk of the revenue office, he could be very valuable to me. "Work for me and supply me information on what our friend John Baites was up to, but double cross me and you will be found late one night with your throat cut." The matter was settled I had a new informer within John Baites office.

Going back to my missing tobacco, I was soon to find out where the it had gone and it may have cost me dearly along with my freedom if the gods once more had not been watching over me and my new informer had not told me what was going on. It was late one evening when there was a knock on my door at home and there stood an old friend of mine George White, I had known George for many years in fact we had worked together on and off over the years and I trusted him well I thought I could trust him but events were to prove me very wrong and there you are I thought I was a good judge of character.

I invited him in and asked him to what do we owe you the pleasure of his visit.

'I have something that might be of interest to you'

'*And what might that be*' I replied

'The ten Hogshead of tobacco you have been asking about'

'*Er yes.* How did you come by it?'

'Well let's just say I have managed to obtain the ten hogshead of tobacco from an old friend who broke into the bonded store and made off with the tobacco along with a few other items'

'*So how much is this going to cost me?*'

'12 shillings per hundred weight'

After about an hour of bargaining we struck a bargain of eight shillings per hundred weight. Arrangements were made where the tobacco was to be delivered and it was not to be delivered directly to the tobacco sheds next to the factory. I needed to carry out further checks as something here was not quite right. The tobacco was too cheap and to be honest, the bargaining was also too easy to win. I was use to fighting the price down against some hard bargainers. It was if he just wanted to get away from me as fast as he could and I felt that something was missing. So I set up a halfway house a place where we normally would hide items before being moved on to their final destination but now it was somewhere we could have items delivered away from the main activities of my business and if I was raided for whatever reason then I would not be implicated and any seizures could be controlled its basically damage limitation.

I left it a month and then I sent word that we were ready for the tobacco to be delivered by horse and cart and by Gorge White himself a known smuggler which in itself should have sounded alarms. A known smuggler delivering goods and goods that I could not full establish its origins and where it had been stored for so long. Looking back I must have been mad. The tobacco was delivered without any problems to the store I had set up and then leaving it for another couples of weeks, I decided to move the tobacco at night and under cover into my main tobacco sheds and there it stayed for about a month with all the paper work in place showing duty paid and to all intense and purpose fully legal and above board. Believing that all was legal and above board, we did not hide or place the tobacco to one side to all intense and purpose everything was above board. Well that's what we thought was the case, until we had a knock on the factory door from the revenue officers and John Baites himself with a big beaming smile was standing on the door step, his opening words being 'come to inspect your store rooms and especially your last delivery' 'mainly the last delivery which we believe is illegal cargo and duty not paid'. My brother was horrified and panicked, he instructed his clerk to keep them occupied whilst he went off and got me. At around 4pm in the afternoon there was a knock on our front door and there standing on the door step was my brother and looking as white as a sheet and out of breath. I looked at him told him to calm down for god sake what's happened. After he had calmed down and got his breath back and had a stiff drink of brandy he told me what had happened and who we had as a visitor from the Revenue inspectors and in particular what they were looking for. I looked across at Charlotte and told her how I checked all the paperwork and it was in order with duty paid etc. but truly in the back of my mind I was still not sure where it had come from or where it had been and through whose hands it had passed. Had my luck run out and they'd finally caught me. Only time would tell.

We did not go straight back but decided to gathered our thoughts and then we decided how we were to handle this delegate situation. We all knew we would be ok we had the paperwork what could be wrong. So after we calmed Sam down we left home heading back slowly to the tobacco factor and there waiting was John Baites who was by now getting more and more annoyed at being left so long, it was now 5.30pm he had been left waiting an hour and half. As we approached the factory, all we could hear was John Baites shouting and raised voices. We walked in through the front door and holding our breath, we walked into the room where John and his fellow officers stood waiting. I turned to John and said to him 'Ok let's get this over with and quickly I have a dinner date I need to attend so turning to my brother I asked him to get the full manifest of all our stock levels showing duty paid. This will show where we got the tobacco from. In reality, the total history of any tobacco we hold in the factory. I informed him we had full traceability of all our stock. John grabbed the manifest from me, we headed into the store shed and started checking the stock levels, and making sure, they matched our records. All matched apart from the ten Hogshead of tobacco, it would be these ten. By now, we had emptied the stock shed as most was being prepared for processing and by now the tobacco had been exposed to the atmosphere and as such, the moisture levels increased so our stock levels showed a higher level than our paperwork showed. It was an old trick used by the smugglers to over dry the tobacco and to pack more tobacco into the barrels and as such you can get more tobacco in to the country for a lower taxes paid, and when you unpack the tobacco the moisture returns and you have a greater amount of tobacco than declared. I had fallen into a trap a trap that of all people should have seen coming. Plead ignorance and so that's what I did, I pleaded I had brought the goods in good faith I had weighed each hogshead of tobacco in turn when it entered the factory and this was entered on to the manifest and I could prove this. My paper work was in order. Then there was the matter of who you bought the goods from and who delivered it to you was a known smuggler, but as I pointed out again and again the paper work was in order and that's all that mattered. At this point I could see a way out and I took it. I turned to John and just told him to leave and vacate the premises unless he could prove we were at fault. He had no evidence we were in the wrong and as such he had not proved anything. He turned and left but he was not a happy person in fact his plan to catch me out was once more in tatters. Before he left he did tell me he would one day get me one way or another, to which my reply was that you need to get up really early to catch me out and anyway I have no idea what you are talking about. John Baites left that evening yet again an unhappy man muttering under his breath how he was going to get me one way or another.

After a quick glass of brandy for medicinal reason you understand, my nerves were in tatters we decided to leave and go home to our wives and families but on the way home we decided to pay George White a visit. We found his cottage it was located on the top edge of the valley just outside Port Douglas and at the top of a very large flight of steps, which by the time I reached his front door. I was out of breath we knocked on the front door. George answered and his greeting was not of a man who had plotted to betray my family and me but of a man who welcomed an old friend into his small but homely cottage. He invited us into his front room, there in the hearth was a roaring fire, and he was in the process of cooking his tea. He pulled out a bottle of wine and three glasses and offered us a drink to which we accepted. Without waiting too long we told George of the tail of the evening's events and how we had been paid a visit by John Baites. To which I asked where he had obtained the tobacco. He assured me he knew nothing of the evening events and that he had obtained the tobacco from somebody in the local Inn who had approached him asking if he would be interested in acting as the agent and then in delivering the tobacco to you. So he told you specifically to come to me and sell me the tobacco at whatever cost to which George replied 'yes'. I looked across to my brother and without any thought told him this is the work of John Baites and that we had been set up. George butted in and told me he even told me how much to sell to you and for that he paid me in dearly in silver and he produced a bag of silver, there must have been around £30-£40 in the bag not a small amount to turn away, that would be about two may be three years' wages in one go and help me along the way.

I asked for George to describe the man in the Inn the man and he described a man very well known to me and in fact a very good friend of mine Doc Tom Brown a really good doctor and a well-educated and knowledgeable person. As our local Doctor I have had used him many a time and he would never accept any payment, payment would always be by a keg of brandy. He could not be seen to accept payment for patching up a smuggler. We bid our farewells to George and told him to stay well out of the way for the time being and that someone will pay for this. We headed back home and decided to pay the Doc a visit the next day, it was late now and was getting dark and the Doc lived on the other side of town about ten miles away which would need us to go by horse and cart.

I rose early the next day telling Charlotte were I was going, who in turn warned me to be careful as we don't know who we are dealing with. Picking up George and Sam on the way we made our way across town and through a small forest or should I say glade, but it was a good place to hide if you were being followed. We had dug out, hollows all along this route and covered them with branches and leaves an easy place to suddenly leave the path way and hide away. Having reached the outskirts of Port Douglas, we found the Doc's cottage. The Doc's cottage was set in a very beautiful spot where the sun would shine through the tress glistening, as it passed through and bounce off the leaves of the trees and just behind the cottage was a stream that wound its way through the countryside with the water eagerly making its way down to the River Oxo and then out to sea. God he was a lucky man to live in such a spot. We knocked on the Doc's front door and within minutes the Doc answered, seeing us on his door step he looked a bit puzzled and asked "What can I do for you all?" "I will get straight to the point, where did you get the ten Hogshead of Tobacco come from?" The Doc stopped and looking a bit worried asked why, to which I conveyed to him the previous night's tale of what had happened and then all of the pieces of the jigsaw fell into place. I was right all along the tobacco had come from John Baites himself. He had removed the tobacco from the bonded store or I thought he had done so without permission and then sold it on without permission through an intimidate which was the Doc. It was to be sold on at such a low price on the understanding that it was to be sold to you John and to you only and being such a low price we knew you would not refuse it, and you would then think you had got a good deal. So what did he do with the proceeds had he kept it or worse handed it into his superiors, now that would upset me. So John Baites was selling on smuggled goods was he. I asked the Doc if he still had the original sale documents, where he informed me that no money was exchanged and no paper work was exchanged 'so tell me how did the tobacco get out from the bonded store', 'it never entered the bonded store, at no time did the tobacco reside within the bonded store, when the tobacco was seized that night the tobacco was removed from the wagons well before it reached the bonded store in Port Douglas and was brought straight to me here. 'I am telling you I had no idea what it was to be used for or to be used against you John. if I had any idea it was being used to get to you then I would have had nothing to do with the transaction. As it was, I only found out about the John Baites' connection after the deal had been done and the goods were delivered into my barn. They arrived late one night, the arrangements were that I was to leave the barn doors open and wait. Then at about 1am I heard the sound of a wagon outside on the cobbles and I decided to get up and take a look outside. All I could see was a group of men unloading ten hogshead of tobacco into my barn and as fast as they came they left. Leaving me instructions and a small keg of brandy for my trouble. Looking at the hand written instructions Its then that I recognised the hand writing as that of John Baites, in my position as the local Doctor I paid a visit to John Baites on more than one occasion and then given written instructions on whom I was to treat and whom I was to charge for my services, it would normally be one of his officers after one of their drunken brawls they would have often gotten into inside one of the local Inns. A common occurrence, which I acknowledged as these brawls or incidents, would have been arranged by myself to keep them busy and out of my way whilst we landed another good cargo of contraband, which the Doc thanked me for as it was good business for him as well.

After finding out as much as we could we left and bid the Doc goodbye thanking him for his help and made our way home. Was this to be the end of the event, no it was not poor George was to bear the brunt of the events of that day and he was visited late one evening and taken away in the middle of the night and was subjected to an horrific attack and one that I wanted nothing to do with. He was found one night buried up to his neck at the water line in the bay of Port Douglas just above high tide. He was found with the top of his head just showing above the waves and the bag of silver in his mouth. His cries for help would not have been heard and his death would have been slow and painful as the tide came in slowly washing in and out over his head till the last moment when the tide rose just covering his face. When he was dug out the marks on his body showed that he had been beaten without mercy with his hand bound behind him so tightly that they had cut into his skin and no way could he have escaped even if he tried. As I said, I wanted nothing of this, even though I knew who had done this terrible dead. Turning against your fellow smuggler was not something you did and even though George had done nothing wrong, this was a warning for anybody else who even thought of informing of your fellow smugglers. My methods of punishment were more subtle and did not involve treatment like this but was just as effective. Worst of all, in reality George had done nothing wrong and I did let the culprits know this and at the same time sent out a warning to all that before such a deed is done again to check their sources and ensure the punishment fitted the crime which in this case it did not. Poor George had done no more than delivered the goods and got caught up in something that in reality was nothing to do with him. If anything the Doc should have been the one to face such treatment and if it was not for me putting a stop to it, then he would have also faced such an act.

The ramifications of Georges murder were to cause a man hunt for the murders not seen before in Port Douglas and may never be seen again. The local constabulary had never had to investigate such a brutal murder before and as such had to request assistance, with assistance coming from London in the form of a constable from Scotland Yard. Between them all no stone was left unturned and with a substantial reward of £200 being offered for any information that would lead to the arrest and conviction of the murders. All in Port Douglas knew who the murders were but no one would tell. The murder of George White was as a result of turning Kings Evidence or all thought he had turned Kings Evidence, so why would anybody help the local authorities in finding his murderer as they too may end up the same way, six feet under. Suspicion was to fall on many in Port Douglas till one sunny day in June when on the outskirts of the town there was great commotion and three men were arrested for the murder of George White. Three local men and all three men we all knew well 'John Brown', David Smith and David White. George's brother surly he did not murder his own brother. But stranger things have happened in the town. The three men were duly charged with the murder of George White and taken away to London to be tried at the Old Bailey. The three men were tried and convicted for the murder of George White and sentenced to be hanged until dead and then their body's to be gibbeted outside Port Douglas. The bodies were stripped naked and left to all to show what would happen to murders. Their bodies were left to rot at the gates to the town and the birds to pick at their bones. Not a very pretty sight to those who entered Port Douglas but a good warning to others. The bodies stayed there for a few weeks after which I spoke to the local constable who agreed for the families to take the bodies and do as they wanted. They were taken down and given a Christian burial in the local church yard attended only by their kinsmen. But in reality, they should not have been buried in the churchyard. Due to their crimes, they should have been buried in unconsicrated ground, but for their relatives who spoke to the vicar and out of compassion he agreed to their request.

I heard nothing more form John Baites with reference to that terrible evening and the events that unfolded afterwards but the relation between us was to grow even worse during the rest of the year to the point he became once more obsessed in trying to catch me but as always I was one step ahead. So instead of going out night after night smuggling I ended up once more financing around half a dozen trips that year and in each case I decided to stay at home and leave the hard work to the younger generation. I am getting to old for all this now, which made Charlotte a lot happier. Although finding out our eldest son was using one of my vessels yes my vessels with my blessing, which made it even worse and I yes his father was financing these trips, which made it even worse when Charlotte his mother found out. I have never ever in my life have seen her so angry and I saw a side of Charlotte that I did not really like. She flew at me and told me a few home truths threatening me with such a gruesome death if her eldest son was caught, her eldest son was following in his father's footsteps, what could be worse than that. She worried enough about me in the early years but her son this was even harder for her to accept, and over the next few months every opportunity I came to hear about it, she just would not let it drop. Women never forget anything either when we argued about this Charlotte would also bring up things that I had done many years before, things I could never remember along with how I broke her favourite dish or how I told her I liked her dress but in reality I hated it. Woman are strange and us men will never understand how their minds work and how they never forget anything only to bring out those long lost points when an argument develops.

But enough of that and back to the story I am telling of yet another event later in the year when John Bates seized cargo, a cargo he lost it again and I gained and John Baites finally lost his mind.

One of the trips I financed that year ended up with us losing the entire cargo. We had landed the goods on a lonely beach, not far from Port Douglas and having landed too late one night, we decided to hide the goods away safely (well, we thought safely) and collect at a later date when we had more time. So we packed the cargo into a cave not far away, hid the entrance from view under bracken and tree branches. We waited for the right moment to collect it but John Bates managed to get to it before we did. But unknown to us he already knew of this hiding place from overhearing one night, a discussion between two know smugglers on how they would use this place to hid a few kegs of brandy. Which he went straight off and seized and unknown to us he had been checking this cave now at least once a week on his travels around the area. Loose tongues cost me money and you know what we do with a loose tongue, cut it out. So as you can imagine this did not amuse me, and we only found out the goods had been seized the same evening when John Baites' motley crew came rolling into the local Inn on a high and started boasting about a large seizure that night. As the night progressed and the drink flowed we obtained were he found the cargo and were it had been taken. We left and gathered up a few reliable me, including the local blacksmith who would be needed to break open the bonded store. We arranged to meet just outside of town and this would be daring raid and as such would need to be done with speed.

There was around twenty of us including my eldest son. We road into town with the horse's shoes clattering on the cobbles as we rode down the street. We turned onto the quay side and there in front of us was the bonded store were my cargo yes my cargo of wine and brandy was lying, following behind us was two horse drawn carts onto which we would load the kegs. We approached the front door the locksmith jumped down from his horse and went to work on the front door, he made short work of it and the door swung open, we entered and as fast as we arrived we had loaded the kegs onto waiting carriages and was making our way out of town. We left at full gallop and the noise of the horse's shoes on the cobble street was deafening and to add to this we also let off a few rounds of musket fire into the air of course. By now we had a crowd of people watching the daring raid and we knew it would not be long before my old friend John Baites and his fellow officers would arrive but they were in the local inn next door drunk as usual, celebrating their great success. However, we also knew how to use the crowd that had gathered to watch our little foray to our advantage. So just before we left I left two kegs of brandy for the crowd with instructions for them to detain the revenue men which they did. Oh and I forgot to say as we left we turned to the night watchmen and informed him 'we had come for what was rightfully mine and nothing else' and of course we did not harm the night-watchman we left him loosely tide up just enough to keep him occupied until we had got away. Of course he got away removing his bindings and ran off to let John Baites know what had happened, apparently the screams of anger could be heard from one side of town to the next and the shame he would endure from this raid I am afraid to say he never ever recovered from. This was the start of his spiral into drink and finally his death late one evening after he got so drunk, the story goes, that he fell off the quay side into the harbour. His body was recovered the next night from one of the local beaches.

The raid on the Revenue store that night was to go down in local history and folk lore on how a group of ragger bonds had outwitted and defeated the local revenue officers and got away with it. We were wearing masks and had our hair whitened so we could not be recognised. We managed to get clean away with what was ours, not the governments but mine and as such all I was doing was re-claiming what was rightfully mine. A reward was posted of £150 for any information that could be used to identify and bring to justice anybody that took part that night in such a daring raid.

John Baites was to be replaced the following year by one of his officers Rupert Brain Thomas who had impressed his superiors so well and had earned the promotion as a result of many a seizure of the odd keg or two, yep ones I had left for him to find to make out he was doing his job so well and to leave me alone to get on with my night time activities without being disturbed. How do you think I have survived so long without being caught, by always being one step ahead of John Baites. Life should be much easier now I had the supervisor to the riding officers for Port Douglas on my pay role, or will it be, would he have too much to lose to be on my pay role as well as the revenue office department's payroll, only time will only tell.

Chapter 24

In the year of our Lord 1770

Life does not get much better though? Even at our age when our children are older and are no longer children but young adults and really should know better. They can still cause us so much pain and suffering and place so much worry on the shoulders of their parents. When one of the twins was to bring us news of a small addition to the family and considering he was still only twenty and not even married, this was too coming as rather a shock to us all especially to his mother and to cause us great disappointment in one of our children. He could not have picked a better time to tell us of his little problem, he told us over dinner late one evening. I can tell you it came as a bit of a shock to find out that we were to become grandparents and at such a young age, a baby in the house that frightens me, we have not had a baby in the house now for many years. He was not married and to the best of our knowledge he was not even seeing anybody or so we thought, well we were wrong there. After gathering my thoughts, I pointed out to him the shame and not to say the damage you may bring to our reputation and standing in Port Douglas and more to the point, what about the poor girl and the shame on the poor girl's family, a baby out of wedlock was no laughing matter. One careless night, one night of passion and two lives are thrown into turmoil and even worse they could be ruined. What the hell were you thinking about? And don't answer that? I agree it takes two and the total blame cannot be taken by our son alone but Bruce should have known better at his age. Although the thought of being grandparents at the age of fifty was also something I did not really want to consider. More to the point we may also have the pleasure of the girl's father knocking on the door and wanting to see Bruce. I then was told who the girl was, and who her father was and finding this out was something I did not want to consider as I can be sure knowing who he was that it would not end with a polite conversation. More than likely it will end up with a confrontation of some sorts and I would end up in the middle of it trying to protect my son. One thing in our favour was my reputation in Port Douglas a reputation that was known throughout the town as somebody not to be messed with and not one that you would want to cross or even get on the wrong side of. But this was different this is a situation that would need to be handle with great care, this was the fault of my son and something that he and he alone needs to sort out and a young lady's life and reputation is now at stake. For once, my reputation throughout the area may not help my son and he may have to take the punishment that no doubt would come his way.

There are many questions which now needed to be answered and the main one was that Bruce has to face up to his responsibilities and quickly and either marry the girl or just support the girl and his child, our grandchild. Mainly he needs to explain himself to us and his family why has he put himself and us his parents in such a position. The real truth was soon to come out and it was not a pleasant one. I would now find out that I might need to pull in as many favours as I could because if we could not sort this out Bruce could end up in court and be forced to support the woman and her child. If he did not, he would end up in the local gaol in which case I doubt for one minute he would last long. On the other hand, when they realize he is such a good sailor he may find he is on route to join His Majesty's Navy where also he would not last long in such a violent and in hospitable place. Whichever way he was in trouble. I made a promise to Charlotte not knowing if I could keep it. That I would sort this mess out some way or other, but now Charlotte trusted me in what I said and over the years if I said something it normally meant I actually could do something, but this time I was not sure, much was out of my control. We sat down in the garden and asked Bruce for the truth and we mean the truth that to say leave nothing out. He began telling us of how his friends decided to have some fun and how they had tricked the girl into coming to some rooms in town they had rented on the pretence that she was to be offered a job at our house as a maid. His mother's reaction to this was not good not at all, I thought she was going to slap Bruce across the face, but instead asking what was he thinking. His friends also knew of the girl's infatuation with our son and it's this infatuation that they played on. When the girl arrived Bruce's friends decided to leave the two of them together on their own and the result was Julia got pregnant not going into too much detail. We asked how old Julia was I am afraid to say she was only seventeen a mere child. I turned back to Bruce and just asked how he could take advantage of such a young girl to which there was no reply and with tears in his eyes he hung his head low in shame. I then pointed out that it was a bit late to be sorry you should have thought about what you were doing and how it was so wrong.

Bruce looked at us and with a tear in his eyes, he asked us "What am I to do?" Looking at his mother who by now was looking on in total disbelief and disappointment of her son and without thinking Charlotte just asked him how could he do this to us, have you no pride.

I looked Bruce in the face and told him he would do the right thing, you will visit the family and explain what happened, take any punishment the father gives out and just marry the girl if she'll have you, and for god's sake face up to your responsibilities, have we not taught you this all through your short life what is right and what is wrong and this was wrong. We sent you to an expensive school to be educated and this is what you do throw your life away for one night of pleasure with a girl you hardly know.

Bruce's reply took his mother and me by surprise, it turns out he knew the girl very well in fact more than just well, and had been seeing her now for about six to eight months and worse still, it's not the first time they had slept together. I could not believe my ears. What the hell had we brought up? I thought he had more sense than that but obviously I was very wrong.

Looking back everything dropped into place now this is why he had kept disappearing during the day taking a picnic down to the beach, or riding off in the evening. We did wonder who he was meeting, and maybe this is why his mind was not on his job, he had made mistakes and cost us dearly especially when he started to sell wine at the wrong price. But this did not impress his mother at all; all she could think of was this poor girl pregnant at such a young age and as for her reputation that was now in tatters. Looking back at Bruce all she could say out loud was, "God it gets worse, I just don't want to know anymore, I need to get out of here and get some fresh air."

By now I was shouting at him. I could not believe what I was hearing, not the first time. "How many times and so how long has this been going on then?" Charlotte by now, was in full floods of tears and turned to Bruce and looking at him just asked. How could you do this to us and after all we have gone through over the last few years. With that Charlotte got up and left the room her last word she said to Bruce before going out was 'You disappoint me' I turned and followed her as I left I turned back to Bruce and told him to think very carefully before doing anything else and to stay in the house for the time being until all the mess is sorted.

I knew where Charlotte was going she had left the house and headed off to a very special place her place where she could be alone and think things through and be close to John the son we lost three or so years previous and sure enough sitting among the dunes in Brandy Bay on her own I found Charlotte. She was sat in the same place that our youngest daughter had gone just after John's death. I sat down beside her placed my arm around her to comfort her and we sat quietly not talking just thinking. After about thirty minutes she looked at me and ask me why? Why us? Have we not suffered enough over the last few years?

By now, it was getting late now, the sun had gone in, and the rain had started to fall so we gathered our things up and headed home to our tea and the rest of the family who by now had realized that something was very very wrong. Tea was served in the dining room and with the family now sat around the table we ate in total silence the atmosphere at the table was terrible you could have cut it with a knife. Looking across the table to Charlotte I threw down my napkin and looked at Bruce and shouted enough I think Bruce you better explain what you done to bring such shame on the family.

As Bruce stood and started to explain there was a sharp knock on the front door I left the room and went to open the front door before one of the maids just in case Julia's father had decided to pay us a visit so late in the day, but no standing on the door step in the pouring rain was Julia soaked through and she was crying well that's not really true she was hysterical. I remember just telling her to get inside child and out of the rain, she was soaked through. Her father had thrown her out onto the street when he had heard she was pregnant, the shame on the family was more than he could bare and the shame on our family was much the same. I could not leave her standing on the door step, this would be even worse for us to bear. We had to show compassion and goodwill to her, we could not turn her away for god sake she was carrying our first grandchild.

Turning to one of the maids who was by now heading over to me to see what was going on. I asked her to assist and take her upstairs to the spare bedroom and to dry her off and then to bring her into the living room so she could warm up by the fire. Hearing the commotion Charlotte came out of the dining room to see what was going on and saw the poor girl standing in the hall way soaked through. She came running over and taking the girl by the hand headed off upstairs to dry the child and get her into some dry cloths. As they headed upstairs the rest of the children stood in the doorway of the dining room with Bruce starting to follow his mother and the mother of his child. His mother stopped turned back and shouted across don't even think of coming near us don't you think you've done enough damage for one day just stay away and I will talk to you later. I was not sure what she was going to say as most things had already been said. Bruce looked across at me for support and I am afraid I lost control and I also shouted across a similar message and stormed off into my study slamming the door behind me, sorry to say I nearly took the paintings off the wall as they shock violently. The whole situation had just taken another turn for the worse; the child was now under our roof and as such under our protection, what the hell do we do next. I sat down in my study and had a drink may be not the best idea but at the time I needed calming down, drink in hand I sat down in front of the fire and for the first time in my life I had no idea what to do. For god sake my son has fathered a child out of wedlock, how can we resolve this problem. For the first time ever this was a situation out of my control the child's father held the key and the solution to the problem. As I sat quietly thinking Charlotte came into the room and sat down next to me and in a soft voice she explained the events of the day and how the child's father had thrown her out and how she had walked around Port Douglas for hours not knowing where to go or what to do and how she came to us as a last resort for help and a hope of talking to Bruce. She had tried earlier but our son had just walked away without saying a word when she told him she was pregnant and carrying his child. This made me even madder sending into a rage I very rarely show and obviously he was not the person we thought he was. He was our son and the person we brought into the world and had taught him to face up to the consequences of his actions and not turn his back on his responsibilities and here he is just doing that turning his back on what is right, he was a coward and no son of mine. That's what hurt me the most, our son had become a disappointment and as such, needed to do what was right, especially before the baby starts to show.

I now know what needed to be done and it needed to be done quickly and in a place where we had the advantage. I sent a message to Julia's father firstly telling him his daughter was safe and well and staying with us for the time being and I suggested that maybe we should meet and try and sort this mess out sooner than later. So we invited Julia's parents to tea the next day Sunday. This should give us enough time to prepare and make things ready. Charlotte did wonder if this was such a good idea to invite Julia's parents round so early. Should we try and wait until the dust had settled before we invited them round. I pointed out to Charlotte that we need to sort this out before the baby is born more to the point before things get any worse that's if we can. So it was agreed we would invite them over for Sunday tea. I disappeared into my study, wrote out the invite and I decided to deliver the invite myself which I thought was for the best and try and defuse the situation the best I could. So I arrived at Julia's parent's cottage, gathered my thoughts and just walked up the path as though there was nothing wrong and knocked on the front door only to be greeted by this rather large and muscly person. I introduced myself not that I really needed to as I was well known throughout Port Douglas and we shock hands; by the way, he nearly crushed my hand with his handshake. He looked me up and down and then invited me in, not sure what to expect I declined and made up some excuse of a previous engagement. The invite was duly accepted after a short but to the point exchange on what he wanted to do to my son for getting his only daughter pregnant. I did point out that that would get us nowhere as he would need all his limbs to be able to make a living to support his future wife and child. So I decided not tell Bruce until about thirty minutes before they were due to arrive. I thought this was for the best so he could not disappear as he had a habit of disappearing to avoid his responsibility. When I did tell him, the look of terror on his face was apparent as he knew the father and what he was capable of. We then explained to Bruce what was to be done and what he was to do and he was to do it quickly. Then as always, we would try and sort his mess out. We seem to keep sorting his mess out. I did have one thought maybe I should just ship him off to some far flung out post of the empire and just wait out the situation and bring him back when the dust had settled but no he has made his bed and he will have to lie in it.

Sunday soon came around which gave Bruce just enough time to come to his senses and do the right thing as we had instructed him to, we told him he was to ask Julia to marry him and then he was to ask her father for Julia's hand in marriage and let's hope this will be an end to it. Julia had taken our advice and had spent the Sunday morning with Bruce mainly so we knew where he was, but at last our son had faced up to, his responsibilities accept the situation and actually ask the girl to marry him. I know at such a young age to be taking on such responsibilities is big thing but I am afraid this is what happens if you are not careful, and let us be honest stupid. At last he was happy the sullen face had gone only to be replaced by a happy smiling young man again, we had our son back again and at the same time gained another daughter. The only thing I wished was the circumstances could have been better.

I was not going to leave my son out to dry as they say. I was always going to help him. it's just that he needed to see it and realize what he had done and face it head on. You cannot walk away from such a situation as this. So as a wedding present I promised him I would provide a home for his new family in Port Douglas and as it so happened a I heard of a small cottage that was up for sale so I bought it and had it prepared for them, and on their wedding day I gave them the key to the front door. But there was much to do before this could be done and firstly we had to appease Julia's parents especially her father.

Whilst Bruce was doing the right thing on Sunday morning, Charlotte instructed the cook what to prepare and for the maids to be shown what was required on them, they would serve the tea and then they could go as we did not want our dirty washing aired in public. Lunchtime came and went and it was soon teatime and a knock on the door and there standing on the doorstep was a very large and muscular person who introduced himself as Julia's father. Well we had already met on more than one occasion as he had acted as a tub man on more than one occasion for me. Standing by his side was a rather petite woman they did not look matched but he introduced her to us as his wife Sarah. This time I avoided the hand shake not wishing to have my hand crushed. They wore their Sunday best and looked rather good actually not sounding snobbish. We invited them both in and we made our way into the back garden, luckily, it was a beautiful summer's day and we thought it might be easier if we sat outside rather than in the grand surroundings of the house. The last thing we wanted was to make them feel out of place, so in the middle of the lawn we had tea laid out. We sat Julia and Bruce to one side next to us and Julia's parents we sat on the other side opposite to Bruce. Julia's father rose from his chair and towered over Bruce and I thought he was going to punch two bails of crap out of Bruce so I moved between them and blocked them and gestured for them to sit down again. Firstly, sending the maids away as I did not want to have them listening in to our affairs and then have it all round the village.

I gestured to Charlotte why do not you take Julia and her mother for a walk in the garden whilst we discuss the issue and try to sort this mess out. When the ladies had left and without any further to do, I turned to Julia's father and started to discuss the situation pointing out that we too were not amused. To which I was told again exactly what he wanted to do with my son and I must admit I could not disagree with him. For god sake, he had got his daughter pregnant, but at the same time, I could not and would not let that happen. I let him have his say and then I explained to him my solution to the problem, they were to be wed and well before the child shows and to help we will pay all of the wedding costs and we will provide a house for them to live in. Within the hour, I found he had agreed and we drank to the marriage of Julia and Bruce.

Just one thing need to be done now and that Bruce had to ask for his daughter's hand in marriage, something I was not looking forward to as I was to leave the two of them to together alone. Bruce had been present through the whole meeting and had kept very-quite as instructed. It was now Bruce's turn to speak and looking across at Bruce he looked terrified I think he must have felt sick to the pit of his stomach and his hands were shaking and were very sweaty. As for his voice well that sounded terrible, he needed a good prompt so without any further to do and before I left them to it I looked across and asked him what he had to say. He made eye contact with me and I thought he was going to burst into tears, and then he got the courage together and asked for his daughter's hand in marriage. There was a long silence whilst Julia's father gave the matter some thought, he let it be known he was not happy but let's be honest he has not much choice considering the state his daughter was in and they needed to be married before the child starts to show. So Permission was duly given and then Julia's father rose from his chair and towered over Bruce. I thought Bruce was going to faint with fright but no they shook hands and then Julia's father gave Bruce a bear hug and looked directly into Bruce's eyes and told him if you hurt my daughter in anyway then you will regret it until you die which might be sooner than you think do you hear me. The look of relief on Bruce's face was a picture I just hope now he has learnt his lesson well.

When the ladies came back, from their walk around the gardens they were surprised how we were laughing and joking together and not trying to kill each other, my charm and diplomacy and luck had come to forth once again. I think they expected to see us all covered in blood and knocking two bails of crap out of each other, but no, I had once more turned the situation from one of confrontation to one of friendship. When we were all seated, I proposed a toast to Bruce and Julia and of course, the little addition, may they live long and prosper.

I declared we now have a wedding to arrange and one that would need to be done quickly and at the same time carefully.

Julia and Bruce obtained a special licence and where to be married in the next month in the local church. The reception was held in a great marquee on our back lawn, with everybody who was anybody invited. It was the first of our children to be wed, even if it was under strange circumstances. The party went on into the early hours of the morning with music, dancing and laughter, and yes I imported the silk to make the wedding dress and if I might say Julia looked rather beautiful. It reminded me of my wedding day when I married the love of my life. much of the wine drank that day came from my wine own cellars or should I say was smuggled into the country. I did chuckle when looking round at the guests on that night if only they knew what they were drinking and were it came from, as always the last laugh is with me. As promised on their wedding day, I handed Bruce the keys to the cottage which would become their home for many years and where they would bring up their children and our grandchildren. In total they had three more children all boys, so they ended up with three boys and one girl. Whom they named Charlotte Sarah Smith after Bruce's and Julia's mother. The three boys where named after me and me and Julia's father, Robert, Michael and Sam my brother.

Chapter 25

The year is 1775 and five years since the marriage of Bruce and Julia and the birth of Charlotte Sarah Smith, yes we were grandparents named after his mother and Julia's mother. The last five years to be honest were uneventful not much happened and if I am honest I become complacent and a bit fool hardy, I started to believe I was invincible and nothing could touch me, which in reality was fare from the truth as I was soon to find out. I financed a few smuggling trips which all went off without a problem and the goods were landed and moved away apart from one which we nearly lost at sea in a storm, when the kegs were not secured correctly and they managed to start moving around the hold crashing into each other, but the crew eventually managed to secure them, saving the ship. I was also to captain the Valiant a few times in those five years and each time, we came back without any problem, we landed the items and each time we were not met with any problems. This being mainly to the fact that the new Revenue Officer, Rupert was a good friend of mine and on my payroll and as such, left me alone to work the coast line unhindered. Like I said, I became complacent and I felt untouchable but I was soon to be brought back to earth with a bang in fact a big bang, my pride would be dented as well as my pocket.

It must have been around March of 1775 when the incident occurred and the events of that night were out of my control. I was helpless and in the hands of god himself. We were due to set sail for Cherbourg and we needed to leave Port Douglas late afternoon. We prepared the Valiant to leave Port Douglas and by the time we left Port Douglas the weather was perfect, hot and sunny with enough wind to fill our sails and take us on our way, a perfect spring day. Well that is what we thought. Our spirits were high and we looked forward to yet another uneventful trip, how wrong were we to be. This was to be one of my most harrowing and dangerous trips I have ever in my life had to endure, and to make it worse, like I said, the situation was out of my control and I was well out of my comfort zone.

The problems started when we were half way home, we had reached Cherbourg loaded up and left with no problem to make our way home. Things were going well until we reached about the middle of the English Channel when from nowhere and I mean nowhere we suddenly realized we were sailing into a bank of fog, very dense fog and soon the whole ship was engulfed in the fog. The temperature suddenly dropped from a pleasant and warm evening to a night were jumpers and jackets were needed but worse we soon found ourselves sailing blind. The fog was so dense we could not even see the other end of the 'Valiant' and we could hardly see our hands in front of our faces. Then without any warning the wind fell from our sails and the sails started to flap like a wounded animal unable to run from the hunter, we found ourselves becalmed in the middle of the English Channel and we were not going anywhere this did not make any sense. We sat there in the Channel bobbing from side to side our sails flapping in what wind there was trying to capture what wind they could and every now and then the sails would fill with wind moving us forwards towards home well I hope it was towards home as we were totally disorientated. I called over to the cabin boy and gave instructions to sound the 'Valliant's' bell every minute with two sharp strikes sending the sound across the by now calm and eerie sea letting all know we were there. The other thing we noticed apart from the sound of our bell it was quite too quite. The hairs on the back of my head stood up and if I am honest I was scared and that is something I had never really experience, something was very wrong here and I just could not put my finger on it. Then out of the gloom appeared the bow of a ship on our starboard side it was a very large square sailed ship I believe it must have passed by missing us by around fifty feet there was no wake or disturbance in sea, the sea was like a millpond, flat as a pancake. As the ship passed by I could just make out her name on her stern 'The Elizabeth Ruth' that name sounder familiar to me but I cannot think why. Apart from my own vessel, the 'The

Elizabeth Ruth' named after my own children. We were within ear shot of this mysterious ship so I shouted across to her but no reply came. The strange thing was the air was so still, there was no sound, nothing as this great ship passed us by. I tried to see if I could not see anybody on board, taking my spyglass, I checked the ship over the best I could. I could see nobody, there was nobody at the helm of the ship steering through the water, and as fast as she appeared, she disappeared back into the fog. Leaving no trace of her behind no wake, nothing it was as though she had never been there. I made a note in my ships log of the encounter, mainly for future reference and just in case I decided to make an inquiry into who she was when we got home. My thoughts then returned to our predicament. We could not locate our position as we could not see the stars and more to the point, we had no wind to fill our sales so we were a drift in the channel and at the mercy of the currents. Anything could come out from the fog and hit us, and sink us, and nobody would know or be the wiser. You do hear stories of ships been sunk whilst deep in a fog bank. I then started thinking about how that ship sailed pass us with no wind in her sails, but their sails were full of wind as she sailed by. We must have been adrift now for about an hour when all of a sudden we felt the wind across our faces and our sails suddenly burst into life. The canvas filling with wind, lifting the bow out of the water as our speed increased. Then the temperature around us visible increased, no longer were we cold. As fast as we entered the bank of fog we suddenly emerged from the bank of fog into a beautiful cloud less night with the brightest starts in the sky I have ever seen. Without a moment's thought the most important thing was to find our position. Using the charts on board and the stars in the sky I plotted our position and course and to my horror I find we were off course and much further down the coast of England than we should be, but how could that be, how could we be further down the English Channel when not under sail. Surly the currents are not that strong.

We were out of it now and that's all that mattered and so pleased were we. We turned back to look towards the fog in disbelief and all we could see for miles was the fog bank. I asked myself what was that we had just experienced and as for that ship that sailed pass us 'The Elizabeth Ruth' it did not look real it seemed as if it was not part of this world if that makes sense. When we reached port, I started asking a few questions about that mysterious vessel and I found out she was a Royal Navy Frigate that was lost at sea twenty or so years previous. She went down in the channel in the area where we were set a drifting with a total loss of crew; nobody knows where she sank or even what really happened to her. I had described this vessel to the letter including her name written on the stern, it was her ok. There was no explanation for what we saw or experienced that night, it was her, I know it was it her, maybe it was a ghost ship I do not know, I had heard of similar stories before and if I am honest I did not believe them, but now having seen what I have seen with my own eyes maybe there is something in what people say.

That night became a talking point within the village of Port Douglas and within the local inn and the tale would be told each time we ended up getting drunk, not that many people actually believed us and thought our tales was a result of a drunken trip across to France. But I know the truth and what I saw that night and I am sure it was the Ghostly ship of 'The Elizabeth Ruth' roaming the seas and drawing sailors to the depths and to their death.

Chapter 26

After that night, I was wary every time I set sail at night and never again did I see or experience such an occurrence. The sudden arrival of such a fog bank and with such speed that it appeared I had never experienced before just seeing the fog roll in it was just incredible. I remember we were under full sale with clear visibility and then suddenly without warning, we were becalmed and engulfed in the fog and I am not sorry to say how sacred we all were. But I am getting older and wiser now and nothing surprises me any more when it comes to the sea and what it can throw at you from out of the blue or should I say the depths.

The year now was 1780 and the country was to be ravaged by yet more storms and that year many where to lose their lives at sea. Even I was to lose a ship with all its crew, hitting us hard knowing the crew so well and also having lost a son to the sea, we knew just what it was like to have a life ripped from us so early in their lives.

Now life was to became much easier for a short while with my old friend Rupert as the Revenue Officer, although I am sorry to say he was moved on after that great storm of 1780. Especially after the word got round of how friendly he was with the local smugglers in fact he married a smugglers daughter which was a no no, being a revenue officer and even worse being the supervisor. But his reign was to only last ten years as the Supervisor of Port Douglas. In those ten years, not one smuggler was caught and prosecuted, well that was not quite true some smugglers were caught but Rupert had a weakness for money and he could be bought quite easily. Those caught in his ten years invariably were set free after they had cross his palm with silver or a keg of brandy. But in his favour and to keep his bosses happy, the bonded store where all the seized cargo ended up was never empty, never full either. We would supply just enough to keep prying eyes away. In addition, I am afraid to say Rupert was not one for paperwork and as such another reason why he was demoted and moved onto another district where he was not known. Now as mentioned before once a week he was supposed to meet up with his fellow officers and check and sign off their diaries, lucky if this was done once every other month let alone each week to such a point that his fellow officers knowing that they were not being checked would stay at home and make up stories of their adventures whilst on patrol. Shame they all did not all get together and ensure their stories matched as they told different stories so much that it became so obvious one day that they had not been out on patrol. The story goes on one occasion that one officer's diary told of how the weather on one night was so bad he could hardly ride around the area without being blown from his horse, whilst another officer claimed the very same night was a clear beautiful night and he could see everything by the moonlight and had nothing to report. This went on for months and months and Rupert knew what was going on but never once did he stop his men and ask what the hell was going on. They had been given a free hand. To cover up what was going on when each diary book was full and to hide the evidence Robert would destroy the records so the irregularities could not be verified. But in the end his supervisors came down one day and carried out some spot checks and all came to light he had been caught out and so he was demoted and moved onto pastures new somewhere in Wales I believe.

We heard later through the grape vine how Rupert had been demoted and was now an ordinary officer once more serving somewhere in Wales not sure where and to be honest I don't really care. He had done well from us all and was now quite a wealthy man. He had no choice but to move lock stock and barrel, the barrel was a present from me for all his help through the years and the barrel was full of brandy. A good one I believe from my last import.

We had a temporary replacement for Robert, one of his four officers was asked to help out and stepped up to the mark as you might say and took on the role of supervisor for a few months whilst a permanent replacement was found. Story goes they had somebody already in mind and we were soon to hear of who our next supervisor was to be, it was not good news, he was to come from London and had been brought in to specifically clean up the area and stop the trading going on along the coast. The amount of landings that had happened in the last ten years had risen ten-fold whilst Rupert was supervisor and had risen to such an extent there must have been at least two landings a night and I should know as most of them were under my control over those ten years. Well they would rise as we had worked the coast unhindered. So had many more of my colleagues, along with others that knew this area was easy pickings and as such had moved into the area. But this new supervisor coming to Port Douglas came with a reputation of being a hardnosed bastard. It would not just only be the smugglers that would fare badly under his reign but also his fellow officers who now would have to work to earn a living and not make up stories whilst sat at home in comfort. They will actually have to go out at night searching the area and try to stop the landings. I predict that there will be blood split under his reign, and it won't just be ours.

May be this was the time to start considering my future and to start to think about handing over the company to my children and take up yet another challenge in my life, the Mayor of Port Douglas. I had been asked enough times to run for Mayor. Like I said, I have been approached many times over the years, but first I needed to turn into a good citizen of Port Douglas. Some people would look up to, not somebody who is known for his heavy handed approach, which I think may be a problem as nearly everybody in Port Douglas knew me too well. I think most of Port Douglas and surrounding area have worked for me at some point in time in their lives, so how can I portray myself as the model citizen suitable to be Mayor of Port Douglas. Well this might be a problem.

Chapter 27

You know tragedy seems to follow me around wherever I go in this year of 1780 was to be no different. Over the last few years, I have had my fair share of family and friends that have died or badly injured. But this year was to hit me even harder than ever with the loss of my very first ship 'The Valiant' and her crew in a storm in 1780. 'The Valiant' left port on the 10th November 1780 on route to the Channel Islands. It was nothing special but a normal run importing some wine legally for our wine cellars, but she never was to return home. She reached the Channel Islands apparently with no problems and left without problems but the storm that was massing in the channel was to take her and her crew to the bottom of the English Channel, and to remind us all that the sea must be respected at all times. Once more her captain did not head my warnings or strict instructions of not to go to sea in a storm or even if a storm is expected. The story of what happened and how the ship was lost will never really be known all we knew is that she never came home. She was reported lost on the 12th November 1780. The remains of the Valiant were found floating in the sea about three miles out from Port Douglas by a local fisherman, who brought some of the remains of the hull home to me. The only reason we knew it was 'The Valiant' was when we looked at the remains of the hull, you could clearly see her name 'Valiant' painted in Red. All we can think is she was swamped by a large wave with the cargo breaking free in her hold, which would have made her very unstable. I suspect and hope the crew would have tried to secure the cargo. Trying to save their ship but this would have been nearly impossible in these conditions not to say also extremely dangerous. The result being that a strong wave may well have smashed into the Valiant side and with the moving cargo in her hold she would have capsized easily, ripping her hull apart along with the cargo being spilled into the sea. She would have stood no chance and then finally swamped by the waves taking the 'Valiant' and her captain and crew down with her

The sea that night was once more, a boiling mass with waves that would have been pounding the ship without mercy. Looking at the waves crashing onto beach at home they must have been at least twenty to thirty feet high out at sea or they could have been even higher, as there was no survivors. No one will ever know. We can only guess by looking at the conditions along the coast and the way the waves were breaking over the sea walls that protected our little harbour. No bodies were ever recovered that night or over the next few weeks giving no closure to their families. The families of the crew clung onto the thought that their loved ones may have made it to safety and dry land only to walk back through the front door and into their arms. But in their hearts, they knew they had lost them forever. A memorial service was held in the local church which I and many local business men contributed towards and I paid for a small memorial stone to be dedicated to the sailors lost that night, giving the grieving family something and somewhere to go and leave flowers or for them to sit and talk to their loved ones. Times would now be hard for the missing sailor's families.

As always I tried my best to look after the families of the crew and captain which is the least I could do as they worked for me and were on out at sea on my business. I did question what were they doing out in such weather. All that sailed with me were told never ever to set sail in such bad weather and to consider their own and their crew's safety first and foremost. I told them if they find themselves in such a position don't be a hero and battle on, make for the nearest port of safe haven and ride the storm out. I also told them not to worry if they were late into port, customers will be cross but at least you will be alive and not like the 'Valiant' and her crew. Something I cared about and beat into each and every captain under my command. The only thing that could explain it was on checking the weather in the Channel Islands when 'The Valiant' left, it was a lovely sunny day with a low wind of around force two to three with no indication of a storm coming down the channel. The only thing I can think of was they must have got caught out and may well have been trying to head inshore and find a safe haven and shelter in one of the many small bays along the coast but alas they did not make it, and we will never ever find out what really happened.

After the loss of 'The Valiant', I lost the will to go to sea. The passion I had once harboured over the years for going to sea had gone. We all know how powerful the sea can be and none more than me as we were reminded once more how we lost our youngest son not so many years back in such a storm, when he was taken from us whilst playing on the beach. I was not frightened of the sea. I had a respect for the sea, which many did not. I know too well what the sea was capable of and how an unforgiving environment a place it can be, where no mercy is shown to anybody or anything.

So that was it, 1780 was the year that saw me loose the will, the will to go to sea and mostly my love of the sea. No longer will I go to sea, and this time I really meant it. I spoke with my solicitor and had agreements drawn up. An agreement in which my children were to take over the running of the family business. My eldest son Roger was to take over the shipping company and my property portfolio, whilst the twins were to take over the wine merchants and I was to enjoy the remaining time I had with my loving wife Charlotte, although Charlotte needed a little persuasion but when I explained what we were to do. Nothing but enjoy our well-earned fortune and live a comfortable and easy life, allowing the children to carry on the family interests. Written into the agreement I made provisions for our own future ensuring we had a steady income, which would allow us to live a comfortable and easy life. Let them have all the pressure and grief that the business will throw at them, we now are going to enjoy ourselves and do all those things I have been unable to do.

Or would we? Let us hope they do not destroy what we have worked so hard to build up, and to satisfy Charlotte it was written into the agreement that no ships of the Robert Bruce Shipping line would be used for smuggling again. So an era came to an end, a time which saw me through my life and kept me alive and young. Times may never have been easy, we worked hard to achieve what we have today and let us hope our children have learnt from us and do not throw away what we have worked so hard to achieve and build.

Chapter 28

A Pardon for Robert Bruce Smith

As the years passed things got harder and harder for the smugglers and sentences were by now also getting harsher on the smugglers with the act of 1781 when if you were caught with firearms or an offensive weapon and you injured a revenue officer then your sentence would certainly be death without the benefit of the clergy. I never did hear of such sentences been given out, but a year later a chance came for me to become an honest citizen of Port Douglas. In 1782, the government had started to turn soft on the smugglers and was realizing just how much money was being lost in taxes due to the smugglers, but as I have said many times we were not criminals and we never thought of ourselves in such a way. We were free traders. There were times when things did turn nasty and injuries did occur but nobody got killed under my reign. Now it was my time to try to make good and as I said, the government was going soft on the smugglers with a new act, which meant that those that could meet the requirements set out within the act could receive a full pardon. The government had tried this before in 1736 with the Act of indemnity, which was a very dangerous act and did not work, but this act was different and the government had learnt a very good lesson this time. The act in 1736 offered a full pardon to all smugglers that came forward who passed on information to the revenue officers that enabled them to arrest and convict a fellow smuggler. Now tell me who is going to do that, turn kings evidence on one of their own. As history has shown nobody but nobody does that and there was very little take up of this offer and those that did, did not live long afterwards. Those that did sell their friends to the authorities invariable died a very long and nasty death with the money they received either found around the body or worse still their mouths sown up and the money jammed within their mouth. Luckily, I did not hear of anybody in Port Douglas taking up the offer.

The act of oblivion in 1782 was different, as England was once more fighting a war far away in the British Empire and the Royal Navy was in need of good sailors. So this time all that was needed for a full pardon was to provide four people to take your place, two able seamen to serve on one of His Majesty's war ships and two able lands men to serve a shore. Now this was to be easy especially with my wealth and influence. I advertised in the local paper and to my surprise, I had a number of responses to the advert, in fact I had so many replies I had a choice. I was to pay a good and fare wage for this good deed, and as well I promised to look after their families, I would move them into one of my many properties allowing them to stay rent free whilst their husbands were away for two years serving their country and in return I would receive a full and total pardon. This meant I really did have to give up smuggling this time, as all previous acts of smuggling would be taken into account if caught breaking the law or caught smuggling again and the punishment would be much more server. The punishment would have been much harder with a longer sentence and hard labour along with the threat of being sent to the plantations in America for a number of years, not something I could face at my age. I am of an age now where more than likely I would not survive such a long trip on a prison ship, as many did not, only to be buried at sea. However, this act would give me a full pardon except for one crime; this did not cover the murder of a revenue officer, which was lucky, as I had not murdered a revenue officer. Other friends of mine also getting to old to carry on smuggling took up the offer and they too found people to take their place and allowing them to be pardoned for their crimes. Those with less severe crimes only needed to find two people one able seamen and one able lands man. We can all now be honest and law abiding citizens, and as I had so many people answer my advert I decided to pass onto my friends their details. I will soon be able to walk around Port Douglas a free and honest man this will be a very strange feeling.

An agreement was reached and four people were found and offered up in exchange for my full pardon, which was duly accepted. The two able seamen I found were sailors and good ones at that. From what I had heard and luckily for me they were both in great debt, I understand heavily in debt and so this was their saviour as you might say, so it was agreed I would pay off their gambling debts as payment and look after their families whilst they were away serving in the navy. The two able lands men were older men and not able to go to sea but fully able to work as able lands men and also luckily they had no family and as such had no one to care for whilst they were away.

For the first time in my life and I could walk around Port Douglas without being under threat of being arrested and with my head held high. An honest man at last and strangely this felt good, no longer a wanted man and no longer afraid each time there was a knock on the door of who may be standing there. Charlotte could not believe I had taken up the offer. She could now face her opponents in the wine circle knowing that she had nothing to hide. Word soon got out that I had taken the offer and been pardoned for my crimes throughout the years and I did think what John Baites would have said I think he would have probable gone mad with rage at knowing he could no longer have the joy of arresting me for smuggling. With that, I smiled and went about my business a free man.

Chapter 29

At the age of sixty-two and entering the twilight years of my life, no longer a smuggler, no longer was I even going to sea and giving my wife Charlotte the excuse to worry herself silly with the thought will I be coming home tonight or worse was I on my way to war in some far-flung place of the British Empire on board one of His Majesty's many warships. As had been the fate of many of my old friends and family. Who all ended up in faraway places thousands of miles from this green and pleasant land we call England. All fighting for a cause we know nothing about and in many cases dying for that same cause, although a few survived and made their home in such places, with the heat being unbearable and rain that never seems to stop. Well nothing, like we see here, well we might see the rain but not the sun. Some made their fortune, as I was to find out when we received a strange but pleasant letter one morning. There was nothing strange in receiving a letter but the strange thing was whom the letter came from, and there was great excitement in the family when we saw the post mark stamped on its front. The letter mark was Barbados, whom do we know in Barbados I could hear as I came through the front door. I walked into the drawing room where there gathered around the table was the family all giggle and laughing like school children in the playground at break time. The room seemed to be full of excitement and tension and there in the middle of the dining room table was this letter addressed to my good-self Mr R B Smith. No one but no one would dare open the letter, I casually walk over picked up the letter and went to leave the room but I am afraid to say I did not reach very far before Charlotte steered me towards the window and gestured for me to sit down in my favourite arm chair, the one by the window. Now this chair was well worn, with holes in the covers and I believe the springs in the base needed attention but I refused to get it mended. It was my father's chair, the one he would spend hours sat in in front of the fire reading a good book. I did as I was told and sat down in my chair with the letter made myself comfortable and proceeded to open the letter. I turned back to the family and with a look of confusion across my face, I asked who we could know in such a faraway place, to which came a very sharp and chorus of replies from all to open it and we will see whom this mysterious person could be. I carefully turned the letter over and examined the seal, not one that I recognised, but the writing it looked somehow familiar there was something about the handwriting it reminded me of someone. Anyway, Charlotte could see that glint in my eye and asked what the matter was to which I replied that the writing was familiar. Well open it she cried with excitement, I glanced across at her and for a moment, I saw that young girl I had fallen in love with and married all those years ago. So without any more to do I broke the seal and unfolded the letter and put my glasses on yes glasses, age was getting to me now. I could hardly believe my eyes as I sat there and read the letter, after reading it I took off my glasses and handed the letter to Charlotte who gave me a look of confusion and standing up she walked to the window and started to read the letter as she got into the letter I could see a tear running down her cheek. As she read more of the letter she turned to me and she burst into tears, and hugged me as tightly as she could. The children by now could not hold back anymore and they asked whom the letter was from too, which she replied your Uncle, my brother whom I have not seen for over twenty-five years and had given up for dead. After that day when he had left Port Douglas late one night, he never returned home. He was caught red handed that evening whilst smuggling a shipload of brandy across the channel from France. Once caught he was placed in gaol and then later that month was convicted of the offence of smuggling and resisting arrest and was shipped off to the Americas to work the plantations for seven years. The letter explained what had happened and how he had survived and worked his time only to be released and allowed to leave America on a ship bound for the Caribbean in particular Barbados, where he befriended another English man who like himself was a convict, a man also transported to the plantations for an act of smuggling. Between them, they worked the sugar plantations earning enough money to purchase a small plot of land naming it Smith point. The plantation grew and grew to the size it is today of several hundred acres with a large plantation house and many workers, mainly slave workers brought in by the slave traders to work the land. Charlotte carries on and explains that their uncle had had enough of Barbados and had sold his half of the plantation to his partner who stayed on to run the plantation whilst your uncle was planning to return with his wife. Having been away for so long, he longed to return to England and his family. Charlotte carried on reading the letter only to realize that he was now married and reading on further she finds he married one of the slave girls and now he has a family two daughters and two sons aged from eleven to twenty and all were on their way home to England and more to the point Port Douglas. He was bringing them all to England. My god what will we do shouted Charlotte excitedly, welcome them with open arms of course I told Charlotte, but the letter says they will be here at Christmas that's six months away this does not leave us much time to prepare for their arrival.

My reply to this was simple what do we need to prepare?

Charlotte seamed more worried on where will they stay? In addition, of course, this house it is not big enough to add such a large family, and we certainly do not have enough time to extend the house and add a few more rooms.

I told Charlotte not to worry about it, we can sort it for god sake we have six months. I left the dining room with Charlotte and the children reading the letter from her brother over and over again and all I could hear was oohs and ahh's as they read and re-read the letter. As I was walking across the hall way and into my office I suddenly remembered an old cottage down by the harbour which I had already heard was on the market it was a wreck but I am sure it could be done up and prepared for Charlottes brother and family to live in. It was next door to

Bruce and his family and he had told me about it a few weeks ago and Bruce was thinking of extending his family or should I say his wife was once more pregnant and as such would need more room. So a perfect opportunity to buy the cottage. So before I could give it much thought I called Charlotte into my office and I told her of the cottage and what I had in mind and suggested we purchased it and make it ready for her brother and his family. Charlotte came over to me sat on my lap gave me a hug and a kiss and asked me how I knew such things and I told her I had heard of the sale whilst down on the harbour drinking in the Inn with Bruce and I got talking to the owner who just mentioned he had a cottage for sale which I told him I knew about it and would yes I be interested. I was always looking out to make a good profit or two and in fact, I had already looked at the cottage on the pretext of purchasing the cottage and then renting it out. I suggested to Charlotte that we both take a look at the cottage and she could tell me what she thought. So we put on our coats and jackets called the children together and made our way into town on foot and down to the harbour where the cottage was. Whilst we were down looking at the cottage, we paid Bruce a visit and informed him of his Uncles arrival. Then we went next door and looked around the cottage. Charlotte took one look at it and with an excited look in her face, which I knew meant she liked it, she kissed me and hugged me and told me how perfect the cottage will be for them. When they have gone we can then sell it on at a profit of course, which at that point I then told Charlotte that Bruce was going to have it. "I tell you what Charlotte I will go now and see Mr Brown and make him an offer." Little did Charlotte know I had already made him an offer that night in the Inn and it had been accepted and was now in the hands of our solicitors who was drawing up the papers. But Charlotte being Charlotte looked me in the eye and knew already I had done the deal and the cottage was already mine. She had to ask me "you have already bought the cottage haven't you and do not forget I can tell when you are lying you sweat and you have that look in your eyes which tells me your lying, it's already ours." She had me once more and I buckled under the questioning and the looks I was now getting. 'Well ok yes it's ours but all it needs is a good lick of paint and some repairs which I will start to organize next week. I must admit Charlotte was not overly happy with me, that I had made such a purchase without her knowledge or for that matter her consent. By now, she was use to me doing such things and anyway the reason she knew the cottage was ours was our solicitors Bentley and Sons had dropped round earlier today asking after me. Charlotte being Charlotte asked Mr Bentley why he needed to see me so without thinking he proceeded to tell Charlotte that he had some papers for me to sign and would return tomorrow. Charlotte then went on to ask what papers does my husband need to sign. At that point, she found out that I had already bought the cottage. I have learnt having been married for so many years that nothing could be hidden from Charlotte, but let us be honest, that applies to most women. I had bought the cottage for Bruce and his family with the arrangement that Bruce was to pay me back on an interest free loan, but plans can change, with Charlotte's brother and family to use the cottage until they are settled and ready to buy their own place.

So preparations were now in place for the arrival of Brian and his family. Christmas this year was going to be one Christmas we will not forget in a hurry and we will be telling this tale for years to come. As for the parties, they will no doubt go on late in to the night and early into the morning.

Thinking back 25 years, I tried to remember what Charlotte's brother looked like. I do remember Charlotte's brother was a good man and very good at what he did but his fault was been caught smuggling. Even worse caught in the very act of smuggling so there was no more to be said. He had no defence when he went to court the following month.

Avoiding being caught is something that I have made into an art and now will never be caught will I. I have my pardon now. I at last have had hung up my sea boots, and yes you are right I did have some regret, in fact many regrets at the start. So I would spend many hours upstairs in the front room of our house just looking out to sea through my spyglass. Watching the little ships heading out to sea and yes I could easily see some of my own ships like the Charlotte and the Elizabeth Ruth, heading out to sea and wondering have I done the right thing. Praying there would be a time when I might venture out again but not these days. I might be able to go out as a passenger thou. When I had been upstairs for some time Charlotte would come upstairs to see where I am and bring me drink. We would then sit there together in silence just looking out to sea and I am sure she knew what I was thinking not that she ever mentioned it. Then she would leave me alone again to my thoughts and dreams.

Now I have so much time on my hands, which I spend these days on less energetic or backbreaking tasks. I must admit my life is no longer as exciting or unpredictable as it used to be but hey I am old man now no longer able to do those things I did when I was younger. Like fighting nature and all that, she could throw at me. l no longer play cat and mouse with my old adversary John Baites who I might add was long dead now bless his soul. Best of all no longer am I getting so wet and cold that when the wind would blow it would cut through to my bones, although I admit I am now suffering. My body is telling me to slow down. Although I do miss the excitement and adrenalin rush you get from seeing the sails filled with wind, the little vessel would heave over, and the bow would cut through the sea like a hot knife through butter. I was now trying to lead an honest and true life; god I did not realize how hard this was going to be.

The family business was now in the hands of our children and I am pleased to say a very good job they were doing in running it too, not that I would ever admit that to them. We still of course had a say in the day-to-day running of the business. We drew a wage from the business each month, which we would carry, on doing until we both die and best of all I still had my office, which there had been many requests to give it up. No way was I giving up my office this was my only link now with my life's work. My life now consisted of now pottering round the garden tending my price roses and keeping the weeds at bay. I did of course keep everybody on their toes, every now and then I would suddenly decide to venture into town uninvited, and I would just drop into the office, much to my children's disgust. They would make me welcome of course but I knew I was no longer required or even welcome. I knew I was just getting in the way, anyway just to make my presence known I would ask many questions about the day's business and nearly always, I would try to change the odd thing or two. I had to let them know it was still my company in name and I was still in control as all major decisions still had to be passed by Charlotte's and myself. Mainly I did have to show them all I still had all my faculties and I knew what was going on around me and that what I said was true and needed to be followed. I remember I would say to them "I am a lot older and wiser than you and I have seen it all, nothing surprises me these days." They might have youth on their sides but I had wisdom on my side, something my father use to tell me and I must admit I would say "yeah yeah" thinking I knew best but alas, father would always be right.

Now I have all this time on my hands apart from when spending time pottering around the garden or even popping into the office. I would sometimes, on a good sunny day, enjoy heading down to the harbour to meet my eldest son as he entered Port and help were I could to unload his cargo. I was always greeted warmly and treated with great respect by all his crew, as many of them mainly the younger ones had been my apprentices and I had taught them the ropes along with everything I know as you might say. As such, they had sailed with me before and knew my ways and me very well. Sometimes Charlotte would accompany me and we would make a day of it. Roger was always pleased to see us both and he knew how I missed the sea, such that one day he called for me and said he had a surprise for me and we both made our way down to the harbour and there tied up along the harbour wall was a small twenty-foot sailing boat. Looking at him, I knew what he wanted to do. After explaining how and where he had obtained the little 'John Bruce' which I was soon to find out that my brother had been ask to build. We boarded her with Rogers help as by now I was not too steady on my feet and we took a pleasure trip around the harbour, one of the best days of my life and for one moment I felt that old feeling of excitement and thrill of being at sea. If only in a small sailing boat going around the harbour, and now we had yet another addition to the fleet, well not one that was going to make any money though, although how about pleasure trips around the harbour to which Roger laughed and asked what will we charge them for the pleasure.

Chapter 30

Christmas of 1782 was soon to come round too fast if I am honest with the impending arrival of Charlotte's brother Brian and family. What will they look like and more to the point Charlotte was more worried she would not recognise him having not seen him for over twenty five years. She told me more than once that she had so much to tell him, a lifetime to fill in with so many years between their last meetings. How many years was it she kept asking me and I must admit I am unable now to remember when and where he was taken, but it must be over twenty five years. Charlotte had many worries as Christmas approached, sleepless nights where I would find her pacing up and down the landing or sat in her rocking chair in the dark at the end of the bed, how will she great him, what will she say to him that's all I could hear her say to herself. The only regret was Charlotte's mother and father would not see their son return home or even see their grandchildren. Although would father have approved to know his only son had married a slave girl and even worse one that he had bought in the local market from the slave traders to work in the fields on his sugar plantation. But I am afraid to say that it will never happen and he will never ever know as he had died many years before and her mother had died before Brian had been taken off to the Americas. Charlotte was also worried about the reception her brother's wife, being of a different background and skin colour, would receive in the village when they arrive. As people can be cruel in not understanding things, which are different from what they are used to, and let us be honest, I suspect no body in Port Douglas has ever seen somebody with such dark skin. But as time would tell Charlotte's as always worried for nothing as when they arrived they were greeted like the return of a long lost relative which if you think about it they were and as for his wife she was accepted without any thought or bad word spoken. Charlotte should have trusted me as I told her the people of Port Douglas are not narrow-minded and accept people for who they are

Charlotte would visit her parent's grave each year to place flowers on their grave and each year she would kneel down by the graves and whilst cleaning and weeding the graves she would talk to them both and tell them all that had happened in the year, but this year was to be a special visit were she would tell them all of the return of their only son, like the return of the prodigal son in the bible.

One month before Christmas of 1782 we had a letter from London and it was short and to the point informing us of the arrival of my brother and his family to London and they had now disembarked from the East Indies clipper 'The Mars' and that they would be catching the next stage coach from London and should be with us in around the Saturday the 14th December. The excitement in the house was electrifying; everybody was so excited that Charlottes long lost brother was coming home.

The cottage we had bought by the harbour was now ready for them in fact everything was ready. The next few days leading up to the stage coach's arrival seemed to last forever and Charlotte was like a cat on hot bricks, she could not relax, she could not sleep. She in fact became unbearable and all I wanted was the 14th of December to arrive and stage coach to deliver the returning brother to Port Douglas. It was also strange as we walked around Port Douglas, as word had got round the village of the return of Charlotte's long lost brother after being away for twenty-five years, and there was a funny feeling in the air, one of excitement. Many people who knew Brian and remembered Brian all knew he was coming home and could not wait to see him again.

As I have told you before the position of our home in Port Douglas were perfect, we could see right out to sea, we can look back inland, and down the main road into Port Douglas and from here, I could see any danger approaching Port Douglas like the arrival of the revenue officers. Today I can see the arrival of one stagecoach from London, but the views across Port Douglas from our house itself were incredible and this is the main reason why I bought the house, its position was perfect for what I was doing in those earlier years. Today though, I still sit upstairs in the attic and keep an eye on what was going on around me, how do you think I keep an eye on my investments like which of my ships are sailing and which ones are returning with a valuable cargo. I might no longer be an active smuggler and I can assure you no one in my family was involved in smuggling so I understood. Unknown to my family who do you think still finances many of the expeditions across the channel me of course. Charlotte is never to know that little fact, as no doubt I would never live that down, and since my pardoned so should nobody else. That will be our little secret, and those that I could trust with my life.

Still I knew what time the stage coach from London was due so I retired to my chair in the attic and watched the main road like I said I had a perfect view across the valley and down the main and only road into Port Douglas. The stage coach was normally on time but for some reason this day it was late, god what a day to be late, every five minutes Charlotte would shout to me 'can you see it'? No came my reply I will tell you when I see it. Then in the distance I saw a plum of dust and a carriage being pulled by four beautiful large white powerful horses, to which I then shouted down, "it's coming, it's coming. It's coming down the main road right now." Without any further ado, I slowly and very carefully got up from my chair, which I was finding harder and harder to do. When up I made my way downstairs to my waiting wife and our house maid who had in her hand my hat and coat along with now my walking stick. I put on my hat and coat carefully and then taking Charlotte by the hand, we made our way on foot into Port Douglas to greet her brother and family. By the time, we got into Port Douglas and down to the harbour, the stagecoach from London had arrived. There was great commotion around the coach and a large gathering of people some shouting and others crying. I turned to Charlotte and with a puzzled look; I asked what was going on. As we approached, we found ourselves pushing our way through the large crowd of people gathered around the carriage. Then we realized what the commotion was it was Brian, Charlottes brother, he was shaking so many hands, getting hugs and kisses from all around, all of this going on whilst his wife and children looked on in total amazement, they did not realize just how many knew him and even liked him. Word soon had got round that he was coming home. Charlotte tried to get his attention and called out his name trying to be heard above the commotion. Brian soon heard that familiar sound of his sister's voice, he turned round and he looked straight across to Charlotte. Charlotte looked across to me enough to say what do I do now. A tear could be seen in the corner of Brian's eye. As for Charlotte well she was in full flood by now, and strange as it might sound but there seemed to be a moment between them were they just looked at each other over the crowded square and then Charlotte just ran towards her brother and flung her arms around his neck and just hugged him, not letting go. After a few minutes, she let go and looked him in the eye and without thinking just shouted at him why did you not write sooner we all thought for the last twenty years you were dead. Not giving him much time to reply she carries on asking one question after another. Brian turns gently grabs Charlotte by the arms and tells her to be quite and all will be explained, and please just stop asking me so many questions and let me introduce you to the family. Charlotte stepped back, composed herself and waved at me to come over and say hello, which of course I did. I shock her brother's hand asking how he was and what the journey to England was like on one of the East India's Clippers, and that we have so much to talk about and catch up on.

Brain pulled Charlotte back and there standing next to the carriage was Brian's wife and children. Brain then started to introduce us to his family, Alison his wife, and his four children, Matilda, Charlotte, Bruce and Robert. Brian pointed out that we named my second daughter after my sister that is you, and my two son's Bruce and Robert after your side of the family Robert. Charlotte stepped forward, embraced them all, and started asking questions again. I looked at Charlotte and told her that was enough questions for now and shall we take them and show them their new home whilst they stay in Port Douglas.

By now, the crowds had dispersed and the excitement had die down leaving us on our own to talk. I gave instructions for their luggage to be taken to the cottage, which would be theirs for as long as they needed it, which it turns out could be much longer than we first thought.

Let's walk Brian and talk and you can remind yourself of what you have missed all these years and I will also show you where you will be staying for the time being or for as long as you would like. As we walked on Charlotte and Alison followed behind and like most women just talked and talked. Charlotte was telling Alison about Port Douglas and what it was like and trying to make Alison feel as welcome as she could. Their children followed behind looking as bewildered and frightened as ever, four young children take from their home, everything they had ever known and dumped in a strange country not knowing anybody or anything of where they were. Even worse, the locals had never seen anybody with such dark skin as theirs, what made it worse was everybody just starred at first and some even asked if the colour washed off. God sake what were they thinking they put the colour on each night, how heart less and inconsiderate people can be, but generally most people accepted them for who they were, Brian's wife and family.

We made our way to the cottage taking over an hour to reach the front door. On route to the cottage, we must have stood around talking for nearly an hour as we stopped every five minutes or so to say hello to old friends. In the end, we reached the cottage, a small but beautiful white washed building big enough for a family with four children. A place they can call home for the time being. I also had time on my hands so I had tendered the garden and planted a few plants in the garden and if I say so, it was a picture of many colours and many smells, a typical English rose garden. I gave them the key to the front door and showed them in and around the cottage and then bid them farewell and left them to make themselves at home. As we left we reminded them they were all invited to come over for tea later on, "let's say 5.30pm. Just before I go you do remember where we live don't you Brian? You passed the house when you came into Port Douglas. Brian turned back to Charlotte and acknowledge her with a smile and replied with a smile "Yes of course I know where you live. I know I have been away a few years but I have not forgotten everything you know." That is something I could never forget. In some respects that is what helped me get through each day, knowing one day I would return here. Still let us get unpacked and get cleaned up and we will be up shortly.

The children then turned, looked at their dad and ran upstairs to decide whose bedroom was to be whose, not without an argument thou which was settled by the two eldest children who just told them which bedrooms they were going to have. Great children I told Brian and you should be proud of them, which of course he was.

As we left, bid our goodbyes and headed home I could see Charlotte was still upset and tears were welling up again in her eyes again. She suddenly noticed I had realised she was still crying, she could not believe Brian was back, back within the family unit. She was more worried for his wife and children and would they all be accepted into the community or would they be treated with contempt, only time would tell. I know the people in Port Douglas and they are good people and they will respect them take my word for it. Charlotte pointed out the children will need to schooled, I told her I had already spoken to the school teacher and there was places for all four of the children and they can start whenever they are ready, god Robert you really have thought of everything haven't you. Well I do try you know me, yes I should know you by now, we have known each other for long enough and that is why I love you so much you are so thoughtful and so considerate.

That year the year of 1782, we had the best Christmas ever. I had gone out and found the biggest tree I could and then we all spent the time decorating it. For once, we had the whole family together. I even persuaded all our children and grandchildren to stay over in the family home on Christmas Eve. It was a squeeze but worth it. For on Christmas day the grandchildren rose early and ran downstairs to open their presents, which they could open one each and leave the rest until later when Brain and his family arrived. It was great to see the house alive again with the sound of children laughing, running around and having fun. The maids started to open the curtains around the house only to find it had snowed. It was a magical sight to see the snow with the children begging their parents to let them go out and play, which they did after breakfast. The first snow at Christmas for a few years, and it was cold as my old bones were soon to find out. That day brought back many memories when the children were younger and the house was always buzzing with excitement and joy. These days it's only Charlotte and myself living in such a great house on our own. The children have flown the nest. One thing we always did at Christmas is the gather the staff up and give them all their Christmas presents, so after breakfast I asked everybody to gather around the tree and I thanked each member of the staff for their service through the year and each one had a small gift. Instructions were also given that after dinner was served that they were to leave us and go and celebrate Christmas themselves, a couple of bottles of fine wine which would be waiting for them on their dining table. Christmas always a special time for us, but this year it was especially special. Although we were to have many more Christmases but none as special as the year of 1782.

Chapter 31

Things were looking up for the family once more Charlotte's brother Brian was back within the family fold along with his new family. Myself well I had my sights on something new and exciting. I had been approached on a number of occasions to become the Mayor of Port Douglas and surrounding areas so why not. I was around sixty-five years old, I needed to put the spark back in my life, and this was a perfect way to do it. Please do not think that my life was boring with Charlotte and the family it was far from anything like that. Charlotte was invigorating and unpredictable and kept me alive, but I needed something to do and this fitted the bill perfectly.

I first had to be elected onto the parish council which was not too difficult to do so in 1785 I put my name forward and was duly elected much to Charlottes surprise and if I truly honest so was I. I carried out my duties as a councillor with pride and became very popular with the locals. They all knew me anyway but not as the honest law abiding councillor which if I am honest made me stand rather proud, something I thought I would never feel, proud to be an honest abiding citizen. It surprised a few of my friends as well. I served on the council for around five years until one day in 1790 I found myself being but forward for the position of Mayor. The councillors met and of course when it came for that vote I had to abstain, as I could not vote for myself now could I and to my surprise I was duly elected in 1790 as Mayor of Port Douglas. Word soon got out and the town crier was sent out to announce that I, Robert Bruce Smith, was now the Mayor of Port Douglas.

The investiture was to take place in the council hall in Port Douglas and all would be welcome and at the investiture, I was duly elected and presented with the badge and chain of office and a bright red cape with black fur along its edge. This all weighed a ton and I had to wear this all day whilst on the Mayors duties.

The current Mayor will finish his term and take on the role of Deputy Mayor throughout my term of office. As he had to do for the next five years as I was re-elected five times in a row until I could do no more and I stepped down.

Something I was really not looking forward to was to make a speech, a speech in which I was to announce a charity that we would support, which in reality would be the poor and less fortunate of Port Douglas something I had been actively involved in all my life and was a serious passion of mine. To help those that were less fortunate than ourselves as I have led a charmed life and a very productive life, and it could so easily have been so different.

The investiture was also to involve attending the Annual Civic Service held within the local church and presided over by yes our own vicar when he was sober. Sometimes if the local Bishop was available then he would take the service. There was a procession after the investiture of the Mayor, which would leave the council buildings and make its way with full pomp and ceremony to the church for the service and I would extend a warm welcome to all the residence of the town who wish to attend the service. Which at times like this the church pews were always full, which these days was a rare sight to see. After the service, we would all make our way back to the council buildings where we would celebrate and dance and laugh deep into the night. Only to wake in the morning with a massive headache and no sympathy from Charlotte. To think I was Mayor for five years on the trot, yes I was mayor for five consecutive years until I was 70. But I must admit I did enjoy it and I made even more friends in high places having to go to London at least once to meet the Prime minister of the time, dammed if I can remember his name thou. As Mayor, I was guest of honour to many a party in the great houses around the area yes I was a somebody now and not just a businessman in Port Douglas and that meant more to me than anything. All I wanted to do was make my family happy and proud, but I cannot ever forget where I came from I came from nothing, from a poor family whose father worked the forest whose mother took washing in to make ends meet and I am not ashamed to admit it in fact I am proud to admit where I came from as you should never forget where you came from. Now I can sit back in my retirement and know my family will want for nothing now and even after, I am gone to meet my maker.

Chapter 32

As the years passed by and I got older, I found even going down to the harbour to meet my son as he came into Port Douglas and then when tied up I would try and help unload. Which is something I loved to do, but even that was getting past me. It was this that made me feel like I was doing something useful and not been a burden on my family. So instead I started to do something I had not done since I was child, I would make my way slowly down to the harbour to meet Roger as he came into port, but this time I would just sit outside the Inn on the harbour front with a drink in one hand and my pipe in the other and just watch the ships coming and going, and once more I tried to guess what they were carrying. But I must be getting old as now I was wrong more times than right apart from the ones that smelt like rotten eggs and those that you could smell before they even reached the harbour wall. Then when Roger had unloaded and finished for the day he would come and join me and we would enjoy a few jars or two and then we would walk me home to Charlotte his mother who would tell us off for drinking and missing our tea, and poor old Roger would then go home and get it in the ear again but this time from his wife.

I keep asking myself were had all the years gone it does not seem that long ago we held our children in our arms and look at them now, all grown up with their own children.

The year now is 1810 and it is at this point that I Roger his eldest son takes over the telling of my father's story. By now, my father was approaching his 90th birthday and mother was, to be truthful I am not sure how old mother was but she was as quick on her feet as she ever was. She also could still tell us off as though we were still children and threaten to put us over her knee if we did not do as we were told. But Father by now was ill and to be truthful he was very ill and had taken to his bed with the doctor calling at least once a week. It was his heart the doctor told us and the result of going out in all weathers, night and day and having worked so hard throughout his life just to ensure his family was well cared for and looked after. As a result, he had ended up a very wealthy man and a highly respected member of the community with being mayor of Port Douglas more than once in his lifetime in fact being Mayor for five years in a row. Something he was very proud of. When he retired, he was given the freedom of the borough, something that to this day he holds dearly. Now he is a frail old man and like I said taken to his bed. It was his heart to start with but what took him in the end was consumption or as it is known Tuberculosis. Near the end, all we could hear was father coughing and fighting to breath and there were the fevers and the night sweats. The doctor ended up visiting daily administering medication and making dad as comfortable as he could and near the end we were warned of what to expect, which I am sorry to say came much sooner than we thought and on the 30th May 1810 with his family by his side my father lost the battle to live and died peacefully in his sleep. We were all prepared for the evitable but nonetheless it still came as a shock and mother took it the hardest after many years of marriage and having lived through the good and the bad times. Mother had not only lost her husband but her best and closets friend her companion in her eyes, she was now alone, but she still had her family around her for support.

The next few days leading up to the funeral were tough for all of the family, sons, daughters, nieces and nephews and by now many grandchildren. On the day of the funeral, we all gathered at the family house, the same house father brought all those years ago. The same house we were born in and as children grew up in, except one-person John who we lost to the sea all those years earlier but who will never forgotten, as in the hall way a picture hangs of John in the garden in his best Sunday suit and in the background is the rest of the family having tea in the garden.

The funeral was arranged for the following week the 5th June with a service at 10am to be held in the local church followed by a private service at the graveside when the body would be interned in the family grave. Yes, this is the same church that father used on hundreds of occasions to hide all of those kegs in the roof space and using many of the graves within the churchyard. What a fitting end for him. A service in the same church that had served him so well but not as a place of worship but a place to hid his contraband with god now looking down on him lying in his coffin.

The service was short and to the point, which is what father, would have wanted and we were surprised at just how many people from the village and surrounding villages attended father's funeral, which just showed how well father was liked throughout Port Douglas. Father had left strict instructions on how the service was to be run and even after his death he was still in control and finally everybody was to celebrate his life and his achievements and under no circumstances was anybody to morn him in any way, one thing he hated in his life most was people being sad, enjoy life he would say and life must go on. Mother followed his request to the letter, arranged an afternoon tea party for after the service, and invited everybody in the village that wanted to attend. My father also left instructions that no one is to wear black he hated black at the best of time and from what I remember he wanted it to be a party just like the ones we use to hold in the garden and so it was, laughing and joking. Except at one stage mother disappeared she was so upset at her loss and needed to be alone for a short while, but she copped remarkable well. She even invited the local Revenue Officers and of course his old adversary John Baites had die all those years before and to add to the tale my father was buried in the grave next to John Baites, the game of cat and mouse could now start over again, but most of all he would see his young son again John.

The funeral came and went and the time came to decide what we were to put onto his grave stone and after great thought and pondering we decided on

Robert Bruce Smith Loving husband to Charlotte Smith
Born 10th April 1720 Died 30th May 1810 aged 90
May his memory live long in our hearts and mind.

The time soon came to the reading of the will and on the 30–08–1810, the family solicitor came over and arranged the reading of the will. The family and those who were mentioned in the will were gathered at the great house and in the living room. When we were all ready, our solicitor started the reading and after two hours of nonstop reading he took his glasses off and pronounced that was the end of the will. It must have been one of the longest wills I have ever heard and in such detail. The estate must have been worth in excess of £500,000 and everybody had been catered for. The shipping company had been losing money and so was sold off about ten years earlier along with the tobacco factory just leaving the wine importers and of course there was a great list of properties that father had brought through the years and which now had been placed in the hands of myself and my brother with the understanding that the whole family in particular mother would be fully supported. Mother was to live in the great house until the day came when she would be re-united with the love of her life her husband Robert. The day to day running of the business which we had been doing so well since father had fallen so ill would now fall under my control being the eldest son. But to be fair to the rest of the family, each and every member of the family would have a say in how Father's business would be run.

Mother never ever got over the loss of dad and was heartbroken until the day she died, she was reunited with Dad about five years later when she also died peacefully in her sleep, she was laid to rest alongside her husband within the family grave, she was once more reunited with her beloved husband and her son John.

Robert Bruce Smith died on the 30th of May 1810 at the age of 90. And Charlotte Smith died on 1st of May 1815. They have now been reunited for eternity.

The author

John Needham, born and raised in Bournmouth
where he lives with his wife and three children. He
started his writing career in 2009 and is enjoying it
more and more. He left school in 1977 and started
his working career at Plessey's, later to become Sie-
mens and in time worked on gas turbines. He then
moved on to London and worked for Tate & Lyle,
travelling the world visiting sugar refineries, finally
ending up in the oil and gas industry. In his spare
time, he likes to write history books, including his
debut novel, A Smuggler's Tale.

The publisher

*He who stops
getting better
stops being good.*

This is the motto of novum publishing, and our focus
is on finding new manuscripts, publishing them and
offering long-term support to the authors.
Our publishing house was founded in 1997, and since
then it has become THE expert for new authors and
has won numerous awards.

**Our editorial team will peruse each manuscript
within a few weeks free of charge and without
obligation.**

You will find more information about
novum publishing and our books on the internet:

w w w . n o v u m - p u b l i s h i n g . c o . u k